A PIECE *of the* WORLD

Novels by Christina Baker Kline

A PIECE *of the* WORLD

(A NOVEL)

Christina Baker Kline

wm

WILLIAM MORROW
An Imprint of HarperCollins*Publishers*

Page 310 serves as a continuation of this copyright page.

HarperCollins books may be purchased for educational, business, or sales promotional use. For information, please e-mail the Special Markets Department at SPsales@harpercollins.com.

FIRST EDITION

Designed by Bonni Leon-Berman

Library of Congress Cataloging-in-Publication Data has been applied for.

ISBN 978-0-06-235626-0 (hardcover)
ISBN 978-0-06-266376-4 (international edition)
ISBN 978-0-06-268594-0 (Books-A-Million signed edition)
ISBN 978-0-06-267550-7 (Target edition)

17 18 19 20 21   RS/LSC   10 9 8 7 6 5 4 3 2

For my father,
who showed me the world

"There was a very strange connection. One of those odd collisions that happen. We were a little alike; I was an unhealthy child that was kept at home. So there was an unsaid feeling between us that was wonderful, an utter naturalness. We'd sit for hours and not say a word, and then she'd say something, and I'd answer her. A reporter once asked her what we talked about. She said, 'Nothing foolish.'"

—*Andrew Wyeth*

A PIECE *of the* WORLD

PROLOGUE

LATER HE TOLD ME HE'D BEEN AFRAID TO SHOW ME THE PAINTING. He thought I wouldn't like the way he portrayed me: dragging myself across the field, fingers clutching dirt, my legs twisted behind. The arid moonscape of wheatgrass and timothy. That dilapidated house in the distance, looming up like a secret that won't stay hidden. Faraway windows, opaque and unreadable. Ruts in the spiky grass made by an invisible vehicle, leading nowhere. Dishwater sky.

People think the painting is a portrait, but it isn't. Not really. He wasn't even in the field; he conjured it from a room in the house, an entirely different angle. He removed rocks and trees and outbuildings. The scale of the barn is wrong. And I am not that frail young thing, but a middle-aged spinster. It's not my body, really, and maybe not even my head.

He did get one thing right: Sometimes a sanctuary, sometimes a prison, that house on the hill has always been my home. I've spent my life yearning toward it, wanting to escape it, paralyzed by its hold on me. (There are many ways to be crippled, I've learned over the years, many forms of paralysis.) My ancestors fled to Maine from Salem, but like anyone who tries to run away from the past, they brought it with them. Something inexorable seeds itself in the place of your origin. You can never escape the bonds of family history, no matter how far you travel. And the skeleton of a house can carry in its bones the marrow of all that came before.

Who are you, Christina Olson? he asked me once.

Nobody had ever asked me that. I had to think about it for a while.

If you really want to know me, I said, we'll have to start with the witches. And then the drowned boys. The shells from distant lands, a whole room full of them. The Swedish sailor marooned in ice. I'll need to tell you about the false smiles of the Harvard man and the hand-wringing of those brilliant Boston doctors, the dory in the haymow and the wheelchair in the sea.

And eventually—though neither of us knew it yet—we'd end up here, in this place, within and without the world of the painting.

THE STRANGER AT THE DOOR

1939

I'm working on a quilt patch in the kitchen on a brilliant July
afternoon, small squares of fabric and a pincushion and scissors on the table beside me, when I hear the hum of a car engine.
Looking out the window toward the cove, I see a station wagon
turn into the field about a hundred yards away. The engine
cuts off and the passenger door swings open and Betsy James
gets out, laughing and exclaiming. I haven't seen her since last
summer. She's wearing a white halter top and denim shorts,
a red bandanna tied around her neck. As I watch her coming
toward the house, I am struck by how different she looks. Her
sweet round face has thinned and lengthened; her chestnut hair
is long and thick around her shoulders, her eyes dark and shin-
ing. A red slash of lipstick. I think of her at nine years old, when
she first came to visit, her small, nimble fingers braiding my hair
as she sat behind me on the stoop. And here she is, seventeen
and suddenly a woman.

"Hey there, Christina," she says at the screen door, out of
breath. "It's been such a long time!"

"Come in," I say from my chair. "You won't mind if I don't
get up?"

"Of course not." When she steps inside, the room smells of

roses. (When did Betsy start wearing perfume?) She sweeps over to my chair and hugs my shoulders. "We arrived a few days ago. I surely am happy to be back."

"You surely look it."

She smiles, spots of color on her cheeks. "How are you and Al?"

"Oh, you know. Fine. The same."

"The same is good, yes?"

I smile. Sure. The same is good.

"What are you making here?"

"Just a little thing. A baby quilt. Lora's pregnant again."

"Such a generous auntie." She reaches down and picks up a quilt square, a piece of calico, pink flowers with green leaves on a brown background. "I recognize this fabric."

"I tore up an old dress."

"I remember it. Small white buttons and a full skirt, right?"

I think of my mother bringing home the Butterick pattern and the iridescent buttons and the calico. I think of Walton seeing me in the dress for the first time. *I am awed by you.* "That was a long time ago."

"Well, it's nice that old dress is getting a new life." Gently she places the square back on the table and sifts through the others: white muslin, navy cotton, chambray faintly marked with ink. "All these bits and pieces. You're making a family heirloom."

"I don't know about that," I say. "It's just a pile of scraps."

"One man's trash . . ." She laughs and glances out the window. "I completely forgot! I came up here for a cup of water, if you don't mind."

"Sit down, I'll get you a glass."

"Oh, it's not for me." She points at the station wagon in the field. "My friend wants to paint a picture of your house, but he needs water to do it."

I squint at the car. A boy is sitting on the roof, looking at the sky. He's got a large white pad of paper in one hand and what looks like a pencil in the other.

"He's N. C. Wyeth's son," Betsy says in a stage whisper, as if someone might hear.

"Who?"

"You know N. C. Wyeth. The famous illustrator? *Treasure Island?*"

Ah, *Treasure Island.* "Al loved that book. I think we still have it somewhere."

"I think every boy in America has it somewhere. Well, his son's an artist too. I just met him today."

"You met him today, and you're riding around in a car with him?"

"Yes, he's—I don't know. He seems trustworthy."

"Your parents don't mind?"

"They don't know." She smiles sheepishly. "He showed up at the house this morning looking for my father, but my parents had gone off for a sail. I answered the door. And here we are."

"That happens sometimes," I say. "Where's he from?"

"Pennsylvania. His family has a summer place up here, in Port Clyde."

"You seem to know an awful lot about him," I say, arching an eyebrow.

She arches an eyebrow back. "I plan to learn more."

Betsy leaves with her cup of water and makes her way back to the station wagon. By the way she's walking, shoulders back and chin forward, I can tell she knows he's watching her. And she likes it. She hands the boy the cup and climbs onto the roof next to him.

"Who was that?" My brother Al is at the back door, wiping his hands on a rag. I can never tell when he's coming; he's as quiet as a fox.

"Betsy. And a boy. He's painting a picture of the house, she said."

"Why would he want to do that?"

I shrug. "People are funny."

"Sure are." Al settles into his rocker, pulling out his pipe and tobacco. He starts tamping and lighting, both of us spying on Betsy and the boy out the window and trying to act like we aren't.

After a while the boy climbs down and sets his pad of paper on the hood of the car. He offers his hand to Betsy, who slides down into his embrace. Even from this distance I can feel the heat between them. They stand there talking for a minute, and then Betsy tugs on his hand, pulling him toward—oh Lord, she's bringing him up to the house. I feel a momentary panic: the floor is dusty, my dress soiled, my hair unkempt. Al's overalls are splashed with mud. It's been a long time since I've worried about being seen through the eyes of a stranger. As they walk toward the house, though, I see the boy gazing at Betsy and realize I don't need to worry. She is all he sees.

He's at the screen, now, on the threshold. Lanky, smiling, quivering with energy, he fills the entire doorway. "What a marvelous house," he murmurs as he opens the screen, craning his neck to look up and around the room. "The light in here is extraordinary."

"Christina, Alvaro, this is Andrew," Betsy says, coming in behind him.

He inclines his head. "Hope you don't mind my crashing in uninvited. Betsy swore it was okay."

"We don't stand on ceremony," my brother says. "I'm Al."

"People after my own heart. And call me Andy, please."

"Well, I'm Christina," I say.

"I call her Christie, but no one else does," Al adds.

"Christina, then," Andy says, settling his gaze on me. I detect no judgment in it, only a kind of anthropological curiosity. Still, his keen attention makes me blush.

Turning to Al, I say quickly, "Remember that book *Treasure Island*? His father did the paintings for it, Betsy said."

"Did he now?" Al's face lights up. "You can't forget those pictures. I probably read that book a dozen times. Might be the only book I ever actually finished, now that I think about it. I wanted to be a pirate."

Andy breaks into a grin. His teeth are large and white, like a movie star's. "So did I. Still do, in fact."

Betsy's holding the oversized drawing pad. As proud as a new mother, she brings it over to show me. "Look what Andy did, Christina, in that short amount of time."

The paper is still damp. In bold strokes Andy reduced the

house to a white box with two gables facing the sea. The fields are green and yellow, with bristly blades of grass poking up here and there. Near-black firs, a purple swipe of mountains, watery clouds. Though the watercolor has been done quickly—there's movement in the brushstrokes, as if the wind is blowing through—it's clear this boy knows what he's doing. The windows are mere suggestions, but you have the peculiar sense that you can see inside. The house seems rooted in the earth.

"It's just a sketch," Andy says, coming up beside me. "I'll keep working at it."

"Looks like a nice place to live," I say. The house is snug and cozy, a fairy-tale version of the one Al and I actually live in, the only hint of its decay in smudges of blue and brown.

Andy laughs. "You tell me." Running two fingers over the paper, he says, "Such stark lines. There's something about this place . . . You've lived here a long time?"

I nod.

"I sense that. That it's a place filled with stories. I'll bet I could paint it for a hundred years and never get tired of it."

"Oh, you'd get tired of it," Al says.

We all laugh.

Andy claps his hands together. "Hey, guess what? Today is my birthday."

"Is it really?" Betsy asks. "You didn't tell me."

He puts his arm around her and tugs her toward him. "Didn't I? I feel like you know everything about me already."

"Not yet," she says.

"What's your age?" I ask him.

"Twenty-two."

"Twenty-two! Betsy's only seventeen."

"A *mature* seventeen," Betsy blurts, color rising to her cheeks.

Andy seems amused. "Well, I've never cared much about age. Or maturity."

"How are you going to celebrate?" I ask.

He raises an eyebrow at Betsy. "I'd say I'm celebrating right now."

BETSY DOESN'T SHOW up again until several weeks later, when she bursts into the kitchen and practically dances across the floor. "Christina, we are engaged," she says breathlessly, clasping my hand.

"Engaged?!"

She nods. "Can you believe it?"

You're so young, I start to say; it's too quick, you hardly know each other . . .

Then I think of my own life. All the years, all the waiting that led to nothing. I saw how the two of them were together. The spark between them. *I feel like you know everything about me already.* "Of course I can," I say.

Ten months later, a postcard arrives. Betsy and Andy are married. When they return to Maine for the summer, I hand Betsy a wedding gift: two pillowcases I made and embroidered with flowers. It took me four days to make the French knots for the daisies and the tiny buttonhole-stitch leaves; my hands, stiff and gnarled, don't work the way they used to.

Betsy looks closely at the embroidery and holds the pillow-cases to her chest. "I will treasure these. They're perfect."

I give her a smile. They're not perfect. The lines are uneven, the flower petals spiky and overlarge; the cotton is marked faintly with the residue of ripped stitches.

Betsy has always been kind.

She shows me photographs from their upstate New York wedding ceremony: Andy in a tuxedo, Betsy in white with gardenias in her hair, both beaming with joy. After their five-day honeymoon, she tells me, she'd assumed they would drive to Canada for the wedding of a close friend, but Andy said he had to get back to work. "He'd told me before we were married that was how it would be," she says. "But I didn't quite believe it until that moment."

"So did you go by yourself?"

She shakes her head. "I stayed with him. This is what I signed up for. The work is everything."

OUT THE KITCHEN window I see Andy trudging up the field toward the house, hitching one leg forward, dragging the other, his gait uneven. Strange that I didn't notice that before. Here he is at the door in paint-flecked boots, a white cotton shirt rolled to the elbow, a sketch pad under his arm. He knocks, two firm raps, and pulls open the screen. "Betsy has some errands to do. Is it okay if I hang around?"

I try to act nonchalant, but my heart is racing. I can't remember the last time I was alone with a man other than Al. "Suit yourself."

He steps inside.

He's taller and handsomer than I remember, with sandy brown hair and piercing blue eyes. There's something equine about the way he tosses his head and shifts his feet. A pulsating thrum.

In the Shell Room he runs his hand along the mantelpiece, brushing off the dust. Picks up Mother's cracked white teapot and turns it around. Cups my grandmother's chambered nautilus in his hand and leafs through the filmy pages of her old black bible. No one has opened my poor drowned uncle Alvaro's sea chest in decades; it screeches when he lifts the lid. Andy picks up a shell-framed portrait of Abraham Lincoln, looks at it closely, sets it down. "You can feel the past in this house," he says. "The layers of generations. It reminds me of *The House of the Seven Gables*. 'So much of mankind's varied experience had passed there that the very timbers were oozy, as with the moisture of a heart.'"

The lines are familiar. I remember reading that novel in school, a long time ago. "We're actually related to Nathaniel Hawthorne," I tell him.

"Interesting. Ah yes—Hathorn." Going to the window, he gestures toward the field. "I saw the tombstones in the graveyard down there. Hawthorne lived in Maine for a while, I believe?"

"I don't know about that," I admit. "Our ancestors came from Massachusetts. Nearly two hundred years ago. Three men, in the middle of winter."

"Where in Massachusetts?"

"Salem."

"Why'd they come up?"

"My grandmother said they were trying to escape the taint of association with their relative John Hathorne. He was chief justice of the witch trials. When they got to Maine they dropped the 'e' at the end of the name."

"To obscure the connection?"

I shrug. "Presumably."

"I'm remembering this now," he says. "Nathaniel Hawthorne left Salem too, and also changed the spelling of the name. But a lot of his stories are reworkings of his own family history. *Your* family history, I suppose. Moral allegories about people determined to root out wickedness in others while denying it in themselves."

"Actually," I tell him, "there's a legend that as one of the condemned witches stood at the scaffold, waiting for the noose, she uttered a curse: 'May God take revenge on the family of John Hathorne.'"

"So your family is cursed!" he says with delight.

"Maybe. Who knows? My grandmother used to say that those Hathorn men brought the witches with them from Salem. She kept the door open between the kitchen and the shed for the witches to come and go."

Looking around the Shell Room, he says, "What do you think? Is it true?"

"I've never seen any," I tell him. "But I keep the door open too."

OVER THE YEARS, certain stories in the history of a family take hold. They're passed from generation to generation, gaining substance and meaning along the way. You have to learn to sift through them, separating fact from conjecture, the likely from the implausible.

Here is what I know: Sometimes the least believable stories are the true ones.

1896–1900

My mother drapes a wrung-out cloth across my forehead. Cold water trickles down my temple onto the pillow, and I turn my head to smear it off. I gaze up into her gray eyes, narrowed in concern, a vertical line between them. Small lines around her puckered lips. I look over at my brother Alvaro standing beside her, two years old, eyes wide and solemn.

She pours water from a white teapot into a glass. "Drink, Christina."

"Smile at her, Katie," my grandmother Tryphena tells her. "Fear is a contagion." She leads Alvaro out of the room, and my mother reaches for my hand, smiling with only her mouth.

I am three years old.

My bones ache. When I close my eyes, I feel like I'm falling. It's not an altogether unpleasant sensation, like sinking into water. Colors behind my eyelids, purple and rust. My face so hot that my mother's hand on my cheek feels icy. I take a deep breath, inhaling the smells of wood smoke and baking bread, and I drift. The house creaks and shifts. Snoring in another room. The ache in my bones drives me back to the surface. When I open my eyes, I can't see anything, but I can tell my mother is gone. I'm so cold it feels like I've never been warm,

my teeth chattering loudly in the quiet. I hear myself whimpering, and it's as if the sound is coming from someone else. I don't
know how long I've been making this noise, but it soothes me, a
distraction from the pain.

The covers lift. My grandmother says, "There, Christina,
hush. I'm here." She slides into bed beside me in her thick flannel nightgown and pulls me toward her. I settle into the curve
of her legs, her bosom pillowy behind my head, her soft fleshy
arm under my neck. She rubs my cold arms, and I fall asleep in
a warm cocoon smelling of talcum powder and linseed oil and
baking soda.

SINCE I CAN remember I've called my grandmother Mamey.
It's the name of a tree that grows in the West Indies, where she
went with my grandfather, Captain Sam Hathorn, on one of
their many excursions. The mamey tree has a short, thick trunk
and only a few large limbs and pointy green leaves, with white
flowers at the ends of the branches, like hands. It blooms all year
long, and its fruit ripens at different times. When my grandparents spent several months on the island of St. Lucia, my grandmother made jam out of the fruit, which tastes like an overripe
raspberry. "The riper it gets, the sweeter it gets. Like me," she
said. "Don't call me Granny. Mamey suits me just fine."

Sometimes I find her sitting alone, gazing out the window
in the Shell Room, our front parlor, where we display the trea-
sures that six generations of sailors brought home in sea chests
from their voyages around the world. I know she's pining for

my grandfather, who died in this house a year before I was born. "It is a terrible thing to find the love of your life, Christina," she says. "You know too well what you're missing when it's gone."

"You have us," I say.

"I loved your grandfather more than all the shells in the Shell Room," she says. "More than all the blades of grass in the field."

MY GRANDFATHER, LIKE his father and grandfather before him, began his life on the sea as a cabin boy and became a ship captain. After marrying my grandmother, he took her with him on his travels, transporting ice from Maine to the Philippines, Australia, Panama, the Virgin Islands, and filling the ship for the return trip with brandy, sugar, spices, and rum. Her stories of their exotic travels have become family legend. She traveled with him for decades, even bringing along their children, three boys and a girl, until, at the height of the Civil War, he insisted they stay home. Confederate privateers were prowling up and down the East Coast like marauding pirates, and no ship was immune.

But my grandfather's caution could not keep his family safe: all three of his boys died young. One succumbed to scarlet fever; his four-year-old namesake, Sammy, drowned one October when Captain Sam was at sea. My grandmother could not bring herself to break the news until March. "Our beloved little boy is no more on earth," she wrote. "While I write, I'm almost blind with tears. No one saw him fall but the little boy who ran to tell his mother. The vital spark has fled. Dear husband, you can better imagine my grief than I can describe to you." Fourteen years later, their teenaged son, Alvaro, working as a seaman on a schooner off the coast of Cape Cod, was swept overboard in a storm. News of his death came by telegram, blunt and impersonal. His body was never found. Alvaro's sea chest arrived on Hathorn Point weeks later, its top intricately carved by his hand. My grandmother, disconsolate, spent hours tracing the outlines with her fingertips, damsels in hoopskirts with revealing décolletage.

MY BEDROOM IS still and bright. Light filters through the lace curtains Mamey crocheted, making intricate shapes on the floor. Dust mites float in slow motion. Stretching out in the bed, I lift my arms from under the sheet. No pain. I'm afraid to move my legs. Afraid to hope that I'm better.

My brother Alvaro swings into the room, hanging on to the doorknob. He stares at me blankly, then shouts, to no one in particular, "Christie's awake!" He gives me a long steady look as he closes the door. I hear him clomping deliberately down the stairs, and then my mother's voice and my grandmother's, the clash of pots far away in the kitchen, and I drift back to sleep. Next thing I know, Al is shaking my shoulder with his spider-monkey hand, saying, "Wake up, lazy," and Mother, trundling through the door with her big pregnant belly, is setting a tray on the round oak table beside the bed. Oatmeal mush and toast and milk. My father a shadow behind her. For the first time in I don't know how long, I feel a pang that must be hunger.

Mother smiles a real smile as she props two pillows behind my head and helps me sit up. Spoons oatmeal into my mouth, waits for me to swallow between slurps. Al says, "Why're you feeding her, she's not a baby," and Mother tells him to hush, but she is laughing and crying at the same time, tears rolling down her cheeks, and has to stop for a moment to wipe her face with her apron.

"Why you crying, Mama?" Al asks.

"Because your sister is going to get well."

I remember her saying this, but it will be years before I understand what it means. It means my mother was afraid I might not get well. They were all afraid—all except Alvaro and me and the unborn baby, each of us busy growing, unaware of how bad things could get. But they knew. My grandmother, with her three dead children. My mother, the only one who survived, her childhood threaded with melancholy, who named her firstborn son after her brother who drowned in the sea.

A DAY PASSES, another, a week. I am going to live, but something isn't right. Lying in the bed, I feel like a rag wrung out and draped to dry. I can't sit up, can barely turn my head. I can't move my legs. My grandmother settles into a chair beside me with her crocheting, looking at me now and then over the top of her rimless spectacles. "There, child. Rest is good. Baby steps."

"Christie's not a baby," Al says. He's lying on the floor pushing his green train engine. "She's bigger than me."

"Yes, she's a big girl. But she needs rest so she can get better."

"Rest is stupid," Al says. He wants me back to normal so we can run to the barn, play hide-and-seek among the hay bales, poke at the gopher holes with a long stick.

I agree. Rest is stupid. I am tired of this narrow bed, the slice of window above it. I want to be outside, running through the grass, climbing up and down the stairs. When I fall asleep, I am careering down the hill, my arms outstretched and my strong legs pumping, grasses whipping against my calves, steady on toward the sea, closing my eyes and tilting my chin toward the sun, moving with ease, without pain, without falling. I wake in my bed to find the sheet damp with sweat.

"What's wrong with me?" I ask my mother as she tucks a fresh sheet around me.

"You are as God made you."

"Why would he make me like this?"

Her eyelids flicker—not quite a flutter, but a startled blink and long shut eye that I've come to recognize: It's the expression she makes when she doesn't know what to say. "We have to trust in his plan."

My grandmother, crocheting in her chair, doesn't say anything. But when Mother goes downstairs with the dirty sheets, she says, "Life is one trial after another. You're just learning that earlier than most."

"But why am I the only one?"

She laughs. "Oh, child, you're not the only one." She tells me about a sailor in their crew with one leg who thumped around deck on a wooden dowel, another with a hunchback that made him scuttle like a crab, one born with six fingers on each hand.

(How quickly that boy could tie knots!) One with a foot like a cabbage, one with scaly skin like a reptile, conjoined twins she once saw on the street . . . People have maladies of all kinds, she says, and if they have any sense, they don't waste time whining about them. "We all have our burdens to bear," she says. "You know what yours is, now. That's good. You'll never be surprised by it."

Mamey tells me a story about when she and Captain Sam were shipwrecked in a storm, cast adrift on a precarious raft in the middle of the ocean, shivering and alone, with scant provisions. The sun set and rose, set and rose; their food and water dwindled. They despaired that they would never be rescued. She tore strips of clothing, tied them to an oar, and managed to prop this wretched flag upright. For weeks, they saw no one. They licked their salt-cracked lips and closed their sunburned lids, resigning themselves to their all-but-certain fates, blessed unconsciousness and death. And then, one evening near sundown, a speck on the horizon materialized into a ship heading directly toward them, drawn by the fluttering rags.

"The most important qualities a human can possess are an iron will and a persevering spirit," Mamey says. She says I inherited those qualities from her, and that in the same way she survived the shipwreck, when all hope was lost, and the deaths of her three boys, when she thought her heart might pulverize like a shell into sand, I will find a way to keep going, no matter what happens. Most people aren't as lucky as I am, she says, to come from such hardy stock.

❦

"SHE WAS FINE until the fever," Mother tells Dr. Heald as I sit on the examining table in his Cushing office. "Now she can barely walk."

He pokes and prods, draws blood, takes my temperature. "Let's see here," he says, grasping my legs. He probes my skin with his fingers, feeling his way down my legs to the bones in my feet. "Yes," he murmurs, "irregularities. Interesting." Grasping my ankles, he tells my mother, "It's hard to say. The feet are deformed. I suspect it's viral. I recommend braces. No guarantee they'll work, but probably worth a try."

My mother presses her lips together. "What's the alternative?"

Dr. Heald winces in an exaggerated way, as if this is as hard for him to say as it is for us to hear. "Well, that's the thing. I don't think there is one."

The braces Dr. Heald puts me in clamp my legs like a medieval torture device, tearing my skin into bloody strips and making me howl in pain. After a week of this, Mother takes me back to Dr. Heald and he removes them. She gasps when she sees my legs, covered with red festering wounds. To this day I bear the scars.

For the rest of my life, I will be wary of doctors. When Dr. Heald comes to the house to check on Mamey or Mother's pregnancy or Papa's cough, I make myself scarce, hiding in the attic, the barn, the four-hole privy in the shed.

❧

ON THE PINE boards of the kitchen floor I practice walking in a straight line.

"One foot in front of the next, like a tightrope walker," my mother instructs, "along the seam."

It's hard to keep my balance; I can only walk on the outsides of my feet. If this really were a tightrope in the circus, Al points out, I would have fallen to my death a dozen times already.

"Steady, now," Mother says. "It's not a race."

"It is a race," Al says. On a parallel seam he steps lightly in a precise choreography of small stockinged feet, and within moments is at the end. He throws up his arms. "I win!"

I pretend to stumble, and as I fall I kick his legs out from under him and he lands hard on his tailbone. "Get out of her way, Alvaro," Mother scolds. Sprawling on the floor, he glowers at me. I glower back. Al is thin and strong, like a strip of steel or the trunk of a sapling. He is naughtier than I am, stealing eggs from the hens and attempting to ride the cows. I feel a pit of something hard and spiky in my stomach. Jealousy. Resentment. And something else: the unexpected pleasure of revenge.

I fall so often that Mother sews cotton pads for my elbows and knees. No matter how much I practice, I can't get my legs to move the way they should. But eventually they're strong enough that I can play hide-and-seek in the barn and chase chickens in the yard. Al doesn't care about my limp. He tugs at me to come with him, climb trees, ride Dandy the old brown mule, scrounge for firewood for a clambake. Mother's always scolding and shushing him to go away, give me peace, but Mamey is silent. She thinks it's good for me, I can tell.

I WAKE IN the dark to the sound of rain drumming the roof and a commotion in my parents' bedroom. Mother groaning, Mamey murmuring. My father's voice and two others I don't recognize in the foyer downstairs. I slip out of bed and into my woolen skirt and thick socks and cling to the rail as I half fall, half slide down the stairs. At the bottom my father is standing with a stout red-faced woman wearing a kerchief over her frizzy hair.

"Go back to bed, Christina," Papa says. "It's the middle of the night."

"Babies pay no attention to the clock," the woman sing-songs. She shrugs off her coat and hands it to my father. I cling to the banister while she lumbers like a badger up the narrow stairs.

I creep up after her and push open the door to Mother's bedroom. Mamey is there, leaning over the bed. I can't see much on the high mahogany four-poster, but I hear Mother moaning.

Mamey turns. "Oh, child," she says with dismay. "This is no place for you."

"It's all right. A girl needs to learn the ways of the world sooner or later," the badger says. She jerks her head at me.

"Why don't you make yourself useful? Tell your father to heat water on the stove."

I look at Mother, thrashing and writhing. "Is she going to be all right?"

The badger scowls. "Your mother is fine and dandy. Did you hear what I said? Boiling water. Baby is on the way."

I make my way down to the kitchen and tell Papa, who puts a pot of water on the black iron Glenwood range. As we wait in the kitchen he teaches me card games, Blackjack and Crazy Eights, to pass the time. The sound of the wind driving rain against the house is like dry beans in a hollow stick. Before morning is over, we hear the high-pitched cry of a healthy baby.

"His name is Samuel," Mother says when I climb onto the bed beside her. "Isn't he perfect?"

"Um-hmm," I say, though I think the baby looks as crab apple–faced as the badger.

"Maybe he'll be an explorer like his grandfather Samuel," Mamey says. "Like all of the seafaring Samuels."

"God forbid," Mother says.

"WHO ARE THE seafaring Samuels?" I ask Mamey later, when Mother and the baby are napping and we're alone in the Shell Room.

"They're your ancestors. The reason you're here," she says.

She tells me the story of how, in 1743, three men from Massachusetts—two brothers, Samuel and William Hathorn, and William's son Alexander—packed their belongings into three carriages for the long journey to the province of Maine in the middle of winter. They arrived at a remote peninsula that for two thousand years had been a meeting ground for Indian tribes and built a tent made of animal skins, sturdy enough to withstand the coming months of snow and ice and muddy thaw. Within a year they felled a swath of forest and built three log cabins. And they gave this spit of land in Cushing, Maine, a name: Hathorn Point.

Fifty years later, Alexander's son Samuel, a sea captain, built a two-story wood-frame house on the foundation of the family's cabin. Samuel married twice, raised six children in the house, and died in his seventies. His son Aaron, also a sea captain, married twice and raised eight children here. When Aaron died and his widow decided to sell the house (opting for a simpler life in town, closer to the bakery and the dry goods store), the seafaring Hathorns were dismayed. Five years later Aaron's son Samuel IV bought the house back, reestablishing the family's hold on the land.

Samuel IV was my grandfather.

All of those sea captains, coming and going for months at a time. Their many wives and children, up and down the narrow stairs. To this day, Mamey says, this old house on Hathorn Point is filled with their ghosts.

WHEN YOUR WORLD is small, you learn every inch of it. You can trace it in the dark; you navigate it in your sleep. Fields of rough grass sloping toward the rocky shore and the sea beyond, nooks and crannies to hide and play in. The soot-black range, always warm, in the kitchen. Geraniums on the windowsill, splayed red like a magician's handkerchief. Feral cats in the barn. Air that smells of pine and seaweed, of chicken roasting in the oven and freshly plowed soil.

One summer afternoon Mother looks at the tide chart in the kitchen and says, "Put on your shoes, Christina, I've got something to show you."

I lace up my brown brogues and follow her down through the field, past the humming cicadas and the swooping crows, and into the family cemetery, my legs steady enough that I can almost keep up. I trail my fingers across the moss-mottled, half-crumbled headstones, their etchings hard to read. The oldest one belongs to Joanne Smalley Hathorn. She died in 1834, when she was thirty-three, the mother of seven young children. When she was dying, Mother tells me, she begged her husband to bury her on the property instead of in the town cemetery several miles away so their children could visit her grave.

Her children were buried here too. All the Hathorns after her are buried here.

We continue to the shore on the southern side of Hathorn Point, above Kissing Cove and Maple Juice Cove, where the estuary of the St. George River flows into Muscongus Bay and the Atlantic Ocean beyond. There's an ancient heap of shells here that Mother says was left by Abenaki Indians who spent long-ago summers on the point. I try to envision what it would've been like here before this house was built, before the three log cabins, before any settlers discovered it. I imagine an Abenaki girl, like me, scouring the rocky shore for shells. From the point you can see way out to sea. Did she keep one eye on the horizon, scanning it for intruders? Did she have any idea how much her life would change when they arrived?

The tide is low. I stumble on the rocks, but Mother doesn't say anything, just stops and waits. Across the muddy flats is Little Island, an acre-wide wilderness of birches and dry grass. She points to it. "We're going there. But we can't stay long, or the tide will strand us." Our path is an obstacle course of seaweed-slick stones. I pick my way along slowly, and even so I trip and fall, scraping my hand on a cluster of barnacles. My feet are damp inside my shoes. Mother glances back at me. "Get up. We're nearly there." When we reach the island, she spreads a wool blanket on the beach where it's dry. Out of her rucksack she takes an egg sandwich on thick-sliced bread, a cucumber, two pieces of fried apple cake. She hands me half the sandwich. "Close your eyes and feel the sun," she says, and I do, leaning back on my elbows, chin toward sky. Eyelids warm and yellow. Trees rustling behind us like starch-stiff skirts. Briny air. "Why would you want to be anywhere else?"

After we eat, we collect shells—pale green anemone puffs and iridescent purple mussels. "Look," Mother says, pointing at a crab emerging from a tide pool, picking its way across the rocks. "All of life is here, in this place." In her own way, she is always trying to teach me something.

TO LIVE ON a farm is to wage an ongoing war with the elements, Mother says. We have to push back against the unruly outdoors to keep chaos at bay. Farmers work in the soil with mules and cows and pigs, and the house must be a sanctuary. If it isn't, we are no better than the animals.

Mother is in constant motion—sweeping, mopping, scouring, baking, wiping, washing, hanging out sheets. She makes bread in the morning using yeast from the hop vine behind the shed. There's always a pot of porridge on the back of the range by the time I come downstairs, with a filmy skin on top that I poke through and feed to the cat when she isn't looking. Sometimes dry oatcakes and boiled eggs. Baby Sam sleeps in a cradle in the corner. When the breakfast dishes are cleared, she starts on the large midday meal: chicken pie or pot roast or fish stew; mashed or boiled potatoes; peas or carrots, fresh or canned, depending on the season. What's left over reappears at supper, transformed into a casserole or a stew.

Mother sings while she works. Her favorite song, "Red Wing," is about an Indian maiden pining for a brave who's gone to battle, growing more despondent as time passes. Tragically, her true love is killed:

Now, the moon shines tonight on pretty Red Wing
The breeze is sighing, the night bird's crying,
For afar 'neath his star her brave is sleeping,
While Red Wing's weeping her heart away.

It's hard for me to understand why Mother likes such a sad song. Mrs. Crowley, my teacher at the Wing School Number 4 in Cushing, says that the Greeks believed witnessing pain in art makes you feel better about your own life. But when I mention this to Mother, she shrugs. "I just like the melody. It makes the housework go faster."

As soon as I'm tall enough to reach the dining room table, my job is to set it. Mother teaches me how with the heavy silver-plate cutlery:

"Fork on the left. L-E-F-T. Four letters, same as 'fork.' F-O-R-K," she says as she shows me, setting the fork beside the plate in its proper place. "Knife and spoon on the right. Five letters. R-I-G-H-T, same as 'knife' and 'spoon.' K-N-I-F-E."

"S-P-O-O-N," I say.

"Yes."

"And glass. G-L-A-S-S. Right?"

"What a clever one!" Mamey calls from the kitchen.

By the time I'm seven I can strip thin ribbons of skin from potatoes with a knife, scrub the pine floors with bleach on my hands and knees, tend the hop vine behind the shed, culling yeast to make bread. Mother shows me how to sew and mend, and though my unruly fingers make it hard to thread a needle, I'm determined. I try again and again, pricking my forefinger, fraying the tip of the thread. "I've never seen such determination," Mamey exclaims, but Mother doesn't say a word until I've succeeded in threading it. Then she says, "Christina, you are nothing if not tenacious."

MAMEY DOESN'T SHARE Mother's fear of dirt. What's the worst that can happen if dust collects in the corners or we leave dishes in the sink? Her favorite things are timeworn: the old Glenwood range, the rocking chair by the window with the fraying cane seat, the handsaw with a broken handle in a corner of the kitchen. Each one of them, she says, with its own story to tell.

Mamey runs her fingers along the shells on the mantelpiece in the Shell Room like an archaeologist uncovering a ruin that springs to life with all the knowledge she holds about it. The shells she discovered in her son Alvaro's sea chest have pride of place here, alongside her black travel-battered bible. Pastel-colored shells of all shapes and sizes line the edges of the floor and the window ledges. Shell-encrusted vases, statues, tintypes, valentines, book covers; miniature views of the family homestead on scallop shells, painted by a long-ago relative; even a shell-framed engraving of President Lincoln.

She hands me her prized shell, the one she found near a coral reef on a beach in Madagascar. It's surprisingly heavy, about eight inches long, silky smooth, with a rust-and-white zebra stripe on top that melts into a creamy white bottom. "It's called a chambered nautilus," she says. "'Nautilus' is Greek for 'sailor.'" She tells me about a poem in which a man finds a broken shell like this one on the shore. Noticing the spiral chambers enlarging in size, he imagines the mollusk inside getting larger and larger, outgrowing one space and moving on to the next.

"'Build thee more stately mansions, O my soul / As the swift seasons roll!'" Mamey recites, spreading her hands in the air. "'Till thou at length art free, / Leaving thine outgrown shell by life's unresting sea.' It's about human nature, you see. You can live for a long time inside the shell you were born in. But one day it'll become too small."

"Then what?" I ask.

"Well, then you'll have to find a larger shell to live in."

I consider this for a moment. "What if it's too small but you still want to live there?"

She sighs. "Gracious, child, what a question. I suppose you'll either have to be brave and find a new home or you'll have to live inside a broken shell."

Mamey shows me how to decorate book covers and vases with tiny shells, overlapping them so they cascade down in a precise flat line. As we glue the shells she reminisces about my grandfather's bravery and adventurousness, how he outsmarted pirates and survived tidal waves and shipwrecks. She tells me again about the flag she made out of strips of cloth when all hope was lost, and the miraculous sight of that faraway freighter that came to their rescue.

"Don't fill the girl's head with those tall tales," Mother scolds, overhearing us from the pantry.

"They're not tall tales, they're real life. You know, you were there."

Mother comes to the door. "You make it all sound grand, when you know it was miserable most of the time."

"It *was* grand," Mamey says. "This girl may never go anywhere. She should at least know that adventure is in her bones."

When Mother leaves the room, shutting the door behind her, Mamey sighs. She says she can't believe she raised a child who traveled all over the world but has been content ever since to let the world come to her. She says Mother would've been a spinster if Papa hadn't walked up the hill and given her an alternative.

I know some of the story. That my mother was the only surviving child and that she clung close to home. After my grandfather retired from the sea, he and Mamey decided to turn their house into a summertime inn for the income, the distraction from grief. They added a third floor with dormers, creating four more bedrooms in the now sixteen-room house, and placed ads in newspapers all along the eastern seaboard. Drawn by word of mouth about the charming inn and its postcard view, visitors streamed north. In the 1880s a whole family could lodge at Hathorn House for $12 a week, including meals.

The inn was a lot of work, more than any of them anticipated, and my mother was needed to help run it. As the years passed, the few eligible bachelors in Cushing married or moved away. By the time she was in her mid-thirties she was well past the point, she thought—everyone thought—of meeting a man and falling in love. She would live in this house and take care of her parents until they were buried in the family plot between the house and the sea.

"There's an old expression," Mamey tells me. "'Daughtering out.' Do you know what it means?"

I shake my head.

"It means no male heirs survived to carry on the family name. Your mother is the last of the Cushing Hathorns. When she dies, the Hathorn name will die with her."

"There's still Hathorn Point."

"Yes, that's true. But this is no longer Hathorn House, is it? Now it's the Olson House. Named for a Swedish sailor six years younger than your mother."

My mind is reeling. "Wait—Papa is younger than Mother?"

"You didn't know that?" When I shake my head again, Mamey laughs. "There's a lot you don't know, child. Johan Olauson was his name then." I mouth the strange words: Yo-han Oh-laow-sun. "Barely spoke a word of English. He was a deckhand on a schooner captained by John Maloney, who lives in that little house down yonder with his wife," she says, gesturing toward the window. "You know who I'm talking about?"

I nod. The captain is a friendly man with a bushy gray mustache and yellow-corn teeth and his wife is a ruddy, broad-faced woman with a bosom that seems of a piece with her middle. I've seen his boat in the cove: The Silver Spray.

"Well, it was February. Eighteen ninety—a bad winter. Endless. They were on their way to Thomaston from New York, delivering fuel wood and coal to lime kilns up there. But when they reached Muscongus Bay and dropped anchor, a storm swept in. It was so cold that ice grew around the ship in the night. There was nothing they could do; they were stranded. After a few days, when the ice was thick enough, they got out and walked across it to shore. This shore. Your father had nowhere to go, so he stayed with Maloney and his wife until the thaw."

"How long was that?"

"Oh, months."

"And the boat was just out there in the ice the whole time?"

"All winter long," she says. "You could see it from this window." She lifts her chin toward the pantry. I can faintly hear the clatter of dishes on the other side of the door. "Well, there he was, in that little cottage all winter, down near the cove, with a clear view of this house up the hill. He must've been bored to death. But he'd learned how to knit in Sweden. He made that blue wool blanket in the parlor while he was staying with them, did you know that?"

"No."

"He did, sitting around the hearth with the Maloneys every night. Anyway, you know how people are: they talk, they tell stories—and oh, those Maloneys like to gossip. They would've told him, no doubt, about how this house was on the verge of daughtering out, and that if Katie married, her husband would inherit the whole thing. I don't know for sure, of course; I can only guess what was said. But he'd been here just a week when he decided he was going to learn English. He walked into town and asked Mrs. Crowley at the Wing School to teach him."

"*My* teacher, Mrs. Crowley?"

"Yes, she was the teacher even then. He went to the schoolhouse every day for lessons. And before the ice thawed, he'd changed his name to John Olson. Then, one day, he made his way up through the field to this house and knocked on the front door, and your mother answered. And that was it. Within a year Captain Sam died and your parents were married. Hathorn House became the Olson House. All of this"—she raises her arms in the air like a music conductor—"was his."

I picture my father sitting with the Maloneys in their cozy cottage, knitting that blanket while they regale him with stories about the white house in the distance: how three Hathorns bestowed their new name on this spit of land, and one built this very house . . . the spinster daughter who lives there now with her parents, their three sons dead, no heir to carry on the family name . . .

"Do you think Papa was . . . in love with Mother?" I ask.

Mamey pats my hand. "I don't know. I really don't. But here's the truth, Christina. There are many ways to love and be loved. Whatever led your father here, this is his life now."

I WANT MORE than anything for Papa to be proud of me, but he has little reason. For one thing, I am a girl. Even worse—I know this already, though no one's ever actually said it to me—I am not beautiful. When no one is around, I sometimes inspect my features in a small cloudy fragment of mirror that's propped against the windowsill in the pantry. Small gray eyes, one bigger than the other; a long pointy nose; thin lips. "It was your mother's beauty that drew me," Papa always says, and though I know now that's only part of the story, there's no question that she is beautiful. High cheekbones, elegant neck, narrow hands and fingers. In her presence I feel ungainly, a waddling duck to her swan.

On top of that, there's my infirmity. When we're around other people, Papa is tense and irritable, afraid that I'll stumble, knock into someone, embarrass him. My lack of grace annoys him. He is always muttering about a cure. He thinks I should've kept the leg braces on; the pain, he says, would've been worth it. But he has no idea what it was like. I would rather suffer for the rest of my life with twisted legs than endure such agony again.

His shame makes me defiant. I don't care that I make him uncomfortable. Mother says it would be better if I weren't so willful and proud. But my pride is all I have.

One afternoon when I am in the kitchen, shelling peas, I hear my parents talking in the foyer. "Will she have to stay there alone?" Mother asks, her voice threaded with worry. "She's only seven years old, John."

"I don't know."

"What will they do to her?"

"We won't know until she's looked at," Papa says.

A finger of fear runs down my back.

"How will we afford it?"

"I'll sell a cow, if I must."

I hobble toward them from the pantry. "I don't want to go."

"You don't even know what—" Papa starts.

"Dr. Heald already tried. There's nothing they can do."

He sighs. "I know you're afraid, Christina, but you have to be brave."

"I'm not going."

"That's enough. It's not up to you," Mother snaps. "You'll do as you're told."

The next morning, as dawn is beginning to seep through the windows, I feel a rough push on my shoulder, a shake. It takes a moment to focus, and then I am staring into my father's eyes.

"Get dressed," he says. "It's time."

I feel the soft shifting weight and dull warmth of the hot water bottle against my feet, like the belly of a puppy. "I don't want to, Papa."

"It's arranged. You know that. You're coming with me," he says in a firm quiet voice.

It's cold and still mostly dark when Papa lifts me into the buggy. He wraps the blue wool blanket he knitted around me and then two more, adjusts a cushion behind my head. The buggy smells of old leather and damp horse. Papa's favorite stallion, Blackie, stamps and whinnies, tossing his long mane, as Papa adjusts his harness.

Papa climbs into the driver's seat, lights his pipe and flicks the reins, and we set off down the hard-packed dirt road, the buggy squeaking as we go. The jostling hurts my joints, but soon enough I adjust to the rhythm, drifting to sleep to the lulling sound, *clomp clomp clomp,* opening my eyes some time later to the cold yellow light of a spring morning. The road is muddy; melting snow has created streams and tributaries. Hardy clusters of crocuses, purple and pink and white, sprout here and there in slush-stained fields. In three hours on the road, we pass only a few people. A stray dog emerges from the woods to trot alongside us for a while, then falls back. Now and then Papa turns around to check on me. I glare at him from my nest of blankets.

Eventually he says, over his shoulder, "This doctor is an expert. I got his name from Dr. Heald. He says he will do only a few tests."

"How long will we be there?"

"I don't know."

"More than one day?"

"I don't know."

"Will he cut me open?"

He glances back at me. "I don't know. No point worrying about that."

The blankets are scratchy against my skin. My stomach feels hollow. "Will you stay with me?"

Papa takes the pipe out of his mouth, tamps it with a finger. Puts it back in and takes a puff. Blackie clip-clops through the mud and we lurch forward.

"Will you?" I insist.

He doesn't answer and doesn't look back again.

It takes six hours to reach Rockland. We eat hard-boiled eggs and currant bread and stop once to rest the horse and relieve ourselves in the woods. The closer we get, the more panicked I become. By the time we arrive, Blackie's back is foamy with sweat. Though it's cold, I'm sweating too. Papa lifts me out of the buggy and sets me down, ties up the horse and attaches its feed bag. He leads me down the street by one hand, holding the address of the doctor in the other.

I am woozy, trembling with fear. "Please don't make me, Papa."

"This doctor could make you well."

"I'm all right the way I am. I don't mind it."

"Do you not want to run and play, like other children?"

"I do run and play."

"It's getting worse."

"I don't care."

"Stop it, Christina. Your mother and I know what's best for you."

"No, you don't!"

"How dare you speak to me with this disrespect?" he hisses, then quickly glances around to see if anyone noticed. I know how much he dreads making a scene.

But I can't help it; I'm crying now. "I'm sorry, Papa. I'm sorry. Don't make me go. Please."

"We are trying to make you better!" he says in a violent whisper. "What are you so afraid of?"

Like a slight tidal pull that presages the onset of a huge wave, my childish protests and rebellions have been only a hint of the feelings that well inside me now. What am I so afraid of? That I'll be treated like a specimen, poked and prodded again, to no end. That the doctor will torture me with racks and braces and splints. That his medical experiments will leave me worse, not better. That Papa will leave and the doctor will keep me here forever, and I'll never be allowed to go home.

That if it doesn't work, Papa will be even more disappointed in me.

"I won't go! You can't make me!" I wail, wrenching away from him and running down the street.

"You are a mulish, pigheaded girl!" he yells bitterly after me.

I hide in an alley behind a barrel that smells of fish, crouching in the dirty slush. Before long my hands are red and numb, and my cheeks are stinging. Every now and then I see Papa stride by, looking for me. One time he stops on the sidewalk and cranes his neck, peering into the dimness, but then he grunts and moves on. After an hour or so, I can't take the bitter cold any longer. Dragging my feet, I make my way back to the buggy. Papa is sitting in the driver's seat, smoking his pipe, the blue wool blanket around his shoulders.

He looks down at me, a grim expression on his face. "Are you ready to go to the doctor?"

I stare back at him. "No."

My father is stern, but he has little tolerance for public displays. I know this about him, in the way you learn to identify the weak parts of the people you live with. He shakes his head, sucking on his pipe. After a few minutes, he turns abruptly, without a word, and jumps down from the buggy. He lifts me into the back, tightens Blackie's harness, and climbs back into the driver's seat. For the entire six-hour ride home he is silent. I gaze at the stark line of the horizon, as severe as a charcoal slash on white paper, the steely sky, a dark spray of crows rising into the air. Bare blue trees just beginning to bud. Everything is ghostly, scrubbed of color, even my hands, marbled like a statue.

When we arrive home, after dark, Mother meets us in the foyer, baby Sam on her hip. "What did they say?" she asks eagerly. "Can they help?"

Papa removes his hat and unwraps his scarf. Mother looks from him to me. I stare at the floor.

"The girl refused."

"What?"

"She refused. There was nothing I could do."

Mother's back stiffens. "I don't understand. You didn't take her to the doctor?"

"She wouldn't go."

"She wouldn't go?" Her voice rises. "*She wouldn't go?* She is a child."

Papa pushes past her, removing his coat as he walks. Sam starts to whimper. "It's her life, Katie."

"Her life," my mother spits. "You are her parent!"

"She threw a terrible scene. I could not make her."

Suddenly she turns to me. "You foolish girl. You have wasted your father's day and risked your entire future. You are going to be a cripple for the rest of your life. Are you happy about that?"

Sam is starting to cry. Miserably I shake my head.

Mother hands the squalling baby to Papa, who bounces him awkwardly in his arms. Crouching down in front of me, she shakes her finger. "You are your own worst enemy, young lady. And you are a coward. It is senseless to mistake fear for bravery." Her warm breath is yeasty on my face. "I feel sorry for you. But that's it. We are done trying to help you. It's your life, as your poor father said."

AFTER THIS, WHEN I wake in the morning, I spread my fingers, working out the stiffness that creeps in overnight. I point my toes, feeling the crimp in my ankles, my calves, the dull sore ache behind my knees. The pain in my joints is like a needy pet that won't leave me alone. But I can't complain. I've forfeited that right.

MY LETTER TO THE WORLD

1940

It's not long before Andy is at the door again. Awkwardly lugging a tripod, sketchbook under one arm, paintbrush like a bit between his teeth. "Would you mind if I set up my easel somewhere out of the way?" he asks, dumping his supplies in the doorway.

"You mean . . . in the house?"

He nods his chin toward the stairs. "I was thinking upstairs. If you're okay with it."

I'm a little shocked at his nerve. Who shows up unannounced at a virtual stranger's house and practically asks to move in? "Well, I . . ."

"I promise to be quiet. You'll hardly know I'm here."

Nobody's been upstairs in years. There are a lot of empty bedrooms. And the truth is, I wouldn't mind the company.

I nod.

"Well, good," he says with a grin. He gathers his supplies. "I'll try to stay out of the way of the witches."

His footsteps are loud as he thumps up the stairs to the second floor. He sets up his easel in the southeast bedroom, the one that once was mine. From the window he can watch the steamers pull away from Port Clyde, heading to Monhegan and the open sea.

Through the floorboards I hear him muttering, tapping his foot. Humming.

Hours later he comes downstairs with paint-stained fingers, the corner of his mouth purple from sticking a brush in it. "The witches and I are cohabiting just fine," he says.

BETSY COMES AND goes. Like us, she knows better than to interrupt Andy while he's working. But unlike us, she has a hard time sitting still. She gets a towel and a bucket of water and washes the dusty windows; she helps me feed the wet laundry through the wringer and hang it on the line. Donning one of my old aprons, she crouches in the dirt and plants a row of lettuce seeds in the vegetable garden.

On warm evenings, when Andy has finished for the day, Betsy shows up with a basket and we picnic down by the grove, where Papa built a fire pit long ago and wedged boards between tree trunks for seats. Al and I watch Betsy and Andy collect driftwood and twigs to make a fire in the circle of rocks. From the campfire, the fields that separate us from the house in the distance look like sand.

One rainy morning Betsy shows up at the door, car keys in hand, and says, "Now, madam, it's your day. Where to?"

I'm not sure I want a day, especially if it means I have to gussy myself up. Looking down at my old housedress, the socks bunched around my ankles, I say, "How about a cup of tea?"

"That would be lovely. When we get back. I want to take you on an adventure, Christina." She strides over to the range and lifts the blue teakettle, inspecting the bottom. "Aha. I thought as much. This old thing is on the verge of rusting through. Let's get you a new one."

"It doesn't even leak, Bets. It works just fine."

She laughs. "This whole house could fall down around your ears and you'd still say it's just fine." She points at my shoe. "Just look at how worn that heel is. And have you seen the moth holes in Al's cap? Come on, my dear. I'm taking you to the department store in Rockland. Senter Crane. They have everything. And don't worry, I'm buying."

I suppose, in some abstract way, I'd noticed the rust on the teakettle. And the shaved heel of my old shoe, and the holes in Al's cap. These things don't bother me. They make me feel comfortable, like a bird in a nest feathered with scraps. But I know that Betsy means well. And truth be told, she seems to need a project. "All right," I relent. "I'll come."

Betsy and Al help me into the station wagon in the drizzle and get me comfortably situated, and then we set off down the long drive to Rockland, half an hour away. At the first stop sign she reaches over and pats my knee. "See? Isn't this fun?"

"It makes you happy, doesn't it, Bets?"

"I like to be busy," she says. "And useful. I think those are pretty basic human desires—don't you?"

I have to ponder this for a minute. Do I? "Well, I used to think so. Now I'm not so sure."

"Idle hands . . ." she says.

"The devil's playground. Is that what you think?"

She laughs. "My Puritan ancestors certainly did."

"Mine too. But maybe they had it wrong." I gaze out the windshield at the fat raindrops that land on the glass only to be whisked away by the wipers.

Betsy glances at me sideways and purses her lips, as if she wants to say something. But instead, with a slight tilt of her chin, she looks back at the road.

OVER LUNCH ONE day—split pea soup with ham, on a blanket in the grass—Betsy tells Al and me that Andy's father doesn't approve of her. He objected to their engagement, warning Andy that marriage would be a distraction and babies even worse. But she doesn't care, she says. She finds N. C. arrogant, bullying, presumptuous. She thinks his colors are gaudy and his characters cartoonish, calculated for the marketplace. "Billboards for Cream of Wheat and Coca-Cola," she says disdainfully.

While she's talking I watch Andy's face. He's gazing at her with a bemused expression. He doesn't nod, but he doesn't protest either.

Betsy tells us that Andy needs to differentiate himself from his father. Take himself more seriously. Push himself harder. Take risks. She thinks he should limit his palette to starker colors, simplify the composition of his images, sharpen his tone. "You're capable of it," she tells him, putting her hand on his shoulder. "You don't even know your own power yet."

"Oh, please, Betsy. I'm just dabbling. I'm going to be a doctor," Andy says.

She rolls her eyes at Al and me. "He just had a one-man

show in Boston and won a prize. I don't know why he thinks he's going to be anything but a painter."

"I like the study of medicine."

"It's not your passion, Andy."

"You're my passion." He wraps his arms around her waist, and she laughs, shrugging him off.

"Go mix your tempera," she says.

MOST MORNINGS ANDY rows over by himself in a dory from Port Clyde, half a mile away. On the way to the house, swinging a tackle box full of paints and brushes, he ducks into the hen yard and emerges with half a dozen eggs, cradling them in one hand like juggling balls. He comes in the side door and chats with Al and me for a little while before heading upstairs.

Andy's eye is drawn to every cracked or faded implement and receptacle and tool, objects that once were used daily and now exist, like relics, to mark a way of life that has passed. Through his perspective I see familiar things anew. The pale pink wallpaper with tiny flowers. The red geraniums blooming in the window in their blue pots. The mahogany banister, the ship captain's barometer in the foyer, an earthenware crock on a shelf in the pantry, the blue pantry door scratched by a long-ago dog.

Some days Andy takes his sketch pad and tackle box to the shed, the barn, the fields. I watch from the kitchen window as he roams the property, loping unevenly down the grass to peer at the words on the headstones in the cemetery, sit on the pebbled shore, gaze at the sudsy waves. When he comes back to the house, I offer him sourdough bread from the oven, sliced ham, haddock chowder, apple skillet cake. He settles on the stoop in the open doorway, cradling a bowl in one hand, and I sit in my chair, and we talk about our lives.

He's the youngest of five, he tells me, with three doting sisters. A twisted right leg and a faulty hip kept him from walking properly as a child, from taking part in sports; you've probably noticed my limp? He was plagued with chest infections. His father was his only teacher. Kept him out of school, apprenticed in his studio. Taught him all about the history of art, how to mix paints and stretch canvases. "I was never like the other kids. Didn't fit in. I was an oddball. A misfit."

No wonder we get along, I think.

"Betsy's told me a lot about you and Al," Andy continues. "How Al chops firewood for everybody on the road. And you make dresses for ladies in town, and even quilts." He points to the tiny flowers on my sleeve. "Did you embroider these?"

"Yes. Forget-me-nots," I add, because it's a little hard to tell.

"Interesting, isn't it, what the mind is capable of," he muses, stretching out his hand and flexing his fingers. "How the body can adapt if your mind refuses to be bowed. Those intricate stitches on the pillowcases you gave us, and here on this blouse . . . It's hard to believe your fingers can do the work, but they can because you will them to." He takes his empty bowl to the counter, swipes a slice of apple cake from the skillet. "You're like me. You get on with it. I admire that."

⁊

IN SKETCH AFTER sketch Andy focuses on the house. Silhouetted against the sky, a blot of smoke rising from a chimney.
Viewed from a drainpipe, the cove, the eye of a seagull overhead. Alone on the hill or surrounded by trees. As large as a
castle, as small as a child's playhouse. Outbuildings appear, dis-
appear. But there are constants: field, house, horizon, sky.

Field, house, horizon, sky.

"Why do you draw the house so much?" I ask him one day
when we're sitting in the kitchen.

"Oh, I don't know," he says, shifting on the stoop. He
stares into space for a moment, drumming his fingers on the
floor. "I'm trying to capture . . . something. The feel of this
place, not the place itself, exactly. D. H. Lawrence—he was a
writer, but also a painter—wrote this line: 'Close to the body
of things, there can be heard the stir that makes us and de-
stroys us.' I want to do that—get close to the body of things.
As close as I can. That means going back to the same material
again and again, digging deeper every time." He laughs, rubbing a hand through his hair. "I sound like a crazy person,
don't I?"

"I just think it would get boring."

"I know, you'd think it would." He shakes his head. "People
say I'm a realist, but truthfully my paintings are never quite . . .
real. I take away what I don't like and put myself in its place."

"What do you mean, yourself?"

"That's my little secret, Christina," he says. "I am always painting myself."

THERE'S A SINGLE bed with a rusty creaking frame—my old bed—in the room upstairs where Andy has set up his easel. When Al finishes his chores in the afternoon, he often goes up there and watches Andy paint for a while before drifting off for a nap.

One day, offhandedly, chatting in the doorway with Al and me before heading upstairs, Andy mentions that he doesn't like being observed. He wants to work in private.

"I'll stop coming up, then," Al says.

"Oh, no, that's not what I'm talking about," Andy says. "I like it when you're there."

"But he's watching," I say. "We're both watching."

Andy laughs, shaking his head. "It's different with you two."

"He's himself around you," Betsy says when I relay this conversation to her. "Because you and Al don't need anything from him. You let him do what he wants."

"It's our entertainment," I tell her. "Not much happens around here, you know."

And it's true. For so long this house was filled to the dormers. I used to wake every morning to a cacophony of sounds coming through the walls and the floorboards: Papa's booming voice, the boys pounding up and down the stairs, Mamey scolding them to slow down, the barking dog and crowing rooster. Then it got so quiet. But now I wake in the morning and think: *Andy is coming today.* The day is transformed, and he hasn't even gotten here yet.

On winter afternoons, when the sun goes down by 3:30 and wind howls through the cracks, we huddle near the woodstove wrapped in blankets, drinking warm milk and tea in the dim light of a whale-oil lamp. Papa shows Al and Sam and me how to make the knots he learned as a sailor: an overhand bow, a clove hitch, a sheet-bend double, a lark's head, a lariat loop. He hands us wooden needles and tries to show us how to knit (though the boys scoff, refusing to learn). He teaches us to whittle whistles and small boats out of wood. We line them up on the mantelpiece, and when the weather warms, we take these boats down to the bay to see whose sails best. I watch my tall, large-limbed father, his blond shaggy head bowed over his miniature boat, muttering to himself in Swedish, coaxing the vessel along in the choppy water. Mamey told me that several months before I was born, Papa's brother Berndt sailed over from Gothenburg to spend the winter here, and the two of them built a crib for me and painted it white. Berndt is the only Olauson who has ever visited us.

On a low shelf in the Shell Room, behind a giant conch, I discover a wooden box filled with a motley collection of objects: a whalebone comb, a horsehair toothbrush, a painted tin soldier from a long-ago children's set, a few rocks and minerals. "Whose is this?" I ask Mamey.

"Your father's."

"What are all these things?"

"You'll have to ask him."

So later that afternoon, when Papa comes in from the milking, I bring him the box. "Mamey said this is yours."

Papa shrugs. "That's nothing. I don't know why I kept it. Just bits and pieces I brought with me from Sweden."

Weighing a black lump of coal in my hand, I ask, "Why did you save this?"

He reaches for it. Rubs his fingers over its metallic ebony planes. "Anthracite," he says. "It's almost pure carbon. Made from decomposed plant and animal life from millions of years ago. I had a teacher once who taught me about rocks and minerals."

"In your village in Sweden?"

He nods. "Gällinge."

"Gällinge," I repeat. The word is strange. *Yah-lee-nyeh.* "So you kept it to remind you of home?"

He blows out a noisy breath. "Perhaps."

"Do you miss it?"

"Not really. I miss some things, I suppose."

"Like . . ."

"Oh, I don't know. A bread called *svartbröd.* With salmon and soured cream. And a fried potato cake called *raggmunk* my sister used to make. Maybe the lingonberries."

"But what about . . . your sister? And your mother?"

And that's when he tells me about the squalid, low-ceilinged two-room hut in the village of Gällinge that his family of ten shared with a cow, their surest hedge against starvation. His father, a drunkard with two moods, brooding and raging, who terrorized him and his seven younger siblings and worked occasionally at a peat farm as a day laborer when he was desperate enough. Papa's own constant stomach-churning hunger. More than once, he says, he avoided jail by eluding police on a long chase through cobbled streets after stealing a rasher of pork, a jug of maple syrup.

From an early age he knew there wasn't much of a future for him in Gällinge; no jobs, none he was qualified for even in the big city of Gothenburg, sixty miles away. Though a quick study, he paid little attention in school, knew how to read only the simplest stories. Never learned a trade. He taught himself to knit so he could help his ma, who earned a few coins making scarves and mittens and hats, but that was no job for a man, he says.

So when he heard about a trading ship bound for New York, he rose in the dark to be the first at the dock at Gothenburg Harbor.

The captain scoffed. *Fifteen years old? Too young to leave your mama.*

But Papa was determined. *She won't miss me,* he told him. *One less mouth to feed, a few more coins for the rest. Sick babies.* The youngest, his brother Sven, not even a year old, had starved to death a month before.

And so he set sail with the captain and his small crew, across and back and around the world. As months turned into years, his past began to recede. He sent money to his mother, and talked, as all the sailors did, about going home, but the more time he spent away from Gällinge, the less he missed it. He didn't miss tripping over his brothers and sisters, not to mention the cow. He didn't miss that dingy hovel with its slop pail in the corner and the rank smell of unwashed bodies. The dank confines of a ship's belly might not have been much of an improvement, but at least you could rise from its depths onto a wide deck and gaze up at a vast sky sprinkled with stars and the yolk of a moon.

IT'S SURPRISING THAT Papa knows as much as he does about farming, given that he grew up in a hovel and spent his twenties at sea. Mother says he's just a quick study at whatever he puts his mind to. He restored the inn to a family home, raises cows and sheep and chickens for milk and meat and wool and eggs. He plants corn and peas and potatoes in the rocky soil, rotating them yearly, and he set up a farm store on the property to sell them. His customers come by boat from Port Clyde and St. George and Pleasant Point, loading their dories with produce and rowing back to where they're from.

Having discovered that seaweed in the fields keeps the ground moist and the weeds down in the summer, Papa corrals Al and Sam and me to collect and distribute it. It takes two of us, our hands encased in thick cotton gloves, to steer a heavy wheelbarrow down to the water's edge at low tide. We rip the kelp from the rocks, pulling up barnacles and crabs and snails, and load the barrow with spongy green strands bubbled at the ends and flat, wide strips fluted like piecrust. The gloves are stiff and unwieldy; it's easier to grab it without them, so we take them off, rinsing our hands in ocean water to wash off the slime. Then we push the wheelbarrow up the hill to the newly furrowed field, where we grab big handfuls of cold kelp, squishing it between our fingers and scattering it down the rows. "Push it back," Papa calls from where he's hoeing. "Don't smother the plants."

Papa is always dreaming up projects to make money. His flock of sheep is growing, and though he sells wool to local people, one season he decides to box up the bulk of it and send it away to be carded and spun and dyed and sold out of state for a higher price. The following summer he constructs a fishing weir with a neighbor in the cove between Bird Point and Hathorn Point. Now that it's winter, he's decided that he will harvest freshwater ice, which can be loaded onto ships and transported easily and cheaply by steamer ship on the nearby sea-lanes to Boston and beyond. He'll store it in an icehouse Captain Sam built that has been standing empty for decades.

Like any crop, ice is delicate and mercurial; bright sun or a sudden storm can ruin it. There's no guarantee, until the ice is received in Boston, that Papa will get paid. He waits until February, when the ice on Vinal's Pond is fourteen to sixteen inches thick, and offers money to other farmers to help him clear the snow with horses and plows. Up before dawn on frigid mornings, they use a workhorse to pull the clearing scraper, a series of boards attached together to create a flat bottom that angles back about eight feet wide, and a three-foot-wide snow scraper to remove heavier, wetter ice. Several men saw through the ice with handsaws fused to long iron T-bar handles, shedding coats and scarves and hats as they warm up. It is hard work, but these men and horses are accustomed to hard work.

When a slab of ice is cut and floating, twelve inches above the syrupy water, the men hold float hooks, long poles with spiky ends, to keep the ice where they want it. After this comes the tedious work of cutting and loading these floats onto flatbed trailers behind horses that will transport them to the icehouse behind the barn. There the blocks will be stacked and stored in sawdust, some set aside to sell to locals and the rest to wait until a carrier bound for Massachusetts is ready in the cove.

The morning of the harvest, after Papa has left the house, I dress in the dark, layering sweaters and trousers over my long underwear and pulling on two pairs of socks. I meet Al in the downstairs hall and we head out into the mist, blowing our breath at each other, and make our way toward Vinal's Pond to watch the horses harnessed to plows trek back and forth on the thick ice, deepening the grooves. Snow falls softly, like flour through a sifter, accumulating in drifts.

We spot Papa in the distance, leading Blackie and the plow. He sees us too. "Stay off the ice!" he shouts. When Al and I reach the edge, we stand silently watching the men do their work. Blackie prances skittishly, tossing his head. He's a nervous horse; I've spent hours in the paddock devising routines to calm him. He's wearing the choke rope I fashioned around his neck several days ago to control him when he gets spooked.

One of the men has broken his float hook in a block of ice, and everyone is distracted, offering suggestions, when I notice that Blackie is sliding in slow motion toward the lip of the ice. All at once there's a high-pitched whinny. His eyes roll in terror as he plunges into the breath-stopping cold, flailing and churning in the water. The plow teeters on the edge. Without thinking, I run toward Papa across the ice.

"Damn it, get back!" Papa yells.

"Grab the choke rope," I call, motioning to my own neck. "Cut off his breath!"

Papa gestures to some of the men, and they join arms, elbow to elbow, Papa in the middle and several holding his belt. He leans far out over the horse's head and grasps the rope, pulling it tight. After a moment, Blackie quiets. Papa manages to pull him up onto the slab by his harness, forelegs first, then belly, and finally his powerful thick haunches. For a moment the horse stands as if frozen, front and back legs apart like a statue. Then he dips his head and shakes his mane, spraying water.

At the supper table that night Papa tells Mamey and Mother that I am the orneriest and most stubborn child he has, and the only reason he didn't wring my neck for running onto the ice is that my quick thinking probably saved Blackie's life. A drowned horse, we all know, would've been a big loss.

"I wonder where she gets that from," Mother says.

IN THE EVENINGS, once or twice a month, local farmers come by the house to drink whiskey and play cards around the dining table. Papa is different from the others, with his quiet ways and his Swedish accent, but the fact that they're all farmers and fishermen is enough of a bond. After Mother and Mamey have gone to bed, Al and I sit on the stairs, just out of sight, and listen to their stories.

The more Richard Wooten drinks, the more he rambles. "There's treasure in that Mystery Tunnel, by God, there is. One of these days, I swear, I'll get my hands on it."

Al and I are fascinated by the legend of Mystery Tunnel. According to local lore a two-hundred-foot tunnel was carved out of rock near Bird Point by early settlers as a place to hide from passing pirates and Abenaki Indians.

"I came this close. *This* close," Richard says. His voice softens, and I have to lean close to the banister to hear. "Pitch black. Not a star in the sky. I sneak down there with a lantern. I'm digging for who knows how long, hours, it's gotta be."

"How many times have you told this story, a hundred?" someone scoffs.

Richard ignores him. "And then I see it: the glint of treasure."

"You do not."

"I do, with my own eyes! And then . . ."

The men grumble and laugh. "Aw, c'mon!" "Now he's just makin' it up."

"Spit it out, Richard," Papa says.

"It disappears. Like—that." I hear the snap of his fingers. "Just as I was reaching for it. It was there and then it was gone."

"Rough luck," one of them shouts. "To treasure!"

"To treasure!"

The next evening Al and I slip out of the house with a candle nub and make our way down to Bird Point. The lip of the tunnel is dark and mysterious; our flickering candle keeps sputtering out. It's eerily silent as we creep along. About fifty feet in, fallen rocks block the path. I feel a strange relief—we probably would've dared ourselves to continue. Would we have found the buried treasure? Or would we have disappeared in the depths of the tunnel, never to be found?

Al and I take our adventures where we can find them. Several weeks later he wakes me up in the middle of the night, a finger to his lips, and whispers, "Follow me." I pull on a housedress over my nightgown and my old leather shoes over my socks and leave the snug cocoon of my bed. As soon as we're outside I see a glowing orange ball several hundred yards out in the harbor, its reflection splashed across the water. Then I realize what it is: a ship on fire.

"Been burning for hours," Al says. "A lime coaster. Headed to Thomaston, no doubt."

"Should we wake Papa?"

"Nah."

"Maybe he could help."

"A dory came ashore with a group of men a while ago. Nothing anybody can do now."

For more than an hour we sit in the grass. The freighter blazes in the dark, its destruction a thing of beauty. I gaze at Al, his face illuminated in the glow. I think about his favorite book, *Treasure Island*, about a boy who runs away to sea in search of buried treasure. Mrs. Crowley, seeing how often Al thumbed through the pages of the copy on her shelf, gave it to him when school let out for the summer. "For our seafaring Alvaro," she wrote on the inside cover in her neat handwriting. "May you embark on many adventures."

Months later, the ribs of that lime coaster are visible when the tide is low. Papa and Al row out to the wreck and strip the hull of its oak planking, and after stacking and weighting them to make them straight, they use them to rebuild the icehouse floor.

EVERY WEEKDAY AL and I walk together to the Wing School Number 4 in Cushing, a mile and a half away. With my unsteady gait it takes a long time to get there. I try to focus on my steps, but I tumble so often that my knees and elbows are constantly bruised and scraped, despite the cotton padding. The sides of my feet are tough and callused.

Al complains the whole way. "Jeez, the cows are faster than you. I could've been there and back by now."

"Go ahead, then," I tell him, but he never does.

It helps if I swing my body forward, using my arms for balance, though even that doesn't always work. When I fall, Al sighs and says, "Come on, now we're really going to be late." But when he pulls me up, he puts all his weight into it.

Sometimes we walk with two neighbor girls, Anne and Mary Connors, but only when their mother insists on it. They cluck their tongues and kick at sticks when I trip and fall behind. "Oh Lord, again?" Mary mutters, and the two of them whisper together so Al and I can't hear.

At school I wait until the cloakroom is empty before taking off my knee pads and armbands and stashing them in my lunch pail. The other kids can be mean. Leslie Brown trips me as I walk up the aisle to get a book, and I crash into Gertrude Gibbons's desk. "Watch it, clumsy," Gertrude says under her breath.

There are things I could say. Few of us at the Wing School Number 4 have picture-perfect lives. Gertrude Gibbons's mother ran off to Portland with a man who worked at the paper mill in Augusta, and never looked back. Leslie's stepfather beats him with a belt. The Connors girls have no father; he didn't go away, he was never here. It's a small town, and we know more about one another than any of us might wish.

One afternoon Al and I are sitting outdoors with our lunch pails under the shade of an elm in the schoolyard when Leslie and another boy begin to circle and taunt. "What's wrong with you? You're not normal, you know that?"

The tips of Al's ears redden, but he stays quiet. He's small and slight, no match for these rough boys with chaw in their cheeks. I don't want him to defend me anyway. I'm more than a year older than he is.

A girl in my grade, Sadie Hamm, strolls over. She's a thin, tough girl, as solid as a sunflower stalk, brown eyed, round faced, with a nimbus of curly sunflower petal hair. Putting her hands on her hips, she juts her chin out at the boys. "That's enough."

"Sadie Bacon," Leslie says with a sneer. "That's your name, right?"

"I don't think you want to play the name game with me, Leslie Brown." Turning to Al and me, Sadie says, "Okay if I join you?"

Al doesn't look too happy about it, but I pat the grass.

Sadie shares her sandwich with me, meatloaf sliced thin on bread with butter. She tells us that she lives with her two older sisters in an apartment above the drugstore, where one sister works behind the counter. She doesn't mention her parents, and I don't ask.

"Mind if I sit with you tomorrow?" she asks.

Al cuts his eyes at me. I ignore him. "Sure you can," I say.

For so long Al has been my only companion. He is as familiar to me as the walls of the kitchen or the path to the barn. It would be nice, I think, to have a friend.

ON LAND AL is shy and awkward. He doesn't talk much. In a crowd of people he acts like he wants to be somewhere, any-where, else. He doesn't know what to do with his hands, which hang like oversized gloves from his wrists. But out on the ocean, when we pull up to one of Papa's blue-and-white buoys bobbing in the water, he is purposeful and self-assured. With a quick yank on the rope he can tell how many lobsters are in the trap far below.

Al has always wanted to be a lobsterman. The summer he turns eight, Papa decides he's old enough to learn. He takes Al out in an old skiff a few afternoons a week, and sometimes I go along for the ride. We row out so far that our white house looks like a speck on the hill. It makes me nervous to be on the open ocean in the small boat—my balance is precarious enough on land. The water is deep and dark around us; the planks are rough, and saltwater pools between the ribs of the boat, pickling my bare feet and dampening the hem of my dress. I fidget and sigh, impatient to get back. But Al is in his element.

Papa hands each of us a handline. It's a simple rig, cotton line coated with linseed oil and wrapped around a piece of wood he whittled on each end to better hold the line. There's a big hook at the end and a lead weight to make it sink. He teaches us to bait the hook with chum he keeps in an old bucket covered by a board. We let our lines down slowly, and then we wait. I don't catch anything, but Al's line is magic. Is it the way he fastens his bait? The way he jigs his line, making the fish believe it's alive? Or is it something else, a serene confidence that fish will come? Half a dozen times there's an almost imperceptible tug on the line between Al's forefinger and thumb, and he in response pulls hard on the line to set his hook and then, hand over hand, hauls in a flapping haddock or cod from the depths of the sea, over the gunwales into our boat.

With the skill of a surgeon, he removes the hook from the

fish and detangles the line. He insists on rowing all the way back by himself. When we land at the dock, he holds up his palms, red and raw, and grins. He's proud of his blisters.

Within a few years Al has restored Papa's old skiff and learned how to build and rig his own traps, fashioning the bows and sills from scraps of lumber, knitting twine for the heads and using rocks as weights to sink them. The traps he builds are better than Papa's, he boasts, and he's right: they brim with lobster. He constructs a fish house behind the barn to store the lobster traps and bait barrels, boat caulking and buoys, fishing nets and nails. Before long, he has taken over the blue-and-white buoys and is selling lobster to customers in Cushing and as far away as Port Clyde.

Al can't wait to be done with book learning. He's just biding his time, he says, counting the days until he can spend every waking moment in his precious boat.

MRS. CROWLEY TOLD ME once—the nicest thing anybody has ever said to me—that I'm one of the brightest students she's ever taught. Long before the others, I have finished my reading and arithmetic. She's always giving me extra work to do and books to read. I appreciate the compliment, but maybe if I could run and play like the other kids, I would be as impatient and distracted as they are. The truth is, when I'm immersed in a book I'm less aware of the pain in my unpredictable arms and legs.

AT SCHOOL WE'RE learning about the Salem Witch Trials. Between 1692 and 1693, Mrs. Crowley tells us, 250 women were accused of witchcraft, 150 imprisoned, and 19 hanged. They could be convicted by "spectral evidence," an accuser's assertion that they appeared in ghostly form, and "witches' marks," moles or warts. Gossip, hearsay, and rumors were admitted as evidence. The chief magistrate, John Hathorne, was notoriously ruthless. He acted more like a prosecutor than an impartial judge.

"He's related to us, you know," Mamey tells me when I relay this lesson after school. The two of us are sitting by the Glenwood range in the kitchen, darning socks. "Remember those three Hathorn men who left Salem in the middle of winter? It was fifty years after the trials. They were running from the shame."

Pulling another sock out of the pile, Mamey tells me about Bridget Bishop, an innkeeper accused of stealing eggs and transforming herself into a cat. Bridget was an eccentric whose colorful clothing—a red bodice covered with lacework, in particular—was believed to be a sign of the devil. After two confessed witches testified that she was part of their coven, she was arrested, thrown into a dank cell, and fed rotten tubers and broth. It took only a few days in those conditions, Mamey says, for a respectable woman to resemble a trapped and desperate animal.

In the courtroom, in front of a jeering crowd, John Hathorne asked her, "How do you know that you are not a witch?"

She answered: "I know nothing of it."

Justice Hathorne narrowed his eyes. Lifted his index finger. When he jabbed it at her, she stepped back as if struck. "Why look you," he said. "You are taken now in a flat lie." He slammed the flat of his hand on the table in front of him—Mamey slams her hand down, demonstrating—and the accusers and spectators erupted in a frenzy.

Bridget Bishop knew it was over, Mamey says. She'd be condemned to death like the others, left to swing on Gallows Hill until someone took pity and cut down her corpse, probably in the middle of the night. Like many of the condemned she was a middle-aged loner, with a house and property that had already been confiscated. Who was there to show support for her? Who would speak to her character? No one.

Eventually the governor of Massachusetts put a stop to the proceedings. One by one the magistrates of the Superior Court recanted, expressing remorse and sorrow about their rush to judgment. John Hathorne alone was silent. He never expressed the slightest regret. Even after his death twenty-five years later—peacefully, in prosperous comfort—his reputation for cold-blooded cruelty lingered.

Mamey tells me about the curse that Bridget Bishop placed on Hathorne's descendants. Well, not a curse, exactly, but a warning, a reckoning. "You have to admire that woman," she says. "Using the only power she possessed to instill the fear of God into him! Or the fear of something. But I believe it. I think your ancestors brought the witches with them from Salem. Their spirits haunt this place."

"For goodness' sake." My mother sighs loudly in the next room. She thinks her mother fills my head with outlandish ideas. She thinks I should pay less attention to Mamey's stories and more attention to my stitches.

WHEN I ASK Papa about the curse, he says he doesn't know about that, but he does know the Hathorns were a notoriously unruly bunch. A fierce, rugged Scots-Irish clan who emigrated to New England from Northern Ireland in the 1600s, they quickly developed a reputation for sadism against their perceived enemies. "Beating Quakers, double-crossing Indians and selling them into slavery—things like that," he says.

"How do you know all this?" I ask.

"I drank some whiskey with your grandfather once, a long time ago," he says.

❧

THE SPRING OF my tenth year, Mother is heavy with child. Mamey and I are doing most of the cooking, which at the tail end of a long winter consists mostly of old root vegetables from the cellar, dried fish and meat from the smoker, stews and chowders. It's so cold and choppy on the water that Papa and Al can't go out in the dory. Sam has a hacking cough and a runny nose. The earth is soggy; if I fall on my way to school, I end up mud soiled and damp skirted all day. None of us have much to be cheerful about.

On the way home from school one wet afternoon I see Papa's buggy on the road ahead of me, a familiar badger shape with a blue bonnet on the seat beside him, and I know Miss Freeley is coming to deliver Mother's baby. When I get home, my brothers and I sit in the kitchen with Papa. Rain pummels the roof and the windows, heavy, slurry, and we can all feel the dampness in our bones. I peel off my socks and drape them over the range. Even the wood smoke from the Glenwood is damp.

The birth is uneventful. Mother is used to this by now. But after Fred is born, she is different. Slow to rise when he needs her. She hands him to Mamey and goes back to bed in the middle of the day. When Fred cries for her milk, Mother turns the other way and Mamey has to stir together cow's milk and water with a sprinkle of sugar. She puts a soapstone in the oven and wraps it in a cloth to put in his crib when he goes down for a nap, but it's no substitute for his mama, she says.

Al and I hurry home from school to take Fred from his crib and rock him in the chair, give him baths in the tin tub. (Before we bathe him he smells sour and damp, like he's been pulled out of a hole in the field. Afterward he smells like a puppy.) We all try to think of ways to cheer Mother up. Mamey makes pound cake with lemon peel, her favorite kind. Papa builds a four-drawer dresser for her linens. Blue is Mother's favorite color, so I decide I'll surprise her by painting some objects around the house a cheerful blue.

Al shakes his head when I tell him my plan. "Painting a chair is not going to help."

"I know," I say, but I hope maybe it will.

I ask Mamey's permission, knowing Papa might not approve. "Splendid," she says and hands me money for paint.

At the A. S. Fales & Sons General Store after school I pick up a gallon of the most vibrant blue on the chart, two horsehair brushes, a tin tray, and a can of turpentine, stashing it in the woods when I'm too tired to carry it all the way home. The next day, when I check the spot where I left it, it isn't there. I'm afraid someone has stolen it, but when I get to the house, it's sitting in the shed. "I still think it's a silly idea," Al says, "but I can't let you do all the work by yourself."

The wet paint is the color of the bluest feather on a bluebird, as shiny as the surface of a lake. With old rags Al and I wipe down the shed doors, the wagon rims and chassis, the sled and hayrack and geranium pots. Once we start painting, it's hard to stop. We go back to Fales for more supplies and return to paint the front and back doors, all of the wagon beds.

When we persuade Mother to come downstairs and see what we've done, she pulls Al and me into a hug.

Slowly, things improve. As the weather warms, Mother and I resume our walks to Little Island at low tide, but now we bring my brothers too. Al runs ahead through the grass; Sam piles starfish in a tide pool. We roam the pebbled beach, searching for shells and stopping for a picnic under the old spruce tree. Mother takes baby Fred out of his sling and lays him on his back on the beach, where he coos and gurgles. I sit on a rock, watching her. She seems better, I think. But now and then I see her staring off into the distance with a blank expression on her face, and it worries me.

WHEN MRS. CROWLEY COPIES a poem by Emily Dickinson on the chalkboard in her neat cursive, the muttering begins.

"Did a six-year-old write that?"

"What are those dashes? Is that proper grammar?"

"My grandpa told me she was just a strange old lady. A spinster," says Gertrude Gibbons, the class know-it-all.

"Emily Dickinson did have a quiet life," Mrs. Crowley says, tucking a strand of gray behind her ear. "A man broke her heart, and she became something of a recluse. She only wore white. Nobody even knew she was a poet; she was admired for her beautiful garden. She would sit for hours at a little desk, but nobody really knew what she was doing. After she died, a folder of her poems was discovered in a drawer. Page after page in her precise script, with very odd notations, as you can see. Hundreds and hundreds of poems."

As I copy the poem on the chalkboard into my notebook I mouth the words to myself:

> I'm Nobody! Who are you?
> Are you—Nobody—too?
> Then there's a pair of us!
> Don't tell! they'd advertise—you know!

"It doesn't even rhyme," Leslie Brown says.

"So what do you think it means?" Mrs. Crowley asks, holding the chalk in the air.

"I dunno. She feels like her life doesn't matter?"

"That's one interpretation. Christina, what do you think?"

"I think she feels like she's different from most people," I say. "And even if they find her strange, she knows she can't be the only one."

Mrs. Crowley smiles. She seems to be about to say something, then changes her mind. "A kindred spirit," she says.

After class I ask her if I can read more poems by this poet I've never heard of. Picking up a small blue hard-backed volume on her desk, she shows me that Emily Dickinson often used "common meter," alternating lines of eight and six syllables, a form more typical of hymns. That she wrote most of her poems in slant rhyme, in which the rhyming words are similar but not exact. And she employed a figure of speech called synecdoche, wherein the part stands in for the whole—"for example, here, in this poem," Mrs. Crowley says, tapping a page and reciting the words aloud: "'The Eyes around—had wrung them dry.' What do you think this refers to?"

"Um . . ." I scan the first few lines of the poem:

> I heard a Fly buzz—when I died—
> The Stillness in the Room
> Was like the Stillness in the Air—
> Between the Heaves of Storm—

"The people standing around the bed, mourning the one who died?"

Mrs. Crowley nods. She hands me the book. "If you'd like, you may take this home for the weekend."

Sitting on the front stoop of my house after school I thumb through the pages, alighting here and there:

> This is my letter to the world
> That never wrote to me—
> The simple news that Nature told—
> With tender majesty . . .

The poems are peculiar and inside out, and I'm not sure I know what they mean. I imagine Emily Dickinson in a white dress, sitting at her desk, head bent over her quill, scratching out these halting fragments. "It's all right if you don't exactly understand," Mrs. Crowley told the class. "What matters is how a poem resonates for you."

What must it have been like to capture these thoughts on paper? Like trapping fireflies, I think.

Mother, seeing me reading on the stoop, dumps a basket of air-dried sheets in my lap. "No time for lollygagging," she says under her breath.

NEAR THE END of eighth grade—the final year of Wing School Number 4, and the last year of any kind of schooling for most of us—Mrs. Crowley takes me aside during a lunch period. "Christina, I can't do this forever," she says. "Would you be interested in staying on for another few years, to get qualified to take over the school? I think you'd make an excellent teacher."

Her words make me glow with pride. But at supper that evening, when I report the conversation to Mother and Papa, I see a look pass between them. "We'll talk about it," Papa says and sends me outside to sit on the stoop.

When he calls me back in, Mother is looking at her plate. Papa says, "I'm sorry, Christina, but you've had more schooling than either of us ever did. Your mother has too much to do. We need your help around here."

My stomach plummets. I try to keep the hard edge of panic out of my voice. "But, Papa, I could go to school only in the mornings. Or stay home when I'm needed."

"Trust me, you'll learn more on this farm than you'll ever learn from a book."

"But I like going to school. I like what I'm learning."

"Book learning doesn't get the chores done."

The next day I plead my case to Mamey. Later I hear her talking to Papa in a low voice in the parlor. "Let her stay in school a few more years," she says. "What can it hurt? Teaching is a fine profession. And let's face it: There's not much else available to her."

"Katie isn't well, you know that. Christina is needed here. *You* need her here."

"We can manage," Mamey says. "If she doesn't do this now, she might end up on this farm for the rest of her life."

"Is that so intolerable? It's the life I chose."

"But that's it, John. You saw the world and then you chose it. She's never been farther than Rockland."

"And remember what a success that was? She couldn't wait to get home."

"She was young and scared."

"The wider world is no place for her."

"For pity's sake, we're not talking about the wider world. We're talking about a small town a mile and a half from here."

"My decision is made, Tryphena."

Telling Mrs. Crowley at recess the next day that I can't stay in school is one of the hardest things I've ever done. She is silent for a moment. Then she says, "You'll be fine, Christina. There will be other opportunities, no doubt." She seems a little teary. I am teary too. She has never touched me before, but now she puts her delicate hand on mine. "I want to say, Christina, that you are . . . unusual. And somehow . . ." Her voice trails off. "Your mind—your curiosity—will be your comfort."

On the last day of school, I am so full of self-pity that I can hardly speak. On my way out the door I linger in front of Mrs. Crowley's globe, ordered from a Sears, Roebuck catalog, and turn it with a finger. The ocean is robin's egg blue, with bumpy raised green and tan parts representing continents. I run my fingers over Taiwan, Tasmania, Texas. These faraway places are as real to me as the treasure buried in Mystery Tunnel. Which is to say: It's hard for me to believe they actually exist.

AFTER I LEAVE school, time stretches ahead like a long, flat road visible for miles. My routine becomes as regular as the tide. I rise before dawn to collect an armload of firewood from the shed, dump it into the bin beside the Glenwood range in the kitchen, and go back for another. Open the heavy black door of the oven, use the poker to stir the ashes, find the faint embers. Add several logs, coax the fire along with kindling, shut the door and press my cold stiff hands against it to warm them. Then I rouse my brothers from bed to feed the chickens and pigs, the horses and the mule. They grumble all the way down the stairs about who scatters the feed, mucks the stalls, collects the eggs. While the boys are in the barn I fix a pot of boiled oats with currants and raisins for their breakfast and make sandwiches of butter and molasses on thick sourdough bread, wrapped in wax paper, for their lunches; gather vegetables and apples from the cellar, a basket looped over my arm as I make my way down the rickety wooden ladder.

Al forgets a book, Sam his pail, Fred his hat. When they're finally out the door, I wash their dishes in the long cast-iron sink in the pantry. Then I start the process of baking bread, pinching off the sourdough starter I keep in the pantry, sprinkling flour over the wooden board. I make beds, empty night jars, limp to the garden to pick squash for a pie. After school, Sam and Fred help Papa in the barn and the fields and Al goes out in his boat. In the late afternoon, when the boys' other chores are done, they work on the fish weir that stretches between Little Island and Pleasant Point. Before supper they have to be reminded to wash, to take their boots off, to come to the table.

I have plenty to think about, I suppose. Will the bread rise properly if I use a different kind of flour? How many servings will one anemic chicken provide? How much money will the wool of eight sheep bring in, after adjusting for expenses? I know how to get the hens to lay more: give them extra salt, keep the henhouse windows clean to let in light, grind lobster shells into their feed. Our healthy hens produce more than our family can consume, so Al and I start selling the eggs. I spend several hours each month sewing bags out of cheesecloth to store them.

Despite my crooked hands, I am becoming a reasonable seamstress. In the afternoons I darn and patch the boys' hard-worn trousers and shirts and socks and spruce up old dresses with new collars and cuffs. Before long I am sewing all my own skirts and blouses and dresses on Mother's treadle Singer in the dining room, with its pretty red, green, and gold fleur-de-lis pattern, its rounded form like an arm bent at the elbow. From her book of patterns I learn to sew a three-panel skirt, and then one with five panels. Buttonholes are hardest; it takes my clumsy fingers ages to get them right.

Mother believes pockets on skirts are inelegant. She shows me how to sew a secret pouch into the lining so no one can see. "A lady doesn't reach into her pocket in view of others," she says.

I find her formality a little silly. It's only us here, and the boys neither notice nor care.

With no running water, we collect rain and melted snow from gutters and downspouts in the large cistern in the cellar and dredge it up using the hand pump in the pantry. Al figures out how to attach a funnel from the downspout to a hose to collect water for the cistern, making the process more efficient. When we run out of water in the cellar, I harness our mule, Dandy, to a wooden drag loaded with two empty barrels, corral one of the boys to help, and lead her to the pasture spring half a mile away to fill them. Laundry, once a week, takes at least one full day, and sometimes two. I boil water on the range and pour it from the large black pot into a wide steel tub, then scrub the laundry on a ribbed washboard and run it through a handwringer before hanging the dripping sheets and shirts and undergarments to dry. It's not easy, with my uneven balance, to pin clothes on the line outside, but I discover that I can detach the rope from the two poles on either end and pin the laundry on it while it's on the ground, then raise the line, with damp clothes hanging from it like a charm bracelet. When it's too snowy to go outside, I hang clothes in the shed. They stay damp for days; the smell of mildew lingers until spring.

I make soap when we need it by combining water with lye and adding oil, then pouring the mixture into molds and letting it dry for several days before turning the bars onto wax paper and putting them in the pantry to cure for a month. I scrub the floors with bleach and well water until my knees and knuckles are red, splotching my dress with white. With my shaky balance, even these ordinary tasks are fraught with peril. My arms and legs are marred and scarred from run-ins with boiling water, toxic bleach, poisonous lye.

When I mutter about these minor injuries, or that too much is expected of me, Al says, "We have a roof over our heads. Some people don't have that much." It helps to remember this, I guess. But it's hard to shake my sadness at having been taken out of school.

Only Mamey understands. "You inherited my curiosity, child," she says. "More's the pity."

As time goes on I find ways to make it bearable. I save three unwanted kittens and choose a runt from a neighbor's cocker spaniel litter and name him Topsy. I order seed packets and plant a flower garden like the one Emily Dickinson kept, with nasturtiums and pansies and daffodils and marigolds. A butterfly utopia, she called it. When my flowers bloom, they lure yellow-and-black monarchs, cabbage whites, teal blue swallowtails.

I find a poem I copied in my notebook:

> Two butterflies went out at Noon
> And waltzed above a Stream,
> Then stepped straight through the Firmament
> And rested on a Beam . . .
> And then together bore away
> Upon a shining Sea . . .

I imagine these butterflies traveling the world, alighting in my garden for a short time before heading off again. Dream that someday I might grow wings and follow, fluttering behind them down the field and across the water.

I try not to think about what I'd be doing if I weren't tied to the farm. Anne and Mary Connors are both continuing their studies, I hear. Anne wants to be a nurse and Mary a teacher. There's talk about her taking over from Mrs. Crowley. When I'm doing errands in Cushing and see one of them from afar, at the hardware store or the post office, I cross to the other side of the road.

WHEN I WAS a child, Mamey would whisper, "You're like me, Christina. Someday you'll explore distant lands." But she has stopped talking like this. Now she just wants me to get out of the house. Unlike my parents, who don't speak of such things, Mamey is always trying to convince me to "mingle," as she calls it. "Pity's sake, you need to be with people your own age!" she says. "Isn't there a social or a picnic you could go to?"

Al has no interest in the dances that are held on Friday evenings at the Acorn Grange Hall in Cushing, so I go with my friend Sadie Hamm. We walk along the rutted path in the semidarkness, linking arms with several other girls. Sadie always breaks the chain when I fall behind, as I often do, stumbling in the ruts. She pretends she wants to gossip, but really she's providing ballast.

Sadie wears dresses with lace-trimmed sleeves and pearl buttons, hand-me-downs from her sisters, she says, but fancier than anything I own. I wear navy blue skirts and white muslin shirt-blouses with buttons at the front. A long dark skirt is forgiving; my misshapen legs aren't as obvious behind its folds. On the way to the dance Sadie sings silly songs and makes a fool of herself, turning cartwheels in her dress. She wears pink lip stain and powder that her sisters bring home from the drugstore in little containers. I envy her free and easy laugh, the way she skips along without fear of stumbling. I wish I dared to speak to the boys at the Grange Hall and get out on the dance floor instead of swaying to the music on the sidelines.

Later, when I'm at home in bed, I conjure entire conversations I might've had with a boy named Robert Allan, whose brown eyes and wavy hair I found so appealing that I could hardly bear to look at him directly, even from across the room.

And then, in my imagining, the music starts. "May I have this dance, Christina?" Robert asks.

"Why, yes," I say.

He extends his hand, and when I take it, he pulls me close, his chest warm against mine. Through my blouse I feel his other hand on the small of my back, guiding me gently, firmly, as he moves forward on his left foot and I step backward with my right: two slow steps, three quick ones, hold. Forward, forward, side to side . . .

I drift to sleep, hearing the music in my head, moving my toes to the rhythm. *Two slow steps, three quick ones, hold. Two slow steps, three quick ones, hold.*

AT EIGHTY, MAMEY seems to float more than ever on the aquamarine oceans of her past, where the sand is as pale and fine as sugar and the smell of tropical flowers lingers on the air. Her eyelids flutter as she dips in and out of dreams, sinking deeper into herself. She can't get warm, no matter how many feather ticks and blankets I pile on. I heat a stone in the oven, her old trick, and slide it under the covers to the foot of her bed.

One day I bring her a conch from the Shell Room, its innards as pink and glistening as an inner lip. Gripping the bony conch, she tells me how she found it on a deserted beach on an expedition to Cape Horn with Captain Sam. Sand under their toes and leafy palm fronds overhead, shielding them from the sun. Siesta on a porch and grilled fish and vegetables for supper.

"Next time I'll take you with me," she says softly.

"I would like that," I say.

MAMEY'S HAIR IS thin and yellowed, her skin as freckled and translucent as a meadowlark egg, her eyes searching, unfocused. Her bones are as delicate as a bird's. Mother comes into her room every day and flits around for half an hour or so, fussing over the bedsheets and picking up soiled linens. "It pains me to look at her," she tells me. Perching on the edge of Mamey's

bed, gazing up at the ceiling, Mother sings one of her own favorite songs, an old gospel tune she learned in church as a child:

> Will there be any stars, any stars in my crown
> When at evening the sun goeth down
> When I wake with the blest in those
> Mansions of rest
> Will there be any stars in my crown?

I wonder what those stars are meant to represent. They must
be proof that you are especially worthy, that you shine a little
brighter than everyone else. But if you wake with the blessed
in heaven, isn't that enough? Haven't you achieved the most
you could've hoped for? The words seem at odds with Mother's personality, her negligible ambitions, her lack of interest
in anything beyond the point. Maybe she believes that the way
she lives is the height of righteousness. Or maybe, as she's said
before, she just likes the melody.

My father comes upstairs now and then and lingers in the
doorway. My brothers drift in and out, rendered speechless in
the presence of such profound dissolution. But I can't really
blame them. Mamey always called my brothers "those boys"
and kept a wide berth from them, while pulling me close.
"Mamey, I'm here," I murmur, stroking her arm and holding
it to my cheek. Her breath on my face smells like scum on a
shallow pond.

When she finally dies, it is after days of not eating and barely
drinking, her skin tightening across sunken cheeks, her breath-

ing becoming raspy and labored. I think of that poem: *the Eyes around—had wrung them dry . . .*

The day we bury her is dreary: a colorless sky, gray-boned trees, old sooty snow. Winter, I think, must be tired of itself. Reverend Cohen of the Cushing Baptist Church, in a eulogy at Mamey's grave in the family cemetery, talks about how she will rejoin the ones she loved who are gone. But as I watch her pine casket descend slowly into the dirt, I try to envision the reunion of a frail eighty-year-old woman with her decades-younger husband and their three sons and am left with the lingering feeling that the places we go in our minds to find comfort have little to do with where our bodies go.

WAITING TO BE FOUND

1942-1943

As the war heats up we see transport ships far out at sea. Soldiers sent down from Belfast roam our property in green jeeps, patrolling the coastline, scanning the horizon with binoculars.

Al is amused. "What do they think is going to happen here?"

When one of the soldiers knocks on the door and asks if I'm aware of any "suspicious activity," I ask him what on earth he means.

"Reports of enemy ships in the area," he says darkly. "The Cushing waterfront has been declared unsafe."

I think of the villainous pirates in *Treasure Island* and their telltale black flag with skull and crossbones. Our enemy—if one is lurking around—probably doesn't announce itself so plainly. "Well, I've seen a lot of activity out there lately. More than usual. But I wouldn't know if it's friend or foe."

"Just keep your eyes open, ma'am."

Soon enough Cushing is subjected to intermittent blackouts and rationing. "This is worse than the Depression," Fred's wife, Lora, exclaims. "There's barely enough gasoline to do my errands."

"Cottage cheese is a sorry substitute for ground beef. I can't for the life of me get Sam to eat it," says my other sister-in-law, Mary.

None of it affects Al and me much. A poster on the wall in the post office instructs citizens to "Use it up—wear it out—make it do!" But that's the way we've always lived. We've never had electricity, so blackouts are nothing new. (They happen every night when we extinguish the oil lamps.) And though we've come to rely on the Fales store for milk and flour and butter, most of what we eat comes from the fields and the orchard and the chicken coops. We still store root vegetables and apples in the cellar and perishables in an icebox under the floorboards in the pantry. Al does his butchering. I boil and crank the laundry as I've always done and hang it in the wind to dry.

It's a cool September day when my nephew John, the oldest son of Sam and Mary, pulls up a chair in my kitchen. A lanky, mild-mannered boy with a lopsided grin, John has been my favorite nephew since he was born in this house twenty years ago.

"I have something to tell you, Aunt Christina." He clasps my hand. "I hitched a ride to Portland yesterday and enlisted in the navy."

"Oh." I feel stricken. "Do you have to? Aren't you needed on the farm?"

"I knew I'd be called up sooner or later. If I'd waited any longer, I'd've been drafted by the army into the infantry. I'd rather do it on my own terms."

"What do your parents have to say about it?"

"They knew it was only a matter of time."

I pause for a moment, absorbing this. "When do you leave?"

"In a week."

"A week!"

He squeezes my hand. "Once you sign on the dotted line, Aunt Christina, you're as good as gone."

For the first time, the war feels starkly real. I put my other hand over his. "Promise you'll write."

"You know I will."

True to his word, every ten days or so a postcard or a pale blue onionskin letter from John arrives at the post office in Cushing. After six long weeks of basic training in Newport, Rhode Island, he is assigned to the USS *Nelson*, a destroyer that escorts aircraft carriers and patrols for enemy ships and submarines. After that the postmarks become larger and more colorful: Hawaii, Casablanca, Trinidad, Dakar, France . . .

Our seafaring ancestors! Mamey would be pleased.

Sam and Mary erect a flagpole in their yard and hang a crisp new American flag for all to see. They are proud of John for serving his country. Mary coordinates scrap-iron drives to collect copper and brass for use in artillery shells and organizes get-togethers with other wives and mothers of servicemen to knit socks and scarves to send to the troops. "Our boy will come back a man," Sam says.

I join Lora's knitting circle and go around the house and barn gathering bits and pieces of metal to send to the war effort. But with John overseas, I sleep fitfully. All I want is for him to come home.

❧

I READ ONCE that the act of observing changes the nature of what is observed. This is certainly true for Al and me. We are more attuned to the beauty of this old house, with its familiar corners, when Andy is here. More appreciative of the view down the yellow fields to the water, constant and yet ever changing, the black crows on the barn roof, the hawk circling overhead. A grain bag, a dented pail, a rope hanging from a rafter: these ordinary objects and implements are transformed by Andy's brush into something timeless and otherworldly.

Sitting at the kitchen window early one morning, I notice that the sweet peas I planted years ago have flourished beyond all reason in their sunny spot beside the back door. Taking a paring knife from the utility drawer and a straw basket from the counter, I make my way to the vine and clip the fragrant blossoms, cream and pink and salmon, letting them tumble into the basket. In the pantry I take Mother's tiny dust-covered crystal vases from a high shelf and wash them in the sink, then fill them with sprigs. I find spots for the vases all over the ground floor: on the kitchen counter, the mantel in the Shell Room, a windowsill in the dining room, even in the four-hole privy in the shed. I set the last vase at the foot of the stairs for Andy to take upstairs.

When he shows up several hours later, I hold my breath as he steps into the hall.

"What's this?" he exclaims. "How glorious!" As he trudges

up the stairs, he calls, "It's going to be a good day, Christina, a very good day indeed."

ONE HOT AFTERNOON I hear Andy pad down the stairs and out the front door. From the window in the kitchen I watch him pacing around barefoot in the grass. Hands on hips, he stares out at the sea. Then he walks slowly back to the house and materializes in the kitchen.

"I just can't see it," he says, rubbing the back of his neck.

"See what?"

He sits heavily on a stool.

"Lemonade?" I offer.

"Sure."

I rise from my chair and grope along the wall to the narrow pantry, using the table, Andy's rocker, and the wall for balance. Normally I'd feel self-conscious, but Andy is so lost in thought he doesn't even notice.

Betsy—seven months pregnant and grumpy in the heat—left a pitcher of fresh-squeezed lemonade on the counter before returning home for a nap. When I lift the glass pitcher with both hands, it wobbles and I splash the liquid all over my arm. Annoyed at myself, I dab at it with a damp dishrag before carefully carrying the glass to Andy.

"Thanks." Absentmindedly he licks the side of his hand where it's sticky from the glass. As I settle back into my chair, he says, "You know, I spend entire days up there just . . .

dreaming. It feels like so much wasted time. But I can't seem to do it any other way." He takes a long swig of lemonade and sets the empty glass on the floor. "Christ, I don't know."

I'm no artist, but I think I understand what he means. "Some things take the time they take. You can't make the hens lay before they're ready." He nods, and I feel emboldened. "Sometimes I want the bread to rise quicker, but if I try to rush it, I ruin it."

Breaking into a grin, he says, "That's true."

I feel a small glow in the pit of my stomach.

"You have an artist's soul, Christina."

"Well, I don't know about that."

"We have more in common than you think," he says.

Later I reflect on the things we have in common and the things we don't. Our stubbornness and our infirmities. Our circumscribed childhoods. His father kept him out of school; we're alike in that way. But N. C. trained him to be a painter and Papa trained me to take care of the house, and there's a world of difference in that.

SOME OF ANDY'S sketches are hurried outlines, a map of the painting to come—a hint of a figure, grasses growing this way and that, geometric slashes of house and barn. Others are precisely shaded and detailed—every strand of hair and fold of fabric, the wood grain on the pantry door. His watercolors are inky greens and browns, the sky merely the white of the paper. Al in his flat-visored cap with his pipe, raking blueberries in the field, sitting on the front doorstep, gathering hay; the fine figure of our dun-colored mare, Tessie, in profile. Andy sketches the scarred wooden table, the white teapot, egg scales, grain bags in the barn, seed corn hanging to dry in a third-floor bedroom. On his canvases these objects look the same, but different. They have a burnished glow.

Andy's father paints in oil, he tells me. But he prefers egg tempera, he says, the method of European masters like Giotto and Botticelli in the late Middle Ages and Early Renaissance. It dries quickly, leaving a muted effect. I watch as he cracks an egg, separates the yolk from the white, and rolls the plump sac gently between his hands to remove the albumen. He pokes the yolk with the tip of a knife, pours the orange liquid into a cup of distilled water, stirs it around with his finger. Adds a chalky powdered pigment to make a paste.

After dipping a small brush into the tempera, he presses out the wetness and color with his fingers and splays the tip to make dry spiky strokes. He layers it over a pale wash of color or pencil and ink on a Masonite fiberboard coated with gesso, a smooth mix of rabbit-skin glue and chalk. Though he works fast, the brushstrokes are painstaking and meticulous, each one distinct. Cross-hatched grass, a dense, dark row of plantings. When wet, the colors are as red as Indian paintbrush, russet as clay, blue as the bay on a summer afternoon, green as a holly leaf. These bright wet colors fade as they dry, leaving a ghostly glow. "Intensity—painting emotions into objects—is the only thing I care about," he says.

Over time Andy's paintings become starker, drained of color, austere. Mostly white and brown and gray and black. "Damn it to hell," Andy murmurs, cocking his head to look at a newly finished watercolor: Al's shadowy figure walking down the rows in his visored cap, the white house and gray barn stark on the horizon. "This is better. Betsy was right."

WHEN HE ISN'T upstairs painting, Andy hovers near me like a bee around honeycomb. He is fascinated with our habits and routines. How are the hens laying, how do you make a perfect loaf of bread without measuring, how do you keep the slugs from the dahlias? What kinds of trees does Al cut for firewood, what type of sail do lobstermen around here use on their boats? How do you collect the water in the cistern? Why are so many things in the house painted the same shade of blue? Why is a dory marooned in the rafters of the shed? Why is that long ladder propped against the house?

"We don't have a telephone," Al explains in his laconic way. "And the closest fire company is nine miles from here. If there's a roof or chimney fire . . ."

"Got it," Andy says.

These questions are easy to answer. But over time his inquiries become more personal. Why do Al and I live here alone, with all these empty rooms? What was it like when it was full of people, before most of the fields went to flower?

At first I'm guarded. "It just turned out that way," I tell him. "Life was busier then."

Andy isn't satisfied with evasions. *Why* did it turn out that way? Did you or Al ever want to live somewhere, anywhere, else?

It's hard to say what's in my head. It's been a long time since anyone cared to ask.

He insists. "I want to know."

So little by little, I open up. I tell him about the trip to Rockland when I refused to see the doctor. The disappearing treasure in Mystery Tunnel. The witches, the sea captains, the ship stranded in ice . . .

What did you miss about going to school?

Why were you so scared of doctors?

He is as gentle as a dog, as curious as a cat.

Who are you, Christina Olson?

In the Shell Room one afternoon Andy finds Papa's wooden box of keepsakes and opens the lid. He strokes the smooth tines of the whalebone comb. Picks up the tiny tin soldier and raises its arms with his forefinger. "Whose is this?"

"My father's. This box is the only thing of his I kept after he died."

"I used to collect toy soldiers," he muses. "When I was a boy, I created a whole battlefield. I still have a row of them lined up on the windowsill in my studio in Pennsylvania." He sets the soldier back in the box and runs a finger over the black lump of anthracite. "Why do you think he held on to this?"

"He liked rocks and minerals, he said."

"This is anthracite, right?"

I nod.

"Coal's glamorous cousin," he says. "In the Civil War—did your father tell you this?—anthracite was used by Confederate blockade runners as fuel for their steamships to avoid giving themselves away. It burns clean. No smoke."

"I've never heard that," I say. But I think: How apt. Papa was never one to give himself away.

"They called them ghost ships. It's a terrifying image, isn't it? These ominous ships materializing out of nowhere." He sets the anthracite back in the box and shuts the lid. "Did he ever go back to Sweden?"

"No. But I'm named after his mother. Anna Christina Olauson."

"Did you know her?"

I shake my head. "It's strange, don't you think—to name your child after a living person you've chosen never to see again?"

"Not so strange," he says. "There's this great line from *The House of the Seven Gables*: 'The world owes all its onward impulses to men ill at ease.' Your father must have felt he had to forge his own path, even if it meant cutting ties to his family. It's brave to resist the pull of the familiar. To be selfish about your own needs. I wrestle with that every day."

SEVERAL MONTHS AFTER Andy and Betsy return to Chadds Ford for the winter, I get a letter from Betsy. In September she gave birth to a sickly child, Nicholas, who needed a lot of special care but seems to be all right. In November Andy was drafted into the army. When he reported for his physical they took one look at his twisted right leg and his flat feet and rejected him on the spot. "He truly feels he's been given a reprieve and is determined to make the most of it," she writes.

A reprieve of one sort, I think. But though I may not have a child of my own, I know all too well how the demands of family life can become consuming. I wonder if, as a father, now, Andy will feel even more torn between the pull of the familiar and the creative impulses that drive him.

1913–1914

I'm in the henhouse early on a warm June morning, gathering eggs, when I hear voices coming closer across the field. We're not expecting visitors. Standing up straight, I lower the warm eggs I'm holding into the pocket of my apron and listen closely.

Ramona Carle—I'd recognize her throaty laugh anywhere.

Ramona, along with her siblings Alvah and Eloise, are summer folk from Massachusetts whose family bought the Seavey homestead down the road several years ago. Alvah is the oldest; Eloise is my age, Ramona a few years younger. They stay in Cushing from Memorial Day to Labor Day. But unlike some other from-aways (with their languid indolence, their impulsive thrill-seeking), the Carles do their best to fit in with the locals. I always look forward to seeing them. They organize egg-in-spoon races at our annual Fourth of July clambake on Hathorn Point, convince everyone to play games like Red Rover and Olly Olly Oxen Free, and bring bags of fireworks to light after dark.

Ramona is my favorite. A friendly, impulsive girl, she is slight and energetic, with hair the color of melted chocolate and eyes as large and shiny as a fawn's. Once, when I was with her in town, an old lady told her she was as cute as a button. (No one has ever said anything remotely like that to me.)

Ducking out of the henhouse with my bounty of eggs and a big smile of anticipation, I nearly run into a man I've never seen before. "Why—hello!" I say.

"Hello!" He's about my age, I think—I've just turned twenty—and about half a foot taller than me, with light-brown hair that flops in front of wide-set blue eyes. He's wearing thin linen pants and a soft white shirt with the sleeves rolled above his elbows.

Self-conscious all of a sudden, I smooth my sleep-matted hair, glancing down at the soiled apron I baked bread in this morning and the wooden clogs I wear to wade through mud.

"Walton Hall," he says, extending his hand.

"Christina Olson." His hand is surprisingly soft. This is a man who has never handled a plow.

"Walton is visiting from Malden," Ramona says. "He and Eloise went to high school together. At the end of the summer he's heading off to Harvard."

"Admit it, you're shocked," Walton says with a small wink. "'Must not be as dull as he looks.'"

"Just because you're going to Harvard doesn't mean you're not dull," I say.

When he smiles, I see that one of his front teeth slightly overlaps the other. He raises an invisible glass in a mock toast. "Good point."

"All right, enough," Ramona says. "Let me remind you, Walton, that an entire household awaits breakfast."

"Ah, yes," he says. "We've come to procure some eggs."

"Right," I say. "How many?"

"Two dozen, yes, Ramona?"

She nods.

"Okay, that'll be fifty cents for the eggs and a penny for the bag," I tell them.

"My word, you drive a hard bargain!"

Ramona rolls her eyes. "You could've asked for fifty cents an egg, Christina. He has no idea what he's talking about."

One by one I slide the eggs into a bag, counting out twenty-four as he teases: "Not that one! It's not oval enough," and "They must all be exactly the same size." He is standing quite close to me and his breath smells of butterscotch. Ramona's talking about the weather, how dull a winter it was and how she counted the days until June, what a beautiful day it is today, but do you think it might take a turn? Will it be calm enough to go out for a sail later on? She wonders what her mother will do with all these eggs if breakfast is over by the time they get back: a soufflé, perhaps? An omelette? A lemon meringue pie?

"Come with us," he says.

Ramona and I both look up.

"What?" I say, confused.

"Come sailing this afternoon, Christina," he says. "The wind will be perfect."

"You might've said that when I was fretting about the weather," Ramona mutters.

I don't usually take off afternoons, especially to sail with strange boys I've only just met. "Thank you, but—I . . . can't. I have to make bread. And my chores . . ."

"Oh, for heaven's sake, come along," Ramona says. "We have to entertain Walton somehow. And bring your brother Sam. He's such fun. I need someone my own age to flirt with."

"I'm sorry, I don't think so."

"My word, you're a hard sell. Look, I'll sign your hall pass," Walton says.

"Hall pass?"

Seeing my puzzlement, Ramona laughs. "They don't have hall passes in one-room schoolhouses, Walton."

"I can't," I say.

He shakes his head and shrugs. "Ah well. Another day, then."

"Maybe."

"That means yes," Ramona tells him with the confidence of a girl accustomed to getting her way. She flashes me a smile. "We'll try again. Soon."

When I return to the house from the brightness of the yard, I lean against the wall in the dim foyer, breathing heavily. What *was* that?

"Did I hear voices?" Mother calls from the kitchen.

I touch my face. Smooth the front of my blouse. Take a deep breath.

"Was somebody here?" she asks when I come in, untying my apron and taking it off.

"Oh," I say, straining for a casual tone, "only Ramona, to buy eggs."

"I could've sworn I heard a male voice."

"Just a friend of the Carles'."

"Ah. Well, the dough's ready for kneading."

"I'll get to it," I say.

OVER THE NEXT few weeks, Ramona and Walton, sometimes with Eloise and Alvah, stop by every other day or so, seeking eggs or milk or a roasting chicken, staying longer each visit. They bring a picnic basket and an old quilt and we sit on the grass, drinking tea steeped in the sun. I come to expect the sight of them sauntering up the field in the late morning or early afternoon. My brothers, with their gentle ways, tend to shy like deer from the summer folk, but the Carles and Walton gradually win them over. When they're finished with chores, Al and Sam often join us on the grass.

One morning, when it's just Walton and Ramona and me, Ramona says, "We're kidnapping you, Christina. It's a perfect day for a sail."

"But—"

"No buts. The farm will manage without you. Alvah is waiting. Off we go."

As we make our way down the path toward the shore I feel Walton's eyes on me from behind. Aware of my awkward gait, I concentrate carefully on my movements. In front of us Ramona chatters away—"The sun is so bright! Mercy, I did not even think of it, but we do not have enough hats; maybe Mother left one or two on the boat"—seemingly unaware that neither Walton nor I say a word in response. And then the very thing

I fear happens: I trip on a root. My legs buckle; I feel myself pitching forward.

Before I can make a sound, an arm is under mine. In a low voice, so Ramona won't hear, Walton says, "What a long path this is."

Though only moments ago I was flushed with anxiety, now I am oddly calm. "Thank you," I whisper.

I have never been this close to a boy who isn't related to me. My senses sharp, I notice everything in the clean morning light: daffodils pale and bowed; guillemots gliding overhead, black, with bright red legs, squeaking like mice; the trees in the distance, red spruce and firs and juniper and slender scotch pines, that frame the field. I taste the salt on my lips from the sea. But mostly I am aware of the warm mammal scent of this boy whose arm is ballast: sweat, perhaps, and the musky smell of his hair, a whiff of aftershave. Sweet butterscotch on his breath.

"I hope you won't think this impertinent, but did you know that the blue flowers in your dress match your eyes exactly?" he murmurs.

"I did not," I manage to answer.

The Carles' boat is a single-mast sloop, with a jib in the front and a large white mainsail attached to the back of the wooden mast. They keep a wooden dinghy on the shore near Kissing Cove, paddles tucked inside, to row out to the sailboat. When we get to the beach, Alvah is waving from the deck of the sloop, about a hundred yards out in the bay. We drag the dinghy to the water. Walton insists on taking the oars and we meander toward the sailboat, this way and that. I have to bite my lips to keep from laughing: his strokes are choppy and inexpert, nothing like Al's rhythmic motion. When we arrive at the boat, Ramona ties the small craft to the buoy, and Walton, taking Alvah's proffered hand, jumps up first so the two of them can assist us.

"Gallant of you, I suppose, but unnecessary," Ramona says, batting away Walton's hand. I don't protest. I need all the help I can get.

Once aboard, I'm more at ease. It is a mild, warm morning, with a gentle wind, and I know how to sail, having learned with Alvaro on his small skiff. Alvah hoists the mainsail, which flaps dramatically in the wind like a sheet on a clothesline, and I pull down firmly on the halyard until it stops. He turns the boat to starboard, weaving away from the wind, lessening the tilt to bring us to a more comfortable sailing angle as we approach open water. I have to warn Walton to duck so he won't get hit in the head by the boom.

He seems surprised and a little impressed that I seem to know what I'm doing. "So many hidden talents!"

It's a miracle I'm any help to Alvah given how distracted I am by the skin on Walton's neck, slightly sunburned just above his collar. The small flaps of his ears turning pink in the sun. The quick flash of his gray-blue eyes.

Alvah, passionate for sailing in the way that boys who grew up on boats with their fathers and grandfathers can be, is happy to do the brunt of the work, and once we're out on the ocean we fall into an easy rhythm. Ramona opens a basket and cuts chunks of bread, slices of cheese, passes around hard-boiled eggs and salt and a tin canteen of water.

In the course of conversation, I learn bits and pieces about Walton's upbringing. His mother is obsessed with social decorum, his father a banker who stays in Boston in a small apartment several nights a week—"when he has to work late. Or at least that's what he tells us," Walton says. I'm not sure what he's implying and fear it's rude to ask; I don't want to look ignorant but also don't want to pry. It's as hard to picture where Walton grew up as it is to imagine life on the moon. I conjure parlor rooms out of Jane Austen, a redbrick mansion, the walls of the dining room adorned with gilt-framed paintings of Harvard-educated ancestors.

He tells me that he had a curved spine, scoliosis, as a child, and had to wear a plaster body cast for a long, hot summer after an operation when he was twelve. While other boys were climbing trees and kicking balls around, he lay in bed reading adventure stories like *Swiss Family Robinson* and *Captains Courageous*. He doesn't say so, but I know he's trying to explain that he understands what it's like to be me.

As the hours pass, the sky drains of warmth. It's not until I notice goose bumps on my arms that I realize I've forgotten a sweater. Without a word, Walton peels off his jacket and drapes it around my shoulders. "Oh," I say with surprise.

"I hope that wasn't too forward of me. You seemed chilly."

"Yes. Thank you. I just—I didn't expect it." In truth, I can't remember the last time anyone noticed my physical discomfort and did something about it. When you live on a farm, everyone is uncomfortable much of the time. Too cold, too warm, dirty, bone tired, banged up, injured by a tool or hot grate—too preoccupied to worry much about each other.

"You're quite an independent girl, aren't you?"

"I suppose I am."

"You've never met anyone like Christina, Walton," Ramona says. "She's not like those silly girls in Malden who don't know how to light a fire or clean a fish."

"Is she a suffragette, like Miss Pankhurst?" he asks in a teasing voice.

I feel woefully ignorant; I don't know what a suffragette is and I've never heard of Miss Pankhurst. I think of all the years Walton spent in school while I was washing and cooking and cleaning. "A suffragette?"

"You know, those ladies starving themselves for the vote," Ramona says. "The ones who think, God forbid, they can do anything a man can do."

"Is that what you think?" Walton asks me.

"Well, I don't know," I say. "Shall we have a competition and find out? We could split logs for firewood, or fix a drainpipe. Or maybe slaughter a chicken?"

"Careful," he says, laughing. "Miss Pankhurst was just sentenced to three years in jail for her treasonous words."

There is, I am almost certain, a spark between us. A flickering. I glance at Ramona. She raises her eyebrows at me and smiles, and I know she senses it too.

ONE DAY WALTON shows up alone on a bicycle. He's wearing a pin-striped sack coat and a straw boater, not the kind of hat any man around here would wear. (For that matter, they don't wear pin-striped sack coats either.) Around my brothers he looks slightly preposterous, like a peacock in a cluster of turkeys.

Holding his hat between his hands, he kneads the brim with his long fingers. "I'm here to do you the favor of relieving you of some eggs. Can you believe they've entrusted me with this important task?" And then, conspiratorially, "Actually, they have no idea I'm here."

"I'll get my coat," I say.

"Don't think you need one," he says. "It's not actually—"

But I've already shut the door.

I stand in the dark hall, my heart thudding in my ears. I don't know how to act. Maybe I should tell him that I'm needed in the—

A rap on the door. "Are you there? All right if I come inside?"

I reach up to the coat pegs and pull down the first thing I find, Sam's heavy wool jacket.

"Christina?" Mother's voice filters down the stairs.

"Getting eggs at the henhouse, Mother." Opening the door, I smile at Walton. He smiles back. I step onto the stoop, putting on the jacket. "Two dozen, yes? You can come with me if you want."

"Butterscotch?" He holds out a piece of amber candy.

"Uh . . . sure."

He unwraps it before handing it to me. "Sweets to the sweet."

"Thanks," I say, blushing.

He gestures for me to lead the way. "Lovely property," he says as we stroll toward the henhouse. "Used to be a lodging house, Ramona said?"

The butterscotch is melting in my mouth. I turn it over with my tongue. "My grandparents took in summer guests. They called it Umbrella Roof Inn."

He squints at the roof. "Umbrella?"

"You're right," I say, laughing a little. "It looks nothing like an umbrella."

"I suppose it keeps the rain out."

"Aren't all roofs supposed to do that?"

Now he's laughing too. "Well, you find out the answer and let me know."

Walton is right; my brother's scratchy jacket is too hot. After I've gathered the eggs, I peel off the jacket and Walton suggests we sit in the grass.

"So what's your favorite color?" he asks.

"Really?"

"Why not?" The butterscotch clicks between his teeth.

"Okay." I've never been asked this question. I have to think about it. The color of a piglet's ear, a summer sky at dusk, Al's beloved roses . . . "Um. Pink."

"Favorite animal."

"My spaniel, Topsy."

"Favorite food."

"I'm famous for my fried apple cake."

"Will you make it for me?"

I nod.

"I'm going to hold you to that. Favorite poet."

This is an easy one. "Emily Dickinson."

"Ah," he says. "'Not knowing when the dawn will come, I open every door.'"

"'Or has it feathers like a bird—'"

"Very good!" he says, clearly surprised that I know it. "'Or billows like a shore.'"

"My teacher gave me a collection of her poems when I left school. That's one of my favorites."

He shakes his head. "I never understood that last part."

"Well . . ." I'm a little hesitant to offer an interpretation. What if he disagrees? "I think . . . I think it means that you should stay open to possibility. However it comes your way."

He nods. "Ah. That makes sense. So are you?"

"Am I what?"

"Open to possibility?"

"I don't know. I hope so. What about you?"

"Trying. It's a struggle."

He tells me that he is going to Harvard to please his father, though he might've preferred the smaller campus of Bowdoin. "But you don't turn down Harvard, do you?"

"Why not?"

"Why not, indeed," he says.

❧

"HE LIKES YOU," Ramona says, eyes sparkling. "He asks me all these questions: how long I've known you, if you have a boyfriend, if your father is very strict. He wants to know what *you* think."

"What I think?"

"About him, silly. What you think about *him*."

It feels like a trick question, as if I'm being asked to respond in a language I don't understand. "I like him. I like many people," I say warily.

Ramona wrinkles her nose. "You do not. You hardly like anyone."

"I hardly know anyone."

"True," she says. "But don't be coy. Does your heart pitter-patter when you think of him?"

"Ramona, honestly."

"Don't act so scandalized. Just answer the question."

"Oh, I don't know. Maybe a little."

"Maybe a little. That's a yes."

As the summer progresses she goes back and forth between Walton and me like a carrier pigeon, carrying scraps of news, impressions, gossip. She is perfectly suited to the task—one of those girls with boundless energy and intelligence and no place to exercise them, like a terrier with a housebound owner.

❧

AT FIRST MOTHER is formal and a little cool with Walton, but slowly he wins her over. I watch how he calibrates his behavior, deferring to her at every turn, calling her Ma'am, presuming nothing. He coaxes her outside for picnics and afternoon sails. "Well, the boy does have excellent manners," she allows at the end of a long afternoon lunch on the shore. "Must've learned them at an expensive school."

One morning Mother surprises me by returning from town with a bolt of calico cloth, a packet of buttons, and a new Butterick pattern. She hands it to me casually, saying, "I thought you could use a new style." I look at the illustration on the cover: a dress with a seven-panel skirt and fitted bodice with small mother-of-pearl buttons. The calico is pretty, flowers with green leaves on a brown-sugar background. I set to work after my chores are done, cutting out each piece of the pattern, pinning the puzzle pieces of delicate tissue to the fabric, marking it with a nub of chalk, trimming along the solid line. I work in the orange light of an oil lamp and several candles as the sun drops from the sky.

Late into the night I sit hunched over Mother's Singer, feeding the fabric through, my foot pumping the treadle. Mother pauses in the doorway on her way to bed. She comes and stands behind me, then reaches down and traces the hem with her finger, smoothing it flat behind the needle.

When I put on the dress the next morning, it skims closely over my hips. In the pantry I hold the small cloudy mirror in my hand, turning it this way and that to get the full effect, but all I can see are bits and pieces.

"That turned out," is all Mother says when she comes into the kitchen to help with the noonday meal. But I can tell she's pleased.

Later in the morning Walton comes to the door with a bouquet of tulips and daffodils. He takes off his straw boater and bows slightly to Mother, who is sifting flour at the table. "Good day, Mrs. Olson."

She nods. "Good day, Walton."

He hands me the bouquet. "What a dress!"

"Mother bought me the fabric and the pattern." I hold out the skirt and turn so he can see all the panels.

"Lovely taste, Mrs. Olson. It's beautiful. But wait, Christina—you made this?"

"Yes, last night."

He grasps a piece of fabric from the full skirt and rubs it between his fingers, touches a mother-of-pearl button on my sleeve. "I am awed by you."

Behind me, Mother says, "Christina can do just about anything she sets her mind to." This rare praise surprises me—she's usually so restrained. But then I remember that my mother was discovered in this house by a stranger at the door. She knows it's possible.

ONE DAY WHEN Walton is visiting I tell him about the Mystery Tunnel—how I think of it as a mysterious and magic place, holding secrets that may never be revealed. "Some think it's filled with buried treasure," I say.

"Show me," he says.

I know my parents won't approve of our going alone, so we make a secret plan: we'll wait until Mother is resting, Papa is at the fishing weir with the boys, and no one will suspect I'm not where I usually am on a Wednesday morning, wringing clothes behind the house and hanging them on the line. He'll come quietly, on foot; and if anyone is nearby, we won't attempt it.

At breakfast, before heading off to the weir, my brothers help me fill the tubs with water. If anyone cared to notice, they might have seen that my dress is starched, my hair neatly braided with a ribbon, my cheeks pink not from exertion but from being pinched between my fingers, as Ramona taught me to do.

Finding me in the yard behind the house after everyone has left, Walton silently takes the heavy, wet clothes from my hands. He begins to feed them through the wringer, turning the crank with one hand and coaxing them along with the other. At the clothesline he lifts the damp pieces from the basket, shakes out the wrinkles, and hands them to me one by one as I pin them on the line. When the basket is empty, he lifts the rope and secures it to the poles.

How thrilling it is—I am suddenly aware—to be playing house.

Hidden among the damp and flapping clothes, Walton reaches for me, pulling me gently toward him. His eyes on mine, he lifts my hand to his mouth and kisses it, then tugs me closer, tilts his head, and kisses me on the mouth. His lips are cool and smooth; I feel his heart pulsing through his shirt. He smells of butterscotch, of spice. It's such a strange and heady experience that I can barely breathe.

When I take the basket back inside the house, I slip out of my apron and smooth my hair, stealing a glimpse of myself in the fragment of mirror in the pantry. What I see looking back at me is a thin-faced girl with a too-large nose and lively if uneven gray eyes. Her features may be plain, but her skin is clear and her eyes are bright. I think of the man waiting for me outside. His hair, I've noticed, has begun to recede. His chest is lightly concave, like a teaspoon, his spine unnaturally stiff from that summer in a cast. When he's agitated he has a slight lisp. It isn't inconceivable to imagine—is it?—that this imperfect man could grow to love me.

We walk silently, single file, in the shadow of the house and barn to the trees beyond the field. At this time of day, with the shadows as they are, we cannot be seen unless someone is actually looking for us. Walton reaches forward and brushes my fingertips, clasps my hand. Several times, making our way down a steep embankment, through a dense cluster of trees, we drop hands, but he finds my fingertips again like a knitter seeking a dropped stitch. When we are out in the open but hidden by the ridge, I pull on his hand playfully and he pulls back, bringing me to a stumbling stop. He is behind me, his breath on my neck, his arm at his side, holding me against him.

"Heaven could not be better than this," he murmurs.

I don't know whether he's talking about the pelt of water stretching out in front of us, the dancing grasses, the rocks with their mantle of inky seaweed—or me. It doesn't matter. This place, this point, is as much a part of me as my hair and nose and eyes.

We are close to the lip of the tunnel. His hands on my waist, Walton turns me around, his forehead against mine.

"I've already discovered the treasure," he says. "All this time you were here, waiting to be found."

WALTON'S ATTENTION IS like a sun high in the sky, so bright, so blinding, that everything else fades in contrast. The voices of my parents, my brothers, the clucking chickens and barking dog, rain on the roof like rice in a can—these noises simmer like a stew in the back of my brain. I am barely aware of them until my mother or a brother shakes my arm and says sharply, "Did you hear what I said?"

Do other people walk around in this state? Did my parents? What a strange idea—that perfectly ordinary people with mundane lives might have once experienced this quickening, this vertiginous unfolding. Their eyes betray no evidence of it.

Mamey used to tell stories about natives on the islands she visited who'd never seen snow and had no language for it. That's how I feel. I have no language, no context, for this.

My friend Sadie says, "You're a goner. You'll move to Boston and we'll never see you again."

"Maybe I'll convince him to live here."

"And do what? He doesn't seem like the farming type."

"He wants to be a journalist, he says. He can write anywhere."

"What's he going to write about? The price of milk?"

But what does Sadie know? Walton seems smitten with our way of life. "This is so different from how I grew up," he says.

"Your knowledge is real. It's practical. Mine is all in my head. I don't know how to foal a calf or skim cream from milk. I'm hopeless at sailing or harnessing a horse to a buggy. Is there nothing you can't do?"

"You're the one who can do, and be, anything you choose," I remind him.

"What I choose," he says, "is to be with you."

It feels as if my life is moving forward at two separate speeds, one at the usual pace, with its predictable rhythms and familiar inhabitants, and the other rushing ahead, a blur of color and sound and sensation. It's clear to me now that for twenty years I have gone through the motions of each day like a dumb animal, neither daring to hope for a different kind of life nor even knowing enough to desire one.

I am determined to keep up with Walton. I ask my brothers to bring the newspapers from town when they go for supplies. I want to learn enough to discuss politics and current events— the flood in Dayton, Ohio, and Irish Home Rule; the federal income tax and the suffragettes demonstrating in Washington; Woodrow Wilson's views on segregation and the assassination of King George of Greece. At the library in Cushing I check out novels by authors Walton has mentioned, Willa Cather and D. H. Lawrence and Edith Wharton, all of which I read through a filter, thinking of him: "She was afraid lest this boy, who, nevertheless, looked something like a Walter Scott hero," Lawrence writes in *Sons and Lovers*, "who could paint and speak French, and knew what algebra meant, and who went by train to Nottingham every day, might consider her simply as the swine-girl, unable to perceive the princess beneath."

I'm afraid that I am the swine girl. But he treats me like a princess. Papa agrees to let me take Blackie and the buggy one afternoon, and I take Walton on a long tour from Broad Cove, with its views of the outer islands, to the quaint shops in East Friendship, to the pristine Ulmer Church in downtown Rockland. We end up in the grass on the hill overlooking Kissing Cove, eating egg salad sandwiches and home-canned pickles, drinking lemonade from a mason jar. As afternoon fades to evening we watch the sun melt into the liquid horizon, a thin disc of moon emerging faintly above. "The stars are so close," he says, pointing up to the black expanse. "Like you could reach up and take one. Hold it in your hand." He pretends to grab one and hand it to me. "When I am in Cambridge and you're here in Cushing, I'll look up at the stars and think of you. Then you won't seem so far away."

THE FINAL WEEK of August is sodden, cloud heavy, with an unwelcome chill that announces the end of summer as abruptly as a dinner host standing at the table to signal the end of the party.

When Walton comes to say good-bye, I am so choked up I can barely speak. I had not realized how dependent I've become on seeing him. "I promise to write," he says, and I promise, too, but he doesn't yet have an address at Harvard, so I will have to wait for him to write first.

Waiting to hear from him is agony. I plod to the post office once a day at noon.

"I'm taking the buggy into town at three o'clock, as always," Al says. "I can pick up the mail."

"I like the fresh air," I tell him.

The postmistress, thin, fussy, meticulous Bertha Dorset, eyes me with curiosity. I soon learn her routines: she keeps stamps in rolls in a tidy drawer and dusts the coin wrappers with a goose feather. Twice a day, according to a checklist on the wall behind her head, she sweeps the floor. At sunset every evening she lowers the flag outside the post office, takes it off the pole, and folds it neatly into a box.

When I arrive, she hands over the mail in our box, bills and circulars, mostly. "That's it for today," she always says.

I nod and try my best to smile.

I feel like I'm living in a jail cell, waiting for release, the strain of listening for the man with the keys making me tense and jittery. After supper one night, as I'm clearing the dishes, my brothers are debating whether to take up the fish weir; it will be destroyed by ice storms if they wait too long, but on the other hand the sardine catch is good so it would be a shame to dismantle it too soon, and I think I might jump out of my skin. I snap at the boys, surprising myself at my own meanness: "For crying out loud, you clodhoppers, pick up your plates! Were you born in a barn?"

There's thin satisfaction in their wounded surprise.

And then one day, long after I've stopped believing there will be a letter, Bertha slides a pile of mail onto the counter, and here it is: a thick white envelope with a red two-cent George Washington stamp, addressed to me. *Christina Olson.*

"Well, look at that. Hope it's good news," she says.

I can barely wait until I'm out of the post office to open the envelope. I settle on a fallen tree just off the road and unfold the thick paper.

"Dearest Christina . . ."

I read hungrily, skipping forward, shuffling pages (two, three, four) to the end—"Yours"—*mine!*—"Walton." My gaze catches on phrases: "summer I will never forget," "the way you shield your eyes from the sun with your hand, the flat collar of your sailor blouse, the blue-black ribbon in your hair," and finally: "All roads lead back to Cushing for me."

I skip forward and back like a bee trying to escape from a hole in a screen. He can't stop thinking about the summer in Maine. The week he was in Malden was tedious and hot; Harvard is lonely after the sailing and picnics and endless adventures. He misses it all: the sloop moored in Kissing Cove, egg sandwiches on just-baked bread, Ramona's silly jokes, clambakes down by Little Island, pink-orange sunsets. But mostly, he writes, he misses me.

The light is different on the walk home, softer, warm on my face. I tilt my chin up and close my eyes, putting one foot after the other in the left-hand rut of the road. I can only walk like this, with my eyes closed, because I know the way by heart.

EVERY WEEK OR ten days a thick letter in a white envelope with a two-cent stamp arrives in the mail. He writes from the library, from the dining hall, from the narrow wooden desk in his dormitory room, by the light of a gas lamp after his rugby-playing, gin-guzzling roommate has gone to sleep. Each envelope, a package of words to feed my word-hungry soul, provides a portal into a world where students linger in wood-paneled classrooms to talk to professors, where entire days can be spent in a library, where what you write and how you write it are all you need to worry about. I imagine myself in his place: strolling across campus, peering up at thick-paned, glowing windows at dusk, going to expensive dinners with friends in Harvard Square, where the waiters wear tuxedos and look down their noses at the unkempt students, and the students don't care.

As the letters pile up I save them under my bed, tied with a pale pink ribbon. In one he writes: "Every night I look up at the great square in the southeast, nearly overhead, and name the stars in it: Broad Cove, Four Corners, East Friendship, and the Ulmer Church, and wish that I were driving around it with you." After supper I open the shed door and step outside, looking up at the vast expanse of stars, and imagine Walton doing the same in Cambridge. Here I am, there he is, connected by sky.

THE CAMEO SHELL

1944–1946

For years, nobody has seemed particularly interested in the young artist who set up a studio in our house. But this summer is different. In town with my sister-in-law, Mary, doing errands, I'm approached by a woman I don't recognize in the canned-goods section of Fales.

"Excuse me. Are you . . . Christina Olson?"

I nod, puzzled. Why would a stranger know who I am?

"I thought so!" she beams. "I'm renting a cottage near here with my family for the week. I've read about you and your brother. Al, is it?"

Mary, who'd wandered over to the next aisle, comes around the corner. "Hello, I'm with Miss Olson. Can I help you?"

"Oh, I'm sorry! I should've cut to the chase. A famous painter is working at your home, I believe? Andrew Wyeth?"

"How do you—" Mary starts.

"I wonder if I might presume on you to get his autograph for me?" the woman wheedles.

"Oh. Well?" Mary asks, looking at me.

I give the woman a tight smile. "No, that's impossible."

Later, when I mention this to Betsy, she wags her head as if she's not surprised. "Sorry about that, Christina. Andy was on the cover of *American Artist* a while back, and we worried it might change things. Evidently it has."

"Did he say anything about Al and me?"

"A little. Not much. He may have mentioned your names. Of course the article reveals that he summers in Cushing, so it probably isn't hard to figure out. I know he regrets saying anything. He really doesn't like being bothered. I'm sure you don't either."

I shrug. I'm not sure how I feel about it.

Several weeks later, sitting in my chair beside the open kitchen window, I watch a baby blue convertible pull up in front of the house. The driver is wearing a cream fedora, the woman beside him a filmy polka-dotted head scarf.

"Toodle-oo!" she calls, waving pink-tipped fingers. "Hello! We're looking for . . ." She bats the man on the arm. "What's his name, honey?"

"Wyeth."

"That's right. Andrew Wyeth." She gives me a pink-lipped smile through the window.

Andy isn't here yet, but I know I'll see him sauntering up the field from Kissing Cove any minute. "Never heard of him," I tell her.

"He's not painting inside this house?"

"Not last time I checked," I say.

She purses her lips, perplexed. "Frank, isn't this the place?"

"I don't know." He sighs. "You tell me."

"I'm pretty sure. That magazine said so."

"I don't know, Mabel."

"I could swear . . ."

Sure enough, as they're chattering away I see Andy coming toward us through the grass, swinging his tackle box of paints. Following my gaze, Mabel cranes her neck in his direction.

"Look, Frank!" she hoots. "That's probably him!"

"That guy?" I say with a forced chuckle. "He's just a local fisherman." I raise my eyebrows at Andy, who sees me and pivots toward the barn. "We let him store his rods up here."

Mabel sticks her lip out in a pout. "Aw, darn it, we came all this way."

"He might sell you some mackerel. I could ask."

"Ew, no thank you," she sniffs, tightening her scarf around her hair. She doesn't bother saying good-bye.

When they've turned their car around and headed off down the drive, Andy emerges from the barn. "Thanks. That was a close one," he says. "I need to keep my big mouth shut."

"Might be a good idea," I tell him. We've had such a closed-off and intimate existence here that civilization has felt very far away. But slowly it's dawning on me that Andy belongs to the world, and not just to us. It's an unsettling realization.

MANY THINGS ARE disquieting these days. In June of 1944 a torpedo zeroed in on John's ship off the coast of Normandy and killed two dozen men. He almost didn't make it out alive; he clawed his way out of the sinking rubble with only the clothes on his back. "The watch I bought in Brooklyn for $100 was smashed to smithereens," he writes, months after the fact. "A day after we were hit, a seagoing tub towed us back to the English Channel, where we were put on a ship to Plymouth. I slept on a coil of rope and nearly froze to death, but I didn't care. I'm just happy to be alive."

Does he come home after this? He does not. He is sent to England, Scotland, Ireland before a short leave in Boston and forty-five days of training in Newport to become a crew member on an aircraft carrier. Then he heads to the South Pacific to fight the Japanese.

Sadie, whose son, Clyde, also joined the naval reserve, tells me, "I'm always on high alert, listening for the sound of an unfamiliar car up the driveway." I know what she means. I wake in the night with a sense of dread that mostly dissipates by morning but is never entirely absent. At random moments in the day and night I think: this could be the moment Sam and Mary arrive on my doorstep with a telegram. But perhaps not if I knead the dough until it's silky. Not if I pluck the chicken until it's smooth of feathers. Not if I sweep the floor and get rid of the cobwebs in the eaves.

EARLY IN THE winter of 1946, Betsy writes with terrible news: Andy's father and his nephew Newell were killed in October by a train in Pennsylvania. Mr. Wyeth was driving the car, which stalled on the tracks. Andy is bereft, she writes, but hasn't shed a tear.

When they return to Maine for the summer, I can see right away how much his father's death has affected him. He is quieter. More serious.

"You know, I think my father might've actually been in love with her," he says when we're alone in the kitchen. Sitting in Al's rocker, he pushes it back and forth abstractedly with his foot. Heel, toe, *creak, squeak.*

I'm confused. "Sorry, Andy—been in love with who?"

He stops rocking. "Caroline. My brother Nat's wife. The mother of Newell, my nephew, the one who was . . . the one in the car."

"Oh—my." I'm having a hard time grasping what he's saying. "Your father and . . . your brother's wife?" I don't know any of these people by name. Andy has never really talked about them.

"Yeah." He rubs his face with his hand, as if trying to erase his features. "Maybe. Who knows. At the very least he was infatuated. My father was that way, you know. 'A man of great and varied passions,'" he says, as if quoting an obituary. "He never made any bones about that. But I think in the end he was miserable."

"Did something happen just before the accident? Did someone—"

"Nothing happened. As far as I know. But I do know death was on his mind. I mean, it was one of his obsessions; you can see it in his work. It's in my work too. But that's not . . ." His voice trails off. It's as if he's talking to himself, hashing out what he feels, trying to settle on an interpretation. "It was strange," he murmurs. "After the accident, we found his painting gear carefully lined up in his studio. All in a row. He's normally like me, his stuff all over the place, you know?"

I think of the tempera splatters and crusted eggshells and petrified paintbrushes all over the house. I know.

"And maybe it was a coincidence, but the bible in his studio was open to a passage on adultery. Or—not a coincidence; I mean, it's not unreasonable to imagine that he was contemplating the consequences of an affair, whatever actually happened. But it doesn't mean he purposely . . ."

"It seems out of character," I say. "From what you've told me. You always described him as so—present."

Andy gives me a sardonic smile. "Who knows what motivates anyone, right? Humans are mysterious creatures." He lifts his shoulders in a shrug. "Maybe it was a heart attack. Or carelessness. Or—something else. We'll probably never know the truth."

"You know you miss him. That's pretty simple, isn't it?"

"Is it?"

I think of my own parents—how sometimes I miss them and sometimes I don't. "I suppose not."

Rocking slowly back and forth, he says, "Before my father died, I just wanted to paint. It's different now. Deeper. I feel all the—I don't know—gravity of it. Something beyond me. I want to put it all down as sharply as possible."

He looks over at me, and I nod. I understand this, I do. I know what it is to carry mixed feelings in the marrow of your bones. To feel shackled to the past even though it's populated by ghosts.

WHEN HIS FATHER died, Andy was working on a life-sized egg tempera of Al leaning against a closed door with an iron latch, next to our old oil lamp. He started it the summer before, trying, in sketch after charcoal sketch, to render on paper the scratched nickel of the lamp and the solid weight of the latch. Then he pulled out his paints and asked Al to pose next to the door in the kitchen hallway. For hours, days, weeks, Al sat against that door as Andy tried, and failed, to translate the vision in his head onto canvas. "It's like trying to pin a butterfly," he said in exasperation. "If I'm not careful, the wings will crumble to dust in my hand."

When Andy left Port Clyde at the end of the summer, the painting still wasn't finished, so he took it back to his winter studio in Chadds Ford. After the accident, he started working on it again. When he returned to Maine, he brought the painting with him and propped it against the fireplace in the Shell Room.

I'm standing near the fireplace looking at the painting one morning when Andy arrives at the front door and lets himself in. Noticing me in the Shell Room from the hall, he comes to stand beside me. "Al hated sitting still like that, didn't he?" Andy says.

I laugh. "He was so bored and fidgety."

"He'll never pose for me again."

"Probably not," I agree.

Half of the picture is in light and half in darkness. The oil lamp casts shadows across Al's face, on the old wooden door, under the iron latch. A newspaper behind the lamp is stained and wrinkled. Al is staring into the middle distance as if deep in thought. His eyes seem clouded with tears.

"Did it turn out how you wanted?" I ask Andy.

Reaching out a hand, he traces the outline of the lamp in the air. "I got the texture of the nickel right. I'm happy about that."

"What about the figure of Al?"

"I kept changing it," he says. "I couldn't capture his expression. I'm still not sure I did."

"Is he . . . crying?"

"You think he's crying?"

I nod.

"I didn't intend that. But . . ." With a rueful smile, he says, "You can practically hear that wailing train whistle, can't you?"

"It looks like Al is listening to it," I say.

He moves closer, studying the canvas. "Then maybe it did turn out all right."

ANDY HAS NEVER asked me to pose for him, but several weeks after this conversation he comes to me and says he'd like to do a portrait. How can I say no? He sits me down in the pantry doorway, arranges my hands in my lap and the sweep of my skirt, and draws sketch after sketch, pen on white paper. From a distance. Up close. My hair, each minute strand, swept back off my neck. With a necklace and without. My hands, this way and that. The doorway empty, without me in it.

Most of the time the only sounds are the scratch of his pen, the great flap of paper as he turns a large sheet. Squinting, he holds out his thumb. He sticks the pen in his mouth, leaving him inky lipped. Mumbles quietly to himself. "That's it, there. The shadow . . ." I have the odd sensation that he's looking at me and through me at the same time.

"I hadn't quite noticed how frail your arms are," he muses after a while. "And those scars. How did you get them?"

I've become so accustomed to dealing with people's reactions to my infirmity—uncertainty about what to say, distaste, even revulsion—that I tend to clam up when anyone mentions it. But Andy is looking at me frankly, without pity. I glance down at the crisscrossing strips on my forearms, some redder than others. "The oven racks. Sometimes they slip a little. Usually I wear long sleeves."

He winces. "Those scars look painful."

"You get used to it." I shrug.

"Maybe you could use some help with the cooking. Betsy knows a girl—"

"I do all right."

Shaking his head, he says, "You do, don't you, Christina? Good for you."

One day he scoops up all the sketches and heads upstairs. For the next few weeks I barely see him. Every morning he comes toward the house through the fields, his thin body swaying off kilter from that wonky hip, his elbows and knees flailing out, wearing blue dungarees and a paint-splattered sweatshirt and old work boots he doesn't bother to lace. He raps twice on the screen door before letting himself in, carrying a canteen of water and a handful of eggs he's swiped from the hens. Exchanges pleasantries with Al and me in the kitchen. Thumps up the stairs in his work boots, muttering to himself.

I don't ask to see what he's doing, but I'm curious.

It's a warm, sunny day in July when Andy comes downstairs and says he's tired and distracted and maybe he'll take the afternoon off and go for a sail. After he leaves, I realize it's a good time to see what he's working on up there. No one is around; I can hoist myself up each stair as slowly as I want. Resting every other step.

Even before I open the door to the bedroom on the second floor I smell the eggs. Pushing the door wide, I see broken shells and dirty rags and cups of colored water scattered all over the floor. I haven't been up here in ages; the wallpaper, I notice, is peeling off the wall in strips. Despite the breeze from an open window, the room is stuffy. I glance quickly at the painting, propped on a flimsy easel in the far corner, and look away.

Pulling myself up onto the single bed—my childhood bed—I lie on my back, staring at the spiderweb fissures in the ceiling. Out of the corner of my eye I can glimpse the rectangle of canvas, but I'm not ready to look at it directly. Andy told me once that hidden in his seemingly realistic paintings are secrets, mysteries, allegories. That he wants to get at the essence of things, no matter how ugly.

I'm afraid to learn what he might see in me.

Finally I can't put it off any longer. Turning on my side, I look at the painting.

I'm not hideous, exactly. But it's a shock nevertheless to see myself through his eyes. On the canvas I'm in profile, looking soberly out toward the cove, hands awkward in my lap, nose long and pointy, mouth downturned. My hair is a deep auburn, my frame thin and slightly off kilter. The pantry doorway is rimmed in dark, half in shadow. The door is cracked and weathered, the grasses wild beyond. My dress is black, with a slash, a deep V, below my white neck.

In the black dress—not what I was wearing—I look somber. Severe. And utterly alone. Alone in the doorway facing the sea. My skin ghostly, spectral. Darkness all around.

Bridget Bishop, waiting to be sentenced.

Waiting for death.

I roll onto my back again. Shadows of the lace curtains, moving in and out with the wind, make the ceiling a roiling sea.

When Andy comes in the next morning, I don't tell him I went upstairs. He says hello, we chat for a few minutes while I stir up drop biscuits, and he walks into the foyer. Stops. Comes back to the kitchen door with his hands on his hips. "You went up."

I spoon the dough onto a flat metal sheet, dollop after dollop.

"You did," he insists.

"How'd you know?"

He sweeps his hand up with a flourish. "Path through the dust all the way to the top. Like the trail of a giant snail."

I laugh drily.

"So what'd you think?"

I shrug. "I don't know about art."

"It's not art. It's just you."

"No, it's not. It's you," I say. "Didn't you tell me that once? That every painting is a self-portrait?"

He whistles. "Ah, you're too shrewd for me. Come on. I want to know what you think."

I'm afraid to tell him. Afraid it will sound vain or self-important. "It's so . . . dark. The shadows. The black dress."

"I wanted to show the contrast with your skin. To highlight you sitting there."

Now that we're having this conversation, I realize that I'm a little angry. "I look like I'm in a coffin with the lid half shut."

He laughs a little, as if he can't believe I might be upset.

I stare at him evenly.

Running his hand through his hair, he says, "I was trying to show your . . ." He hesitates. "Dignity. Solemnity."

"Well, I guess that's the problem. I don't think of myself as solemn. I didn't think you did, either."

"I don't. Not really. It's just a moment. And it's not really 'you.' Or 'me.' Despite what you think." His voice trails off. Seeing me struggle with the heavy oven door, he comes over and opens it for me, then slides the baking tray of biscuits in. "I think it's about the house. The mood of it." He shuts the oven door. "Do you know what I mean?"

"You make it seem so . . ." I cast about for the right word. "I don't know. Lonely."

He sighs. "Isn't it, sometimes?"

For a moment there's silence between us. I reach for a dishrag and wipe my floury hands.

"So how do you think of yourself?" he asks.

"What?"

"You said you don't think of yourself as solemn. So how do you think of yourself?"

It's a good question. How do I think of myself?

The answer surprises us both.

"I think of myself as a girl," I say.

1914–1917

Everybody in town seems to know about the envelopes postmarked Massachusetts. I can tell that Bertha Dorset has been gossiping by the way she smirks and lifts her eyebrows when she hands me the mail. When I mention it in a letter to Walton, he writes, "I'm sorry that anyone should bother you with their curiosity," and offers to use Ramona as a foil—she can address the envelopes from Boston, he says. "Then they wouldn't know that I was writing. But I'm afraid they would hear of it some other way."

I decide not to let it bother me. People will always talk. At least now they have good reason.

In one of his letters, Walton says that he has tried, and failed, to grow sweet peas, his favorite flower, in his Cambridge apartment. In April, months before he is due to return, I send away for mail-order sweet pea seeds and ask Al to build a trellis. When the packet arrives, I soak the seeds overnight in water, drain them and chip one end with a sharp blade, then plant them in the manure-rich dirt. I feel like Jack anticipating his beanstalk.

Sprigs sprout, grow into skinny stalks, and race up the lattice. By mid-June, when strawberries are ready to harvest, the sweet peas begin to flower. Though Walton has written to let me know the week he'll be back, and though Sam reports an in-town sighting, I am startled to see him coming up the path on a warm morning with a cluster of sweet peas in his hand and a wide grin on his face.

"You're a sight for sore eyes!" he says when he arrives at the kitchen door, pulling me into a quick embrace. Handing me the bouquet, he says, "I know how much you like sweet peas," and I want to say, no, you're the one who likes them; you know how much I like *you*. But I am oddly touched that he has conflated his feelings with mine.

"I have a surprise," I tell him and make him close his eyes before leading him to the trellis. "Open."

He gives me a rueful look. "I'm sorry. Owls to Athens."

"Great minds," I say. "I grew these for you."

"For me?"

I nod.

He moves closer, grasps my hand. "There's enough beauty here to lure me without sweet peas."

Welcome back, I think.

I'VE NEVER PAID much attention to how I look, but all of a sudden I'm acutely aware of it. I notice the soiled patch on my blue chambray dress, the frayed sleeves of my muslin blouse, the dirty hem of my skirt. I run my fingers through my hair, separating it into oily strands. The entire family bathes on the third Monday of each month in the same water in the kitchen, oldest to youngest (though in the summer the boys, never much for

baths to begin with, get by with a swim in the lake or the ocean).
Every few days I wash my face and under my arms with a wet
cloth dunked in a pot of water warmed on the range. But that, I
decide, isn't enough. I drag the old galvanized tin tub from the
woodshed, with Al's help, and we fill pots with water from the
pump in the pantry and carry them to the range to heat. When
the water's close to boiling, we dump it in the tub and add buck-
ets of cold water. Then I send him out of the room.

In the tub I rub castile soap across my arms, my legs, my
pale stomach, the downy fur under my arms and between my
legs. Dipping my head, I wet my hair and run my soapy hands
through it, my fingers strange on my scalp, like someone else's.
After rinsing my hair, I pour apple cider vinegar into a cupped
hand, as Mother taught me, and run it through the strands until
they squeak. The water is soothing on my knotted muscles and
floating arms, free of gravity's pull. My legs are floating too.
When I was younger, I would bathe in the pond with my brothers sometimes, reveling in the weightlessness, the momentary
release from pain. Now the bath is the only place I can find this
relief. I shut my eyes, savoring it.

Leaning back against the cold tub, I fantasize about what it
would be like to leave this place. I envision the moment as if I'm
a character in a story: A young woman rises while the rest of the
house is asleep, gathers some items into a bundle, makes her way
down the stairs as quietly as she can (as she is accustomed to do,
waking before the others to stoke the fire and prepare breakfast). She laces her shoes in the shadows of the front hall and
opens the door to the outside. Light on her feet as a ballerina,

weightless as a butterfly, she slips down the steps and around the corner, beyond the house and the barn to the automobile that waits out of sight, a young man behind the wheel. (Walton, of course. Who else would it be?) He takes her bag, tosses it over the seat. In her bag: a chambered nautilus, an empty picture frame decorated with shells that awaits a moment worth remembering. Almost everything else she leaves behind, bits and pieces of a life outgrown. Whatever she'll need in the future can be found where she's going.

AS THE SUMMER progresses we fall into our routines from the year before: boating with the Carles, clambakes on the rocks by Kissing Cove, picnics in the meadow. One day, as we're meandering down to Bird Point, he says, "It would be terrific if you could come to Boston this fall."

I feel a surge of pleasure. "I would like to."

"You could stay with the Carles, I'm sure. And . . ." He hesitates, and I hold my breath, hoping he'll make the invitation more personal—"perhaps you might see a doctor for your affliction while you're there."

I stop walking in surprise. We haven't ever explicitly talked about my condition, though I've come to rely on his arm under mine. "You want me to see a doctor?"

"These country physicians are well meaning, no doubt, but I doubt they're conversant in the latest advances. Wouldn't you like to find out what's wrong with you?"

"Wrong with me?" I stammer. My skin feels cold.

He taps his forehead with two fingers. "Forgive me, Christina. 'What ails you,' I should have said. You don't complain, but I can imagine how much you suffer. As one who cares about you . . ." His voice trails off again, and he grasps my hand. "I'd like to see if something can be done."

These concerns are reasonable, even logical. So why do his gentle entreaties make me want to put my hands over my ears and beg him to stop? "You are kind to want to improve my welfare," I tell him, striving for a neutral tone.

"Not at all. I only want for you to be well. So will you consider it?"

"I would prefer not to."

"Said Bartleby." He flashes a smile, breaking the tension.

Bartleby. From the recesses of my school brain I dredge the reference: the obstinate scrivener. I smile back.

"I only want what's best for you, you know."

"You're what's best for me," I say.

AUGUST IS EXQUISITE agony. I want each day to last forever. I am fretful, fevered, perpetually irritated by everyone but Walton, to whom I'm determined to show my best self. It's a peculiar kind of dissatisfaction, a bittersweet nostalgia for a moment not yet past. Even in the midst of a pleasurable outing I'm aware of how ephemeral it is. The water is warm but will cool. The ocean is a sheet of glass, but wind is picking up, far across the horizon. The bonfire is roaring but will dwindle. Walton is beside me, his arm around my shoulder, but all too soon he will be gone.

On our final evening as a group, sitting on the beach, making conversation, Walton mentions the almanac's prediction of a hard winter ahead, and Ramona says, "Will Christina ever know anything except a hard winter?" She doesn't look at him when she says it, but we all know what she's asking: if, and when, Walton is going to offer a way out.

He seems oblivious. "Christina's not like us, Ramona. She likes the cold Maine winters. Isn't that so?" he asks me, squeezing my shoulders.

I look at Ramona, who shakes her head slightly and rolls her eyes. But neither of us says anything more.

FLOWERS FADE, FREEZE in an early frost, wither on the vine. Trees burst into flame and burn themselves out. Leaves crumble to ash. All the things about life on the farm that once contented me now fill me with impatience. It has become harder to tolerate the months after summer ends, the plodding regularity of my daily chores, the inevitable descent into darkness and cold. I feel as if I'm on a narrow path through familiar woods, a path that goes around and around with no end in sight.

I spend the early fall canning and preserving and pickling: tomatoes, cucumbers, strawberries, blueberries. Shelving the jars in the shed. Alvaro slaughters a pig, and we carve and cure and smoke every last bit of it, from hoof to curly tail. We trowel up and store unlovely root vegetables, rutabagas and turnips and parsnips and beets. Pluck apples and lay them out on a long table in the cellar for the long winter ahead.

I have too much time to think. I torment myself. All I do is work and think. I feel like the mollusk in Mamey's nautilus, grown too big for its shell. A woman my age, I think, should be laboring for her own husband and children. All around me, friends and classmates are becoming engaged and getting married. The boys I went to school with are settling into lives as farmers and fishermen and shopkeepers. The girls, Sadie and Gertrude among them, are setting up house and having babies.

When I trudge through my tasks, Mother chides me—"Pick up your feet, my girl; life is not as tragic as all that"—and Al looks at me sideways, and I know what they're thinking, that it might have been better if Walton had never come along.

But Walton's letters are hot-air balloons, lifting me out of melancholy. He writes about his classes, his teachers, his thoughts about his future career. Though he's been training as a journalist, news about the war raging in Europe dominates the papers, making it a hard time to break into domestic reporting, he says. He has decided to shift his sights to teaching. Teachers are always needed, whether a war is raging or the stock market is falling. It's not lost on me that he could be a teacher anywhere— even in Cushing, Maine.

WINTER PASSES AS slowly as a glacier melts. Christmas and New Year's provide momentary distraction before we settle into months of ice and snow. Walking back from the post office in the late-afternoon gloom of a February day, I am tucking Walton's letter inside my coat when my shoe catches on a protruding chip of ice and I crash to the ground. I prop myself on an elbow, noting with strange detachment my torn stockings, the thin coating of blood on my shin, a throbbing pain in my right hand, the one I used to break my fall. Tentatively I extend my left arm and begin to hoist myself up. I pat my jacket. The letter must have flown from my pocket when I fell. I feel around on the ground, muddying my skirt even further, my blood pinking the ice. Several yards away I spy the envelope and limp over to it. Empty. The sky is darkening, the air is cold, my shin is throbbing, and still I continue, as desperate as an opium addict; I can't leave until I find it. And then I see the folded pages, fluttering in the ditch.

When I reach them, I find that the ink has run; the letter—mud spattered, water soaked—appears to have been written in a diabolical code designed to drive the recipient insane. I can only identify every fourth or fifth word or phrase (*entertaining . . . I am glad to say . . . beginning to enjoy*), and after straining to make out the letters with increasing exasperation, I hold the pages flat against my dress, inside my coat, hoping they'll be legible when dry. The walk home is slow and painful. When I step into the house, I open my coat to find the bodice of my chambray dress tattooed with ink. A permanent reminder of how important his words have become to me.

SUMMER AGAIN. WHEN I answer the door one June morning in 1915 to find Walton standing there, he gives me a huge smile and presents me with a package of butterscotch candies. "Sweets to the sweet," he says.

"That's an old line," I tell him. "You've said it before."

He laughs. "I obviously have a limited repertoire."

Soon we fall back into our familiar routines, seeing each other nearly every day. We stroll the property, sail in the afternoon, picnic in early evening with the Carles and my brothers Al and Sam down by the grove. I see Ramona watching as Walton and I go off together to collect driftwood and twigs to make a fire in the circle of rocks, as he pulls me behind a tree and kisses me. At the end of the evening we sit on the rough benches Papa made and watch the cinders crumble and settle. The sky changes from blue to purple to rose to red as the sun sinks like an ember into the sea.

When Walton gets up to talk to Alvah on the other side of the fire pit, Ramona comes to sit beside me. "I need to ask," she says quietly. "Has Walton discussed the nature of his commitment to you?"

I knew this question was coming. I've been dreading it.

"Not exactly," I tell her. "I think our commitment is—understood."

"Understood by whom?"

"By both of us."

"Does he say *anything*?"

"Well, he needs to establish himself before—"

"I am prying, forgive me. I've tried to keep my mouth shut. But my goodness, this is the third year."

It's not like she's articulating anything I haven't thought myself, but her words feel like a punch in the gut. Walton is a scholar, I want to say, studying the classics and philosophy; he cannot make any decisions until he is done with school. Nobody seems to understand this.

I'm not sure I understand it myself.

"It's really not your business, Ramona," I say stiffly.

"It's not, you're right."

We sit in silence, the air between us bristling with words unsaid.

After a few moments, she sighs. "Look, Christina. Be careful. That's all I'm saying."

I know Ramona means well. But this is like telling a person who has leapt off a cliff to be careful. I am already in midair.

IN LATE AUGUST, Walton and I make a plan to sail alone to Thomaston. Since my conversation with Ramona I've been acutely aware of how deftly he evades any talk of commitment. Maybe she's right; I need to raise the issue directly.

I resolve to do it on our sail.

It's early evening, and the air is laced with cool. He stands behind me, unfurling a big wool blanket and wrapping it around our shoulders as I steer.

"Walton—" I begin nervously.

"Christina."

"I don't want you to leave."

"I don't want to leave," he says, wrapping his hand over mine.

I slide my hand out from under his. "But you have things to look forward to. All I have is months of winter. And waiting."

"Ah, my poor Persephone," he murmurs, kissing my hair, my shoulder.

This irritates me further. I pull away a bit. For a few moments we are quiet. I listen to the mournful yawp of seagulls overhead, as large as geese.

"I want to ask you something," I say finally.

"Ask."

"Or—well—tell you."

"Go ahead."

"I love . . ." I start, but my courage fades. "Being with you."

He pulls the blanket tighter around me, enveloping us in a cocoon. "I love being with you."

"But . . . what are we—what are you—"

His hands move up my sides, resting on my ribs. I arch my back, leaning into him, and his hands move to the front, cupping my breasts gently through the fabric. "Oh, Christina," he breathes. "Some things don't need explanation. Do they?"

I decide I will not ask him, press him, insist. I tell myself it's not the time. But the fact is, I am afraid. Afraid that I will push him away, and that this—whatever it is—will end.

❧

AL AND I are clearing the dishes from supper one evening when he says, "So what do you think is going to happen?"

"What?"

He's bent over the plates, scraping leftover potatoes and yams and applesauce into a bucket for the pigs. "You think Walton Hall is going to marry you?"

"I don't know. I haven't thought about it." But Al must know this is a lie.

"All I'm saying is . . ." He is strained and awkward, unaccustomed to the intimacy of speaking his mind.

"'All I'm saying is,'" I mock him impatiently. "Stop hemming and hawing. Spit it out."

"I've never seen you like this."

"Like what."

"As if reason has left you."

"Honestly." Feeling a flare of annoyance, I handle the pots recklessly, clanging them into each other.

"I'm concerned for you," he says.

"Well, don't be."

For a few minutes we work silently, clearing the table, scooping the cutlery into a bowl, pouring warm water from the kettle into a pan for the dishes. As I go through the familiar motions I get even angrier. How dare he—this cautious man-child who has never been in love—pass judgment on Walton's motives and my own good sense? Al knows as much about the nature of our relationship as he does about sewing a dress.

"What do you think?" I blurt finally. "That I am an imbecile? That I have not a thought in my head?"

"It's not you I worry about."

"Well, you needn't worry. I can take care of myself. And besides—as if it's any of your business—Walton has been honorable in every way."

Al lowers a stack of plates into the washing pan. "Of course he has. He likes the diversion. He doesn't want to give it up."

Clutching a fistful of forks, I turn to him. For a brief moment I contemplate striking him with them, but instead I take a deep breath and say, "How dare you."

"Come on, Christie, I don't mean to . . ." Again his voice falters, and I can see, given how unnatural it must feel for him to confront me, how important he considers this. And yet I find him irritatingly simplistic. All the things I ordinarily admire about Al now strike me as deficits: his loyalty no more than fear of the unknown; his decency, merely naïveté; his sense of morality, prim judgment. (How quickly, with a slight twist in perception, do people's strengths become flaws!)

"What I'm saying is that . . ." He swallows. "His options are many."

It's no use trying to explain to Alvaro what love is. So I say, "You might say the same about Papa, when he courted Mother."

An ironic look flits across his face. "How's that?"

"He could've worked on any ship. Traveled all over the world. But he settled here, with her."

"Mother had a big house and hundreds of acres." He flings

his hand toward the window. "You know what this house, the *Olson* House, used to be called."

I splash the cutlery in the dishwater impatiently. "Did you ever consider that maybe Papa fell in love?"

"Sure. Maybe. Just remember—you have three brothers. This house isn't yours to inherit."

"Walton isn't after this house."

"Okay." He dries his hands on a dish towel and hangs it on a hook. "I'm just saying you should be careful. It's not right for him to keep you on a tether."

"I'm not on a tether," I tell him sharply. "Anyway, I'd rather be with Walton for three months in the summer than any of these local boys all year-round."

One morning after gathering eggs, a few weeks later, I step across the threshold into the house and hear my parents' voices in the Shell Room, a place they rarely enter. I stand very still in the foyer, cupping the eggs, still warm from the hens, in my hands.

"She's no beauty, but she works hard. I think she'd make a fine companion," Papa is saying.

"She would," Mother says. "But I'm beginning to wonder if he's toying with her."

My face tingles as I realize they're talking about me. I lean against the wall, straining to hear.

"Who knows? Perhaps he wants to run a farm."

Mother laughs, a dry bark. "That one? No."

"What does he want with her, then?"

"Who knows? To fill his idle time, I suspect."

"Maybe he really does love her, Katie."

"I fear . . ." Mother's voice trails off. "That he will not marry her."

Papa says, "I fear it too."

My cheeks are aflame, my heart beating in my ears. In my trembling hands, the eggs jostle and shift, and though I try to contain them they slip between my fingers and drop to the floor, one after the other, splattering smears of yellow and viscous white across the entryway.

Mother appears in the doorway, looking stricken. "I'll get a rag." She ducks away and comes back; crouching, she mops the floor around my feet. Both of us are silent. I'm aware of nothing but my own humiliation, the shock of hearing my silent fears put into words. The screen door slams and I watch Papa go past the window, ducking his head on his way to the barn.

IN SEPTEMBER, WHEN Walton is back at school, he writes, "I think that night we made the trip to Thomaston was the happiest I ever spent. How could you steer, under the circumstances? I believe I was to blame." He is homesick for Cushing. Homesick for me. "This was the best summer of my life. A large part of that I owe to you," he writes, signing his letter, "With love, Walton."

I feel as if a wall of the house has detached from the rest and fallen gently to the ground. I can see a way out, a clear path to the open sea.

WITH WALTON AND the Carles around all summer I don't need anyone else; my brothers and I buzz around them, moths to their vivid flame. But after they leave, I am lonely. When Gertrude Gibbons, a girl I never particularly liked at school who has grown into a mildly tolerable adult, invites me to a Wednesday night sewing circle run by a professional seamstress, Catherine Bailey, I reluctantly agree. Gertrude, too, makes her own dresses, and between sessions of the group we start sewing together in the evenings sometimes, when the chores are done. It's a way to pass the time.

On a cool November evening, I take my sewing to Gertrude's house in a sack slung over my shoulder, a two-mile walk. All day it's been raining; the road is damp, and I have to walk slowly and carefully to avoid muddy puddles.

"Finally!" Gertrude exclaims when she answers my knock. Round faced and ruddy, with an ample bosom that strains the buttons on her dress, she's chewing a molasses cookie. Her large black dog barks and leaps. "Down, Oscar, down!" she scolds. "Come in, for mercy's sake."

A cat is curled on an upholstered chair. "Shoo, Tom," Gertrude says, flapping her hands, and the cat reluctantly obliges. "Sit here," she tells me. "Cookie? Fresh baked."

"I'm fine for now, thanks."

"That's how you stay so thin!" she says. "You're abstemious

like my sister. I try, honestly I do, but I don't know how anyone can resist a warm molasses cookie."

The house is snug; embers glow in the fireplace. Gertrude tosses on another log while I get settled. Her parents are away, visiting relatives in Thomaston, she says; her brother is out with friends. Oscar sprawls in front of the hearth, his eggplant stomach soon rising up and down in contented sleep.

We chat about the large yield this season of potatoes and turnips; I tell her about the fox that stole three hens out of our coop, and how Al trapped and killed it. She wants to know my famous fried apple cake recipe and I explain it step-by-step: how you peel and thinly slice the apples, fry the slices over a low flame in a heavy black skillet, adding a stream of molasses until the apples are soft in the middle and crispy on the edges, then turn the skillet over onto a platter. (I don't tell her that I can no longer turn the skillet on my own and have to ask one of my brothers to do it.)

The skirt I'm working on is beige cotton, with pleats and pockets. Before I came to Gertrude's I pressed the fabric with a hot iron, one inch all the way around, and now I'm using a slip stitch to hem it. My stitches are small and neat, partly because I have to concentrate so hard to get them right. Gertrude's are sloppy. She is easily distracted, full of gossip she's been waiting to share. Emily Jones had a stillborn baby early in the summer and she still hasn't left the house, poor girl. Earl Standin has a drinking problem. His pregnant wife showed up at Fales with a shiner last week, claiming she walked into a pole. Sarah Stewart married a blacksmith from Rockland she met at a social, but rumor has it she's in love with his brother.

"So what do you hear?" she asks.

I hold up the fabric and frown, pretending to be vexed by a missed stitch. The more she natters on, the less I want to say. I know she is eager for details about Walton, but I hold them close, not trusting that she won't chew them into cud. She waits patiently, her sewing in her lap.

"You are a sphinx, Christina Olson," she says finally.

"I'm just a bore," I say. "Nobody tells me anything."

"What about that Ramona Carle and that Harland Woodbury? I hear he's sweet on her."

A man named Harland Woodbury did, in fact, travel up from Boston to visit Ramona this summer in Cushing. But after he left, Ramona made fun of his chubby cheeks and porkpie hat. "Don't know a thing about it," I tell Gertrude.

She gives me a sly look. "Well, I heard something you might be able to shed light on." She licks her index finger and rubs the frayed edge of her thread into a point. "I heard," she says, threading her needle, "that a certain young man from Harvard can't make up his mind."

A flush moves through me, starting at the top of my head, like heatstroke. My fingers tremble. I put down the cloth so Gertrude won't see.

"Surely you're aware that a man like that . . ." she says gently, as if to a child. She sighs.

"Like what?" I ask sharply, and immediately regret engaging her at all.

"You know. Educated, from away." She reaches over and pats my leg. "So just—what's the saying—don't put all your goods on one ship."

"Okay, Gertrude."

"I know you're private, Christina. And you don't want to talk about this. But I could not, in good conscience, let the moment pass without telling you what I think."

I nod and keep my mouth shut. If I don't speak, she can't answer.

MAKING MY WAY home from Gertrude's house I am distracted, lost in thought, when my foot sinks into a rut in the road and I tumble forward. As I fall I try to pivot sideways to protect the parcel I'm carrying containing my half-finished dress, landing with a thud on my right side. I feel a searing jolt of pain in my right leg. Both of my forearms are skinned. As soon as I brush the gravelly dirt off, blood springs to the surface. My leg is twisted under me, my foot splayed in an unnatural direction. The parcel is torn and muddied.

It's no use calling for help; no one will hear. If my leg is broken, if I can't get up, it will probably be morning before anyone finds me. How stupid was I to venture out like this on a cold night by myself—and for what?

I moan, feeling sorry for myself. People make dumb mistakes all the time, and that's the end of them. A man in Thomaston was found frozen to death last winter in the woods, either because he was disoriented or had a heart attack. People go out in skiffs in cloudy weather, swim in the ocean when there's an undertow, fall asleep with candles burning. Go out alone and break a leg in the middle of nowhere on a frigid November night.

I reach down to touch my right thigh. The kneecap. I bend my leg and feel a sharp jab. Ah, there. The ankle.

Papa urged me to take his walking stick when I left the house, but I refused.

I'm so tired of this mutinous body that doesn't move the way it should. Or the low thrumming ache that's never entirely absent. Of having to concentrate on my steps so I don't fall, of my ever-present scabs and bruises. I'm tired of pretending that I'm the same as everyone else. But to admit what it's really like to live in this skin would mean giving up, and I'm not ready to do that.

"Your pride will be the end of you," Mother often says. Perhaps she's right.

I tuck the parcel into my waistband and struggle to my knees. Bunching my skirt beneath me to buffer my skin from the ground, I drag myself toward the side of the road, moving gingerly to avoid putting pressure on my ankle. I squint toward a clump of birches about a dozen feet away, looking for a stick to use as a cane. After pulling myself to my feet, I stagger to the cluster of trees, picking my way over rocks and ruts, and feel around with my hands. Here. Too short, but it'll do. Limping back to the road, I lean heavily on the stick, grimacing through the pain.

An hour ago I couldn't wait to leave Gertrude's house, but now going back there is my only option. I hobble slowly down the road. When I see her front porch, I breathe a sigh of relief. I pull myself up the three front steps, leaving a sludgy trail, and pause in front of the door. The lights are off. I pound on the door with the side of my closed fist. No answer. I rap hard on the window beside the door with my knuckles.

From deep inside the house I hear footsteps. Through the window I see the glow of a lamp. Then Gertrude's frightened voice on the other side of the door: "Who's there?"

"It's me. Christina."

The door opens and I lurch inside.

"Mercy!" Gertrude flaps her arms like a bird trying to land on a rock. "What happened?"

"I fell on the road. I think my ankle may be broken."

"Oh dear. You are covered in mud," she says with dismay.

"I'm sorry. I'm sorry to bother you." Hot tears spring to my eyes, tears of relief and exhaustion and bitterness—that I can't walk right, that I am back at this house, that, damn her, Gertrude may be right: Walton will never marry me, I will be stuck in this place for the rest of my life, sewing with this wretched woman. I turn my face so she doesn't see the tears streaking through the grime.

Gertrude sighs and shakes her head. "Stay right there. Let me find a cloth so you don't ruin the rug."

"I BROKE MY ankle coming back from Gertrude Gibbons's house," I write to Walton. "It was foolish. I never should have been alone on that road in the dark."

"I am glad to hear you're on the mend, and dearly hope you'll be more prudent in the future," he writes back. "Yours faithfully—."

I scan the letter several times, trying to hear his voice between the lines. But the words are stiff and formal. No matter how often I read them, they sound like an admonition.

I'M APPREHENSIVE ABOUT seeing Walton for the first time after the long winter apart, but he gives me a warm hug and a kiss on the cheek. "I have a present for you," he says, drawing a large shell from the inside pocket of his seersucker jacket and placing it on the table in front of us. "I thought you might add it to your collection."

The shell is shiny and garishly colored—orange red, with bulky knobs on top that get smaller toward the edges.

I pick it up. It's as smooth and heavy as a glass paperweight. "Oh. Where did you find this?"

"I bought it. In a specialty shop in Cambridge." He smiles. "From Hawaii, I believe. It's called a cameo shell. At least that's what the card on the shelf said. It'll look nice in the Shell Room, don't you think?"

I nod. "Sure."

He touches my arm. "You don't like it."

"No, it's—interesting." But I'm disappointed that he doesn't know me well enough to understand that this gaudy bauble from a specialty shop doesn't belong in the Shell Room, filled with discoveries from expeditions. I wish he'd lied and told me he found it on a beach.

I set the cameo shell on the mantelpiece in the Shell Room, but it looks out of place, like an artificial flower in a garden. After a few weeks, I put it in a drawer.

AS THE SUMMER of 1916 progresses, Walton acts exactly as he always has: solicitous, courtly, quick with a smile and an ironic aside. But I am acutely aware that like a slip of paper in the wind, something in his nature eludes my grasp. Even when I ask direct questions, he is evasive, offering only vague generalities about his life in Boston, his family, his plans for the future.

One early July morning Walton and I are making our way through the high grass to Hathorn Point to harvest mussels for dinner when I notice that he's not saying much. He seems uncomfortable, fiddling with his sleeve as he walks.

"What is it? Walton, tell me."

"It's just . . ." He shakes his head as if dislodging a thought. "My parents. Thinking they know what's best for me."

I know his parents live in Malden, near the Carles. As far as I'm aware they've never come up for a visit. "Did you get a letter?"

He bends down, swipes an errant stick from the grass, and snaps it in half with a small, sharp movement. "Yes. A long, tedious letter. Saying it's time for me to grow up, to take a job in Boston in the summers and stop frittering away my time up here with the Carles." He snaps the stick halves in half again before flinging all the tiny pieces onto the ground.

"Is this about . . . me?"

He shoves his hands in his pockets. His grievance has taken on a theatrical air, as if exaggerated for my benefit. "It's not personal," he says brusquely. "They claim to be concerned about my future. They don't want me to limit myself."

My heart skitters ahead of my words. "What—what do they mean by that?"

"It's absurd," he says. "Keeping up appearances. Harvard, all that. The right job. The right wife."

"Meaning . . ." I ask in as neutral a tone as I can muster.

He shrugs. "Oh, who knows. They want me to marry someone"—he lifts forked fingers to convey that he's quoting— "'educated' and 'from a good family.' Which means, naturally, a family they've heard of. A Boston family, preferably. A family that will bolster their social standing. Because that's the important thing."

I find myself shrinking into silence. Of course Walton's parents don't want their Harvard-educated son marrying a girl who didn't even go to secondary school.

"You're upset," Walton says, patting my arm. "But you shouldn't be. This isn't about you. They don't really know about you."

This shocks me into words. "You've never mentioned me?"

"Of course I've mentioned you," he says quickly. "I just don't think they realize quite what . . . quite how much you mean to me."

"Do they know that we are . . ." The word *sweethearts* springs to mind, but I'm afraid it will sound cloying, presumptuous.

He shrugs. "I try not to talk to my parents about much of anything."

"So they don't know that we've been . . . seeing each other for four years?"

"I'm not sure what they know, and I don't care," he says dismissively. "Let's put this aside and enjoy the morning, shall we? I'm sorry I brought it up."

I nod, but the conversation has dampened my mood. It's only later, going over it in my head, that I realize he didn't answer my question.

THE DAY BEFORE Walton and the Carles are to return to Massachusetts, we make a plan to go to the Acorn Grange Hall in Cushing for a dance. Walton shows up earlier than expected with Eloise and Ramona and finds me in the yard behind the house, struggling with a load of laundry. It's wash day, and I can't leave until all the clothes are on the line.

"Go ahead, I'll be along soon," I tell them. I'm hot and perspiring, still wearing my old frock and apron.

"I'll help her finish," he says to the others. "We'll catch up with you."

Eloise and Ramona leave the house with Al and Sam in a clamorous gaggle. I watch them as they make their way down the road—Al and Sam tall and awkward, bending like reeds toward the pretty sisters.

Walton helps me wring the damp pieces, his strong hands far more efficient than mine. He hoists the straw basket to his hip and we make our way to the clothesline; then, crouching, he takes each piece of damp clothing from the basket, shakes it, and hands it to me, and I pin it to the rope. The intimacy of this ordinary task feels bittersweet.

Walton waits on the back stoop while I go inside to change into a clean white blouse and navy skirt. "You look nice," he says when I appear. As we stroll toward the Grange Hall, he rummages in his pocket. I hear the familiar crinkle of wax paper. He pops a butterscotch candy into his mouth.

"Do you have one for me?" I ask.

"Of course." He stops and takes out another, unwraps it, and puts it on my tongue. He rubs my arms. "Autumn in the air already," he muses. "Are you cold? Do you need my jacket?"

"I'm perfect," I say a little stiffly.

"I know you're perfect. I was asking if you're chilly." He smiles, and I can tell he's trying to lighten my mood.

I suck on the candy for a moment. "You're leaving."

"Not for a few days."

"Soon."

"Too soon," he concedes, lacing his fingers through mine.

For a few minutes we walk along in silence. Then I venture, "Teachers are needed all over. Even in Maine."

He squeezes my hand gently but says nothing. Above our heads a riot of birdsong erupts, piercing the quiet. We both look up. The dense tree cover, leaf lush, gives nothing away. Then, suddenly swooping across the road, a dark flurry.

"I've never seen so many crows," he remarks.

"Actually, they're blackbirds."

"Ah. What would I do without you to correct me?" He pulls on my hand playfully, and then, realizing he's yanking me off balance, tucks his arm around my waist. "Such a clever girl," he murmurs in my ear. Then he slows and stops in the road.

I'm not sure what he's doing. "What is it?"

He puts a finger to his lips and tugs me gently down the embankment into a copse of blue-black spruce. In the shadows he cups my warm face in his cool hands. "You are truly something, Christina."

I look into his pale eyes, trying to decipher what he's saying. He gazes back implacably. "I can't tell if you're sad to be leaving," I say, a petulant tone creeping into my voice.

"Of course I am. But admit it—you'll be a bit relieved. 'Finally summer's over, I have my life back.'"

I shake my head.

He shakes his head, mimicking me. "No?"

"No. I—"

He kisses me on the mouth, gathers me closer, kisses my bony shoulder, the hollow of my neck. He runs his hand down my bodice, hesitates for a moment, then continues all the way to the folds of my skirt. I am dizzy with surprise. He pushes me back against the bark of a tree. I feel its knots pressing into my back as he leans into me, running a hand down my side, another under my blouse, up the slight curve of my breast. His mouth on mine jams my head awkwardly against the trunk, an uncomfortable and yet not altogether unpleasant experience.

The butterscotch clicks in my mouth. "I'd better spit this out, or I might choke," I say.

He laughs. "Me too."

I don't care that it's unladylike; I spit it on the grass.

Now his hand is between my legs, lost in the fabric. I feel him cup me there in a proprietary way, and I push my hips toward him, feeling his hardness between us. My skin is alive, every nerve ending pulsing. His breathing ragged, insistent. This is what I want. This passion. This certainty. This clear sign of his desire. Right now I would do anything, anything he asks.

And then—a sound on the road. Walton jerks his head up, alert as a bird dog. "What is that?" he breathes.

I cock my head. Feel a low rumbling in my soles. "An automobile, I think."

The sky is dark now. I can barely see his face.

He pulls back, then sways into me, clutching my shoulders. "Oh, Christina," he murmurs. "You make me want you."

The darkness emboldens me. "I'm yours."

Still holding my shoulders, he rests his head on my breastbone like a nudging sheep. When he sighs, I feel his warm breath on my chest. "I know." Then he looks up into my eyes with a startling intensity. "We must be together. Beyond"—he waves an arm, indicating the trees, the road, the sky—"all this."

My heart leaps. "Oh, Walton. Do you mean it?"

"I do. I promise."

Though everything in my nature fights against it, I'm determined to find out what he means. Swallowing hard, I ask, "What do you promise?"

"That we will be together. There are things I need to— resolve. You must come to Boston, and meet my parents. But I promise you, Christina, yes."

Blue-black spruce shushing overhead, gravelly dirt under my thin-soled shoes, the smell of pine, a Necco wafer of moon in the sky. Some sense memories fade as soon as they're past. Others are etched in your mind for the rest of your life. This, I already know, is one of those.

When we get to the Grange Hall, Ramona and Eloise are chatting and dancing with whatever stray boys they can round up, gaily pulling them out of chairs. The makeshift band, fiddle and piano and standing bass, is composed of some of the boys I grew up with, Billy Grover and Michael Verzaleno and Walter Brown. They play raucous, sloppy versions of "The Maple Leaf Rag" and "It's a Long Way to Tipperary." Walton croons in my ear: "Leave the Strand and Piccadilly, or you'll be to blame, for love has fairly drove me silly—hoping you're the same!"

When they start to play "Danny Boy," I listen to the words as if I've never heard them before, as if they were written just for me.

> The summer's gone, and all the roses dying,
> It's you, it's you must go and I must bide . . .
> It's I'll be here in sunshine or in shadow—
> Oh, Danny boy, oh Danny boy, I love you so

We dance nose to nose, Walton's hand low on my waist, a tacit reminder of our moment in the woods. "I'll miss this," he says. "I'll miss you."

My voice chokes in my throat. I don't trust myself to speak.

After the last song, we make our way home on the dark road with the others. My legs are tired, but melancholy makes me even slower, like a dog on a leash being pulled where it doesn't want to go. Walton puts his arm around me and we fall back, away from the others. At the turnoff for the Carles' we linger by the gate. I lean my head on his shoulder.

"I wish I could reach up and grab a faraway star and put it on your finger," Walton says. Running a finger over my lips, he bends down to kiss me. I feel in his kiss the weight of his promise.

TEN DAYS LATER I receive a letter postmarked Massachusetts. "Remember a week ago tonight? I shall remember it until I see you again," he writes. "What promises I make, I keep."

DECEMBER IS AS gray as my mood. I haven't received a letter from Walton since September.

Though it's cold, there's little snow. A cat has been hiding under the house, a butterscotch tiger-striped Maine coon with enormous ginger eyes. I tempt it out with a bowl of milk. Shivering, it laps the milk hungrily, and when the bowl is empty, I lift it onto my lap. A female. Her skin is loose around her bones; it's like cradling a bag of hollow pipes. She licks my chin with a sea-urchin tongue and settles on my lap with a purr. I name her Lolly. She's the only bright spot of my entire month.

For Christmas I give my brothers plaid shirts I've sewn out of flannel while they were working outside. Mother knits socks and hats. Papa makes no pretense of giving presents; he says the roof over our heads is present enough. Sam gives me a baking tray, Fred puts a ribbon on a new straw broom, Al carves a set of wooden spoons. Walton sends a thick cream-colored card foil-stamped with a green wreath and a red bow, addressed to The Olson Family. "Sending you warm wishes in this cold season. Happy Christmas and God Bless!" He signs it "Walton Hall."

Instead of displaying his card, as I've done in past years, I take it upstairs to my room. I take the stack of his letters from the shelf where I keep them, untie the pale pink ribbon, and sit on my bed, opening the letters and reading each one. *All roads lead back to Cushing for me. What promises I make, I keep. With love.* I hold the Christmas card between my hands so tightly that it rips a little. Slowly, I tear it down the middle, then rip the pieces again and again until they're as small as butterscotch candies, as two-cent stamps, as faraway stars in the sky.

I WRITE TO Walton after the holidays, wishing him a happy 1917, telling him about the presents I received from my brothers and the flannel shirts I sewed. I describe the suckling pig we roasted in a pit Al built in the yard, the blueberry compote and fried apple cake, the chicken stew with squash dumplings and the drink Sam concocts on New Year's Eve: rum, molasses, and cloves in a mug with boiling water, blended with a cinnamon stick. Whaler's Toddy, it's called. I strive to convey the flavor of our humble rituals, the camaraderie and clamor of a house filled with boys, a feeling of well-being and holiday cheer that isn't so much exaggerated in the telling as enhanced. I do my best to avoid a plaintive undertow.

I don't understand. Why haven't you written?

Days pass, weeks. Months. I thought I was used to waiting. This is a new kind of hell. My soul feels coated with tar.

I berate myself for the letter I sent, filled with mindless chatter about our simple rituals. What I have to share is paltry, insignificant, domestic. And yet it's all I have to give.

As winter turns to spring I slog to the post office, zigzagging through the snow and slush. Bills, flyers, the *Saturday Evening Post*. "Nothing for you today, Christina," Bertha Dorset says, her prim voice threaded with pity. I want to lunge across the counter and throttle her until her face purples and she gasps for breath. But I take the mail and smile.

Even when the snow melts and the crocuses bloom I am cold, always cold, no matter how many blankets I pile on my bed. In the middle of the night, I listen to the wind screaming through gaps in the wall. I remember a story I read once about a woman who goes mad trapped inside her house and comes to believe that she lives behind the wallpaper. I am beginning to wonder if I will stay in this house forever, creeping up and down the stairs like the woman in that story.

IT IS A warm morning in May when I see Ramona out the kitchen window, striding toward the house across the grass, head down, shoulders squared. I've thought about this day all winter. I sink into my old chair beside the red geraniums. Lolly springs onto my lap and I stroke her back. Ordinarily I would get up, put a kettle on for tea, stand in the doorway to welcome her, but I can't rally the energy to cover the conversation that I know is coming with the rituals of a friendly visit.

Ramona isn't surprised to find me in the kitchen. "Hello, Christina. Mind if I come in?" Her smile is wobbly. Stepping across the threshold into the gloom, she squints. "So good to see you."

I muster a smile in response. "You too."

"Did I catch you in the middle of something?"

"Just the usual."

"You look well."

I know I don't. I'm wearing an old apron over a plain checked dress. "I wasn't expecting company." I start to untie the back of the apron.

"Oh, please don't change," she says, adding quickly, "It's just me."

"I'm done with the lunch dishes. About to take it off anyway."

She watches me wrestle with the tie in the back. I can tell she wants to help but knows I wouldn't like it.

For a moment she hesitates in the middle of the floor. She's clutching a paper bag and wearing a style of dress I haven't seen before, yellow and white checkerboard patterned with full white sleeves and three tortoiseshell buttons, a drapey white collar, and a wide waistband. Pale stockings and white leather shoes. Her hair is pulled back in a bun with a yellow ribbon.

"That's a nice dress," I say, though her outfit makes me think she must be stopping through on her way to somewhere more exciting.

"Oh, thank you. It's summery, don't you think?"

"I guess."

As if suddenly remembering, she says, "I brought you something! Mama had a crate sent from Florida." She takes three large oranges out of her bag and sets them on the table. "I'd love to get down to Florida one of these days. I can just see myself lying on a beach on a towel with a big straw hat. Wouldn't that be nice?"

"Maybe so."

"How about we go together? In the winter sometime, when it's so dang cold."

I shrug. "I'm not keen on burning in the sun."

"I forget about your Swedish skin," she says. "Why don't I peel us an orange and I can dream about Florida and you enjoy a healthy treat?"

"Well, I just ate lunch . . ." I begin, then relent. "All right."

She digs into an orange with her thumbs and peels back the thick cratered crust, carefully picks off the white veins. Pulling it apart, she hands me a slice. "Cheers!"

The orange is so sweet, so juicy, that I almost forget how nervous I am.

When we've polished it off, Ramona pulls Al's rocker toward the table and sits down. "I love this old rocker," she says. "So lived in." She rubs the arms where the black paint has worn through to wood.

It's only now, with her hands draped over the arms of the rocker, that I notice a sparkle on her finger—a ring. "My goodness, is that—?"

She blushes deeply, then leans forward and thrusts her splayed fingers toward me. "Yes! Can you believe it? Engaged. I wondered when you'd notice." The false cheer in her voice is evidence of how awkward this is for both of us. "I would've written to let you know, but it happened only a few weeks ago."

The ring, with a sizable central diamond encircled by a pattern of tiny diamond chips, is more ornate than any I've ever seen. I tell her honestly, "It's beautiful. From Harland, I assume?"

She laughs. "Of course Harland. It got quite serious quite suddenly. We plan to marry in the fall, just a small family wedding. There's lots to do, goodness! But I'm so glad to be back here now. And to see you."

"Well." I think of portly Harland in his funny short-brimmed hat. "Congratulations."

"Thank you. It means the world to have your blessing." Spying Lolly sidling through the doorway, she cries, "Oh, what a pretty cat! So big."

"She's a Maine coon. They're little tigers."

"Here, kitty." She clucks her tongue and snaps her fingers.

Lolly freezes, looks back and forth between us.

"She won't come," I say. "She's stubborn and shy. Like me." As if to demonstrate, the cat streaks across the floor and leaps onto my lap.

Ramona smiles. "You're not shy. You just like who you like. That cat's the same way."

Lolly arches into my hand, insisting that I stroke her, and for a few moments her steady purring is the only sound in the room.

A faint citrus scent lingers in the air.

Finally Ramona sighs. "I have been fretting about how to bring this up. Walton . . . I don't . . ." She shakes her head, twists one of the large buttons on her dress. "He's a dear, I adore him, but he can be so *exasperating*."

I can't follow what she's saying. Walton is a dear? She adores him? "He stopped writing," I say.

"I know, he told me."

I grip Lolly's back so hard that she meows and sinks a claw into my palm, then squirms out of my lap. A bead of blood springs to the surface of my hand. I wipe it on my skirt, leaving a pink smear.

"It was abominable of him. I kept telling him so. And—well—cruel."

Though I knew this moment was coming, not a single fiber of my being wants to be having this conversation. "Ramona—"

"Let me bumble through this, horrible as it is—I have to. Walton loves you—loved you, I suppose. Oh, Christina." She sighs. "Every word out of my mouth is as painful for me to say

as it must be for you to hear, and I don't want to do this, but . . ."
She stops. Then blurts: "Walton is engaged to be married."

Walton is. Engaged. To be. Married. Am I missing something? Engaged to be married to me? I look at her blankly.

Walton is engaged to be married.

To someone else.

In all the ways I've thought about his silence, considered its sources, this possibility never occurred to me. But why not? It makes the most logical sense. He stopped writing abruptly. Of course—of course—he met someone else.

I feel as if I am emptied out, filled with thick, heavy air. I can't think or see; it fills me to my eyes. I try to remember what Walton looks like. A straw boater with a black grosgrain ribbon. A linen jacket. Soft girlish hands. But I can't envision his face.

"Christina? Are you all right?" Ramona's face is stretched into a ghastly expression. I look into her eyes. It's as if I'm watching her through a scrim.

"Why." A tiny word, one syllable, not even a question.

She sighs. "I've asked myself a million times, and Walton too; I've begged him for an answer that makes sense. I don't even know if *he* knows, except . . ." Her voice trails off.

"Except . . ."

"Except." She twists in her chair. "The distance. And his parents."

"His parents."

"He told you, he said. That they—disapproved."

"He didn't say that."

"He didn't?"

Leaning back in the chair, I close my eyes. Maybe he did.

"His mother is an awful woman. A striver. She wanted—wants—a certain kind of life for her golden boy. And she kept bringing around the daughter of a friend, a girl at Smith, and I just think after a while he thought, what's the use, I can't fight it anymore; the easiest thing is to give in."

"The easiest thing," I echo.

"I suppose she's not a bad sort, really. She's all right." Ramona shrugs. "Though of course I never said that to him; I only told him how vexed I was, how disappointed. On your behalf."

By the way she's telling me this I can see that she has spent time with this woman, that they have all been out together. "What is her name."

"Marilyn. Marilyn Wales."

I contemplate this for a moment. A real person, with a name. "He never even . . . wrote to explain."

"I know. It makes me so angry. We argued about it. I told him it was unconscionably rude. He said he couldn't do it; he begged me to write to you myself, to tell you, and honestly I refused."

I feel as if I'm being whipped, every word a lash. "You knew I was waiting," I say slowly, my voice rising, "and you wouldn't put me out of my misery?"

"Christina?" Mother calls from upstairs. "Everything all right?"

I look steadily at Ramona and she looks back, her eyes filling with tears. "I am so sorry," she says.

"Everything is fine, Mother," I call back.

"Who's there?"

"Ramona Carle."

My mother is silent.

"He didn't deserve you," Ramona whispers.

I shake my head.

"Yes, he's smart, and he can be charming, but quite honestly he is a weak man. I see that now."

"Stop," I say. "Just stop."

Leaning forward in the rocker, Ramona says, "Christina, listen to me. There will be other fish in the sea."

"No, there won't."

"There will. We'll find you a great catch."

"I have hung up my rod," I say.

This seems to break the tension. Ramona smiles. (It was hard for her to be this serious! She isn't constitutionally cut out for it.) "For now. There'll be more expeditions."

"Not in this leaky boat."

She laughs a little. "You are as stubborn as a Maine coon, Christina Olson."

"Maybe so," I tell her. "Maybe I am."

WHEN I GO to bed, I never want to get up. There's an ache deep in my bones that won't go away; I jolt awake in the night sobbing in pain. Nothing will ever get better. It will only get worse. I pull the blue wool blanket Papa made tighter around me and finally drift to sleep. When I wake several hours later in the astringent light of morning, I bury my face in my pillow.

Al comes into my room. I can hear him, see him, though my eyes are shut and I pretend to be asleep. "Christina," he says softly.

I don't answer.

"I found some bread and jam for breakfast. Sam and Fred are in the barn. I'll bring eggs to Mother and Papa when chores are finished."

I sigh, tacit acknowledgment that I hear him.

Behind my eyelashes I see him look down, hands on hips. "Are you sick?"

"Yes."

"Do you need a doctor?"

"No." I open my eyes, but I can't rouse myself to an expression. He looks back at me steadily. I don't remember ever holding his gaze like this.

"I would like to kill him," he says. "I really would."

My bed feels like a shallow grave.

I TAKE THE stack of letters from Walton, tied with their pale pink ribbon, and place them in a box. Part of me wants to set them on fire and watch them burn. But I can't bring myself to do it.

At the top of the first flight of stairs is a small closet door on the side wall. When no one is around, I slide the box into a dark corner of the closet. I don't want to see his letters. I just want proof that they exist.

IN TOWN NOBODY says a word about it, at least not to me. But I see the pity in their eyes. I hear the whispers: *She was abandoned, you know.* Their sympathy fills me with a shame so deep that I can understand why someone might sail off to a distant land, never to return to where he's from.

GETTING READY FOR a late afternoon sail with my brothers on a warm June day, I tuck the shell Walton gave me into my pocket. On the sloop I stroke it with my fingers, probing its rough crevices and silky exterior. It's the perfect weight and shape to nestle in my palm. Toward the end of the trip, as the sun dips in the sky, I move to the back of the small sailboat and sit alone, peering down at the scalloped water. How easy it would be to slip over the side and sink to the bottom of the ocean. Blackness, only blackness, and merciful unconsciousness. I taste the tears running down my face, salty sweet in my mouth. Before long, no doubt, my brothers will marry, my parents will weaken and die, and I will be alone in the house on the hill, with nothing to look forward to but the slow change of seasons, my own aging and infirmity, the house turning to dust.

Walton and I sat together at the back of the boat just like this. *I adore you,* he whispered in my ear. How devoted he was; he couldn't get enough of me, loved only me. Only me. His solid shoulder against mine, his long finger pointing toward the sky, the constellations, all the names I learned so eagerly: Orion the Hunter, Cassiopeia, Hercules, Pegasus. I look up now at the darkening sky, as solid as slate. The stars are washed away, present only in memory.

Closing my eyes, I lean over the side, the salt spray on my face mingling with tears. I weigh the shell in my palm—this cameo shell that has no place with the others. A store-bought trinket with no history, no story. I knew, deep down, when he gave it to me that he didn't understand anything about me. Why didn't I recognize it as a warning?

I feel a hand on my arm and open my eyes. "Nice night, isn't it," Al says mildly. "Careful back here. It's slippery."

"I'm all right."

He tightens his grip on my arm. "Come sit with me."

"In a minute."

"Did anyone ever tell you you're as stubborn as a mule?"

I laugh a little. "Once or twice."

We gaze out into the dusk. On the shore, faint lights glow in the windows of a faraway house. Our house. "I'll stay here with you, then," he says.

"You don't need to do that, Al."

"Wouldn't want anything to happen. Couldn't forgive myself if it did."

The weight of sorrow presses on my chest. I grip the shell, feeling its blunt knobs. Then I let it slip from my fingers. It makes a small splash.

"What was that?"

"Nothing important."

The shell sinks quickly. I'll never have to look at it again, or hold it in my hand.

WHAT PROMISES I MAKE

1946

"Hel-loo? Chris-tina?" A woman's artificially high voice comes through the screen.

"In here," I say. "Who is it?"

The woman pulls open the door and steps into the kitchen like she's stepping onto a sinking ship. She's of indeterminate middle age, wearing a worsted wool suit and stockings and pumps and carrying a casserole. "I'm Violet Evans. From the Cushing Baptist Church? We have a hospitality club, and—well—we've put you on our list for a stop-in visit once a week."

My back stiffens. "I don't know about any list."

She smiles with aggrieved patience. "Well, there is one."

"What for?"

"Shut-ins, mostly."

"I'm not a shut-in."

"Umm-hmm," she says, glancing around. She holds up the dish. "Well. I brought you chipped beef and noodles." She squints into the gloom. It's late afternoon, and I haven't lit a lamp yet. Until she came inside, I hadn't really noticed how dark it is in here. "Maybe we could switch on a light?"

"No electricity. I'll find a lamp if you'll wait a moment."

"Oh—don't go to any bother for me. I won't stay long." She

steps gingerly across the floor and sets the casserole on top of the range. "I spilled a little on my skirt, I'm afraid. Can you point me toward your sink?"

Reluctantly I direct her to the pantry. I know what's coming.

"Why, this is—a pump!" she says with a little surprised laugh, just as I knew she would. "My heavens, you don't have indoor plumbing?"

Obviously we don't. "We've always managed fine without it."

"Well," she says again. She stands in the middle of the floor like a deer poised to bolt. "I hope you and your brother like chipped beef."

"I'm sure he'll eat it."

I know she expects me to act more appreciative. But I didn't ask for this casserole, and I don't particularly care for chipped beef. I don't like her haughty manner, as if she's afraid she'll catch a disease by sitting in a chair. And something in my nature bridles at the expectation that I must be grateful for charity I didn't ask for. Perhaps because it tends to be accompanied by a kind of condescending judgment, a sense that the giver believes I've brought my condition—a condition I'm not complaining about, mind you—on myself.

Even Betsy, who understands me, is always wanting to improve my lot. She washes the dishes with her delicate hands and puts the crockery back in the wrong places. I find the broom behind the door and the dishrag drying on the back stoop. One day she showed up with a pile of blankets and sheets and plunked them on the table in the dining room. "Let me take those old rags you sleep on," she said. "I think it's time you had some fresh linens, don't you?" (Everyone knows I'm proud. Betsy's the only one I'll tolerate speaking to me like this.) She gathered up my bedcovers—which, it's true, had seen better days, especially the threadbare blue blanket Papa knitted—and hauled them outside, tossing them in the back of the station wagon to take to the dump.

"Don't worry about the Pyrex," the woman from the Baptist church assures me. "I'll collect it next week."

"You don't need to keep doing this. Really. We get along just fine."

She leans over and pats my hand. "We're glad to help, Christina. It's part of our mission."

I know this woman from the Baptist church means well, and I also know she'll sleep well tonight, believing she's done her Christian duty. But eating her chipped beef and noodles will leave a bitter taste in my mouth.

MOST SUMMER DAYS, around midmorning, when heat thickens over the fields like a gelatin, Andy is at the door. There's a new intensity to his demeanor; his son Nicky is almost three years old and Betsy is pregnant again, due in a month. Andy needs, he says, to produce some work that will support his growing family.

Sketch pad, paint-smeared fingers, eggs in his pocket. He kicks his boots off and roams around the house and fields in his bare feet. Makes his way to the second floor and moves from one bedroom to another, trudges up another flight to a long-closed room. I can hear him opening windows on the third floor that haven't been cracked in years, grunting at the effort.

I think of his presence up there as a paperweight holding down this wispy old house, pinning it to the field so it doesn't blow away.

Andy doesn't usually bring anything, or offer to help. He doesn't register alarm at the way we live. He doesn't see us as a project that needs fixing. He doesn't perch on a chair, or linger in a doorway, with the air of someone who wants to leave, who's already halfway out the door. He just settles in and observes.

All the things that most people fret about, Andy likes. The scratches made by the dog on the blue shed door. The cracks in the white teapot. The frayed lace curtains and the cobwebbed glass in the windows. He understands why I'm content to spend my days sitting in the chair in the kitchen, feet up on the blue-painted stool, looking out at the sea, getting up to stir the soup now and then or water the plants, and letting this old house settle into the earth. There's more grandeur in the bleached bones of a storm-rubbed house, he declares, than in drab tidiness.

Andy sketches Al doing his chores, picking vegetables and raking blueberries, tending the horse and cow, feeding the pig. Me sitting in the kitchen beside the red geraniums. Through his eyes I am newly aware of all the parts of this place, seen and unseen: late-afternoon shadows in the kitchen, fields returned to flower, the flat nails that secure the weathered clapboards, the drip of water from the rusty cistern, cold blue light through a cracked window.

The lace curtains Mamey crocheted, now torn and tattered,

blow in an eternal wind. She is here, I'm sure of it, watching her life and stories transform, as stories will, into something else on Andy's canvas.

ONE CLOUDY DAY Andy blows through the door with a grim expression and stomps up the stairs without stopping to chat as he usually does. I hear him banging around up there, slamming doors, swearing to himself.

After an hour or so of this, he plods back down to the kitchen and sinks into a chair. Mashing his palms over his eyes, he says, "Betsy is going to be the ruin of me."

Andy can be dramatic, but I've never heard him complain about Betsy. I don't know what to say.

"She's decided she wants to restore an old cottage on Bradford Point for us to live in. Without even consulting me, I might add. Damn it all to hell."

This doesn't strike me as entirely unreasonable. Betsy told me they're living in a horse barn on her parents' property. "Do you like the cottage?"

"It's all right."

"Can you afford to fix it up?"

He shrugs. Yes.

"Does she want you to help?"

"Not really."

"Then . . . .?"

He gives his shaggy head a violent shake. "I don't want to be shackled to a house. The way we're living is perfectly adequate."

"You live in a barn, Andy. In two horse stalls, Betsy said."

"They're fixed up. It's not like we're sleeping on hay bales."

"With one child and another on the way."

"Nicky likes it!" he says.

"Hmm. Well . . . I think I can understand why Betsy might not want to live in a barn."

Picking at a patch of dried paint on his arm, Andy mutters, "This is what happened to my father. Houses and boats and cars and a dock that needed constant repairs. . . . You get in too deep, start hemorrhaging money, and then you're making decisions based on what will sell, what the market wants, and you're ruined. Goddamn *ruined*. This is how it starts."

"Fixing up a cottage isn't quite the same as all that."

Andy narrows his eyes and gives me a curious smile. Except for my unhappiness with his portrait, I've never really disagreed with him. I can tell it startles him.

"I've known Betsy since she was a girl," I say. "She doesn't care about material things."

"Sure she does. Not as much as some women, maybe. But I would never have married those women. You bet she cares. She wants a nice house and a new car . . ." He sighs heavily.

"She's not like that."

"You don't know, Christina."

"I've known her a lot longer than you have."

"Well, that's true," he concedes.

"Did she tell you how we met?"

"Sure, she was bored one summer and started coming to visit."

"Not just to visit. She knocked on the door one day—she was only nine or ten—and came in, and looked around, and set to work washing dishes. Then she started showing up every day or so to help out around the house. She didn't want anything for it. She was just being . . . herself. She used to braid my hair . . ." I think about Betsy pulling the clips from my long hair and working through it with a wide comb, patiently teasing out tangles. My eyes closed, head tilted back, the sky orange inside my lids. The strands of hair caught in her brush threaded with silver. Her small hands strong and firm as she separated my hair into three strands and wove them together.

Andy sighs. "Look, I'm not saying she isn't a lovely person. Of course she is. But girls grow into women, and women want certain things. And I don't want to think about any of that. I just want to paint."

"You do paint," I say with rising impatience. "All the time."

"It's the pressure I'm talking about. It's hard not to be—influenced."

"But you aren't. You wouldn't be. It's all about the work, you always say that. *She* always says that."

He sits there for a minute, drumming his fingers on his knee. I can tell there's more he wants to say that he isn't sure how to articulate. "My father loved all that stuff, you know. The trappings of fame. It just makes me angry."

"What makes you angry? That he valued that stuff, you mean?"

"Yeah. No. I don't know." He stands abruptly and goes to the window. "I was almost hit by the same train that killed him, did you know that? At the same intersection, several years ago. I was driving along, thinking about something else, and I looked up and jammed the brakes at the last second and the train went firing past. So I know what it was like for him to see that train bearing down. The horror of it. The futility of realizing there's nothing you can do." He hesitates, then adds, "And I'm filled with rage. At—at losing him. Losing him too soon."

Ah, all right, I think.

"I'm angry at losing him, but I'm also angry at the waste," he says. "The time wasted, the energy squandered on meaningless possessions, the compromises . . . I don't want to make the same mistakes."

I think of the mistakes my own father made toward the end of his life. I know how the death of a parent can be both a release and a reckoning.

"You won't."

"I'm about to."

"Let me make you a cup of tea," I say.

He shakes his head. "No. I'm going back up. Rage is good for the work. I'll pour it in. And sorrow, and love, all mixed together." Standing in the doorway, gripping the frame, he says, "Poor Betsy, it's not her fault. She wanted a normal life and she got me instead."

"I think she knew what she was in for."

"Well, if she didn't, she does now," he says.

1917–1922

For the first time in years, the summer days hold more hours than I know what to do with. I order wallpaper from a catalog in the Fales store and enlist Mother's help in transforming the rooms downstairs. (If this is to be my home, let it at least be papered with small pink flowers on a field of white.) Mother persuades me to join groups I've previously disdained—the Friendly Club, the Helpful Women's Club, the South Cushing Baptist Church sewing circle, with their ice cream socials and apron sales and weekly meetings. I borrow books from the library that Walton didn't recommend. (*Ethan Frome* in particular, with its bleak New England winters, its agonizing compromises and tragic mistakes, keeps me up at night.) I take sewing orders for dresses and nightgowns and slips from ladies in town. I even agree to go to the Grange Hall on a Friday night with Ramona and Eloise and my brothers, though when I hear the cheerful piano and fiddle music wafting through the trees as we get closer—"Tiger Rag" and "Lady of the Lake"—I want to vanish into the woods.

As soon as we arrive, everyone disperses. "You poor dear!" Gertrude Gibbons yelps from across the room when she spots me. She rushes over and grabs my hand. "We were all so sorry to hear."

"I'm fine, Gertrude," I say, attempting to fend her off.

"Oh, I know you have to say that," she stage whispers. "You are so *brave*, Christina."

"I'm not."

She squeezes my hand. "You are, you are! After all you've been through. I would crawl into a hole."

"No, you wouldn't."

"I would! I would just collapse. You are so . . ." She sticks her lip out in a pretend pout. "You always make the best of things. I admire that *so much*."

And just like that, I've had enough. I close my eyes, take a breath, open them. "Well, see, now, I admire *you*."

She puts a hand on her chest. "Really?"

"Yes. I think it would be hard to have such a slender sister, when you try so desperately to watch your weight. That doesn't seem fair at all."

She stands erect. Pulls her stomach in. Bites her lip. "I hardly think—"

"It must be very difficult." Reaching out, I pat her shoulder. "Everybody says so."

I know I'm being unkind, but I can't help myself. And I don't regret it when I see the hurt look on her face. My heart is shattered, and all that's left are jagged shards.

MOTHER HAS BEGUN spending entire days in her bedroom with the shades drawn. Dr. Heald comes and goes, trying to figure out what is wrong. I hover in the shadows out of his way. "It appears that she has a progressive kidney disease and possibly a heart condition," he tells us finally. "She needs to rest. When she feels up to it, she can venture out into the sunshine."

She has good days and bad. On bad days, she doesn't come out of her room. (When she calls for tea, I make my way up the stairs slowly, rattling the teacup in its saucer, splashing the hot liquid on my hand.) On good days, she appears after I've finished washing the breakfast dishes and sits with me in the kitchen. Now and then, when she's feeling particularly well, we'll take a picnic to Little Island, timing our walks to the ebb of the tide. We are quite a pair: a sickly woman short of breath and a lame girl lurching alongside.

Mother keeps Mamey's black bible, worn and faded from years of travel, on the table beside her bed, and often thumbs through its gossamer pages. Now and then she murmurs the words aloud she knows by heart: *We rejoice in our sufferings, knowing that suffering produces endurance, and endurance produces character, and character produces hope . . . For this light momentary affliction is preparing us for an eternal weight of glory beyond all comparison . . .*

One morning I come to the barn to bring Papa a jug of water and find him slumped against the mule in its stall, a strange grimace on his face. Startled, I drop the cup and stumble forward.

"Help me, Christina," he gasps, reaching out a hand. "I can't get up." His muscles constrict and spasm; his legs are so painful, he says, that he can barely move them. When I finally get him into the house, he lies on the floor of the kitchen and kneads his calves, trying to dull the pain.

Al goes to fetch Dr. Heald. After examining Papa, he announces that it must be arthritis, and there's not much he can do.

With Mother in and out of bed and Papa increasingly infirm, the duties of the household fall even more heavily on my brothers and me. We have no choice, or the whole farm will slide into entropy—animals unfed, the cows needing milking, tasks doubled for the next day. To get it all done I have to dim my brain, turn it down by notches like the flat-turn knob on a gas lantern, leaving only a nub of flame.

AS SUMMER TURNS to fall, envelopes with two-cent stamps postmarked Boston begin to arrive for me at the post office again. Ramona's "small family wedding," she reports, has grown, predictably, into a more lavish affair. Her dress will be modern, despite her mother's objections—a white satin V-neck with a skirt just below the knee, a wide satin belt, and a bridal cap veil (not, God forbid, her grandmother's, with its crumbling yellowed lace). "If suffragettes can picket the White House, I can express my emancipation from long skirts and old veils," Ramona declares. She will carry a bouquet of irises like the bride on the cover of *Hearst's* magazine.

The invitation—on thick cream card stock, hand-painted with pastel flowers—arrives in an oversized cream envelope. I stand in the road and read the words etched in florid black script:

Mr. and Mrs. Herbert Carle
Respectfully request the honor of your presence
At the marriage ceremony of their daughter
Ramona Jane
And Harland Woodbury . . .

Equally respectfully, on notebook paper, I decline to attend. My brothers are busy with the harvest and I must prepare for the holidays, but we all send our best wishes to the happy couple. (And later a silverplate tea service marked down on sale at a home goods shop in Thomaston.)

After the wedding, held in early November, I receive a honeymoon postcard postmarked Newport—"Such magnificent houses! All the ladies here wear furs"—and, a few weeks later, a note describing the sunny apartment in a new brick building that the newlyweds are renting in Boston. "You must come and visit in early spring. I know Al will be busy with the planting, so bring dear Sam," Ramona writes. "He needs an adventure, and so do you. It's neither haying nor holiday season, so no excuses. A few weeks only! Nothing will be disrupted."

The idea of traveling to Boston under such vastly different circumstances than the one I envisioned sends me to bed with a headache for the afternoon.

"YOU KNOW WE can't possibly go," I tell Sam when he confronts me with the letter, which I foolishly left open on the dining room table.

"Why not?"

"The distance . . . my infirmity—"

"Nonsense," Sam says. "I've never been anywhere. Nor have you. We're going."

Looking at tall, handsome Sam, with his strong jaw and aquiline nose and piercing gray eyes, I think of all those seafaring Samuels he was named after, setting off to explore the world. Sam is twenty years old. Ramona is right—he needs an adventure. "You go," I urge him.

"Not without you."

"But—Al can't manage the farm on his own."

"He's not on his own. Fred is here. And Papa will help."

I give him a skeptical look. Papa hasn't been much help for a while now.

"Al will be fine. I'm not taking no for an answer."

So it is that early on a March morning in 1918, despite my trepidation, Al drives us through the fog to Thomaston, where Sam and I will catch a train bound for North Union Station in Boston. The staircases and ticket lines, narrow hallways and train platforms are a bewildering obstacle course for both of us, made even more difficult by my tight new shoes. Sam carries both suitcases and an overcoat and still manages to keep a firm arm under mine, steadying me as we slowly make our way toward the gate. When we finally get to our railway car, we collapse onto the red leather seats.

A few minutes after we've left the station, Sam asks, "Got anything to eat?"

I had packed a few dry biscuits in my bag, but when I pull

them out, they crumble in my hand. Just as I'm thinking we might have to wait until Boston, the conductor, a red-faced man with a bristly mustache, happens along to collect our tickets. Sam fumbles through his jacket for them. "Let me guess," the conductor says. "First time on a train?"

I nod.

"Thought so." He leans over the seat. "Lavatories are in the next car . . ." He points a meaty finger toward the right. "And the dining room is four cars down. You can get a hot meal or a cup of tea. Or whiskey, if you prefer," he says, chuckling. His breath is briny, like lobster.

"Thank you," I say. But after he moves along, I tell Sam, "I don't think we should. We need to budget." We've brought $80 for the entire visit; the round-trip fare has already eaten up $5.58 each. But I'm also reluctant to make a spectacle of myself, jerking back and forth.

"What we need to do is eat," Sam says.

"You go and bring me something small."

Sam knows what I'm thinking. Four long cars. He stands with a flourish and holds out his arm. I take a deep breath and rise to my feet. But now there's another question: Do we take our things with us so they won't be stolen, or do we leave them here? An elderly woman with a face like a cellar apple leans forward in her seat across the aisle. "Don't worry, dears, I'll watch your bags."

The swaying of the train actually disguises my infirmity. Accustomed to having to work to keep my balance, I adjust to it more quickly than Sam, who weaves from side to side like a drunkard.

In the dining car, we eat ham sandwiches and drink tea with milk and sugar, gazing out at the rushing dark. For years I've dreamed of this moment—or rather, a moment like this. How different it is from my imaginings! My ankles are cold, my feet pinched in these new shoes, the air sour with tobacco smoke and body odor, the bread stale, the tea weak and bitter.

And yet—here I am, going somewhere new. How shockingly easy it was to pick up and go, to buy a ticket and board a train and head off into the unknown.

Portland, Portsmouth, Newburyport. We slow into stations one after another that never have meant more to me than words on a map. When we arrive in Salem, I think about our ancestor who lived here. I imagine Bridget Bishop standing on the scaffold, trying desperately to use the sentence against her to her own advantage. *If you truly believe I'm a witch,* she must have thought, *then you must also believe I have the power to harm you.* I've always assumed that John Hathorne trumped up those charges against rebels and misfits as a way of enforcing social codes. But now I wonder: What if he really did believe those women were capable of ensnaring his soul?

When we pull into South Station, it's dark and cold and we must take three different trains to get to the Carles'—one of them elevated, which requires dragging our bags up and down stairs. With Sam's arm under mine I concentrate on my steps, one foot up, the next one down. When I dreamed of a life with Walton, I hadn't thought about what it would be like to navigate city living. Everything comes back to this body, this faulty carapace. How I wish I could crack it open and leave it behind.

DESPITE MY TREPIDATION about being in Boston, it's exciting to be in a new place and easy enough to pretend that everything is all right—to chat amiably with Ramona as she fries eggs for breakfast, exclaim over her wedding gifts and the charming view of the cobblestoned street from the apartment window, play card games in the evenings at a square folding table in the living room with her and Harland and Sam. (Though I can't help flinching when Harland suggests we play Old Maid.)

But just under the surface, my heart feels raw, painful to the touch. Beneath my smiles and nods and exclamations, I drift through each day like a ghost, silently keening for what might have been. Here, in Harvard Yard, Walton and I might have rested on a park bench. At Jordan Marsh Department Store we would have selected furniture and dishes. On the banks of the Charles we'd spread a quilt for a picnic and I'd lean back against his chest, watching the rowers go by. At night I fall into bed exhausted, overwhelmed by a grief so overwhelming that I can hardly breathe.

In spite of my best efforts, Ramona isn't fooled. One morning she says, apropos of nothing, "It was brave of you to come." The two of us are sitting at the breakfast nook eating soft-boiled eggs in china cups and toast propped in a silver rack. Sam and Harland have gone for a stroll.

"I'm happy to be here."

She takes a sip of coffee. "I'm glad. It couldn't have been an easy decision to make the trip."

"No," I admit. "But Sam insisted."

"I know. He told me. But—you are having a nice time, aren't you?"

I nod, buttering my toast. "Of course, a lovely time."

"I want to tell you, Christina . . ." She sets down her spoon. "You must be wondering. Walton lives in Malden. He rarely comes into the city these days."

I look in her eyes. "I was wondering."

"I hope that sets your mind at ease."

"Does he know I'm here?"

"I told him. I felt I had to. In case . . ."

"It makes sense. You're friends." I can hear the bitter edge in my voice.

She bites her lip. "Family friends. From childhood. It's hard to just cut people off . . . even though . . ." Shaking her head, she says, "I don't know how to explain it. I feel like a traitor. I know how painful it was for you. He behaved abominably."

Ramona seems so sincerely distressed that I feel a trickle of empathy for her. "You don't have to explain. I understand."

"Do you?" she says hopefully.

"The past is past."

I know it's what she wants to hear. She smiles, clearly relieved. "I'm so glad you feel that way. I do too! And by the way, I know you said you aren't interested, but Boston is filled with eligible bachelors."

"Ramona—"

She flaps her hand. "Yes, yes, I know, you've hung up your rod. You can't blame a girl for trying."

A FEW DAYS later, Ramona says, "I can't imagine it's easy for you, Christina dear, all this perambulating around."

She's right. Every inch of Boston has been treacherous for me, from the cobblestoned streets to the crowded sidewalks. She and Sam and even bumbling Harland steer me into the elevator and down the steps, offering steady arms for our afternoon strolls. Even so, I trip and stumble. "I truly appreciate your help," I tell her.

"Oh, well—it's nothing. But it does seem, perhaps, that your situation is more acute than it used to be. I see you wincing sometimes. Are you in pain?"

I shrug. The pain has become part of me, just something I live with, like my pale eyelashes and skimmed-milk skin. But when I wake in the morning now, it takes several minutes of stretching and kneading before I can move my hands. And my feet often feel mired in glue; I can't walk more than four or five steps on my own without losing my balance.

"Christina, Walton told me he had a conversation with you about this some time ago. He said he urged you to come to Boston to see if something could be done."

I feel my face flush. "He didn't have any business—"

She raises a finger. "This is not about Walton. I spoke with a doctor—a very good doctor—at Boston City Hospital, and he thinks they might be able to help. It wouldn't be right away. Not this visit. We'd need to make an appointment. All I'm asking is for you to consider it. Look"—she sighs—"don't you want to have a normal life, with normal opportunities? You refused before, and . . ."

Her unsaid words linger on the air. I know what she's implying: that my unwillingness to consider treatment may have cost me the relationship. I feel a surge of anger. Yes—this was exactly what I feared at the time. That Walton's feelings for me were conditional. That he was telling me to get better, or else.

But the anger subsides as quickly as it arose. It would be nice to have a normal life. I'm tired of pretending to be strong, of hiding the fact that even the smallest chores exhaust me. I'm tired of the bruises and scrapes and the pitying looks of people on the street. Maybe this doctor could actually help me. Who knows? Maybe he can even make me well.

"All right," I tell Ramona. "I'll consider it."

She smiles. "Good! We just might get that leaky boat of yours patched up after all."

NEWSPAPERS ARE FILLED with dispatches from the front. *The Boston Globe* reports that the United States is sending nearly ten thousand soldiers to France every day. In Cushing we heard occasional stories about boys who enlisted, or, after the Selective Service Act was passed last year, were drafted. (My farmer brothers, like many in our area, were exempt.) We listened to radio reports. But here the news is not an abstract event, happening far away. Walking across Harvard Yard, Sam and I come upon several thousand young men in blue regulation sailor suits, new recruits attending Radio School. Boston Common is lined with Red Cross tents, where volunteers collect and pack supplies to ship overseas.

When the suffragettes who've been picketing in front of the White House for more than two years are disparaged in opinion columns, Ramona and Eloise are incensed and talk about it at length. They know the names of some of the ladies, the arguments for why women should be given the vote. They talk about these events as if they have a stake in the outcome. As if they have a right—an obligation, even—to an opinion.

"But this has nothing to do with us," I say.

"It has everything to do with us," Ramona replies indignantly.

None of the tasks that fill my days in Cushing are relevant in Ramona's world. It's as if she's playing house in her four-room apartment overlooking the street, four flights up, with no one to take care of but her well-meaning but slightly ham-fisted husband and plenty of money with which to do it. How different my life would be with electric lights and an indoor toilet, hot water that comes out of a faucet in the kitchen and the lavatory, gas burners on the stovetop that ignite with the flick of a match, cast-iron radiators that heat every room. If I weren't spending all my time stoking the fire, maybe I, too, would know what's going on in the wider world. Ramona attends the opera, the latest plays; she browses in the millinery store and the ladies' shops. She has a girl (Ramona calls her that, though she's older than us) who comes in twice a week to take the laundry, scrub the floors, change the bedding, dust the breakfront, and wash the dishes while Ramona sits at the table in her dressing gown reading the *Boston Herald*.

Ramona refuses to step outside without a hat and a dress in the latest style, freshly starched and ironed. I—who have two plain dresses, two skirts, two blouses, and two slightly crumpled hats to choose from—spend a lot of time waiting for her to get ready. "Oh, Christina, you must be exasperated," she says with a sigh, hurrying out of her bedroom, pinning on one of her many hats in front of the hall mirror while I idle by the door. "All this folderol, primping and pin curls and hatpins—I expend so much energy worrying about how I look! You just are who you are. I envy that."

I don't believe her. She is living the life she wants to lead. But I don't really envy her, either. Even without an infirmity it would be hard to adjust to these narrow streets clotted with buildings and pedestrians and endure incessantly clanging streetcars, blaring horns, squealing brakes, music drifting from doorways, human chatter. The Boston sky, watered down by lamplight, is never completely dark. I miss the thick, star-sprayed blackness of Hathorn Point at night, the soft glow of gaslight, the moments of absolute quiet, the view of our yellow fields and the cove and the sea in the distance, the horizon line beyond.

RAMONA AND EVEN Harland, bless him, are more than generous, but when it's time to leave, I am ready to go. The day of our departure is brilliantly sunny. Snow is melting into puddles in the streets. Yellow and purple crocuses in the park have burst overnight through the slush. I'm in my tiny bedroom, tucking my few belongings into my suitcase, when there's a rap at the door. "It's Sam. May I come in?"

"Sure."

When he opens the door, I look up. His eyes are sparkling and he has a huge grin on his face. "So are you nearly ready?"

"Yes. Are you?"

"Not quite."

"Well, hurry up then." I hold up a long skirt and fold it in half. "We don't want to miss the train."

He wavers in the doorway, half in the room and half out, his hand on the knob. "I'm not ready to go back."

I look up in surprise. "What?"

He presses his forehead against the door and sighs. "I've been thinking. If I'm going to spend my life in a tiny place in the middle of godforsaken nowhere, I want at least to see something of the world."

"Isn't that what we've been doing?"

"I think I'm just getting started," he says.

I'm having trouble wrapping my mind around this. "So— you want to stay on with Ramona and Harland? Have you asked them if they mind?"

"Actually, Herbert Carle has offered me a position as a mail clerk in his company and a room in their house. So I wouldn't need to stay here."

It dawns on me slowly that he's been hatching this idea for a while. "Why haven't you told me about this?"

"I'm telling you now."

"But what will . . . how will . . ."

"You'll be fine," he says, as if reading my mind. "I'm going to escort you to the station. And then I'll turn right around and go to work."

"Well, what about the farm?"

"Al and Fred can manage. Anyway, it'll be good for Fred to step up and help out more—he's been the baby of the family for too long."

I feel stung. "You've thought this through."

"I have."

"Without even consulting me."

He squirms in the doorway like a dog being scolded. "I was afraid you wouldn't approve."

"It's not that I don't approve. It's that I . . . I . . ." What is it, exactly? "I suppose it's that I feel . . ."

"Abandoned," he says. It's as if we both realize it at the same time.

My eyes fill with tears.

"Oh, Christina," he says, coming over and putting a hand on my arm. "I've only been thinking of myself. I wasn't thinking of you at all."

"Of course you weren't," I say, choking on the words. I know I'm being melodramatic, but I can't help myself. "Why should you? Why should anyone?" Turning away from him, I reach for a folded handkerchief in my suitcase and weep into it, my shoulders shaking.

Sam steps back. He's never seen me like this. "I'm being selfish," he says. "I'll come home with you on the train."

After a few moments, I take a deep breath and dab my eyes with the handkerchief. Outside the window I hear the clatter of a streetcar, a honking car. I think of Mamey's wanderlust. Her desire to see the wider world. Her frustration that no one in the family seemed to share her ambitions. Why shouldn't Sam stay in Boston? He has his entire life ahead of him.

"No," I say.

"No . . . ?"

"You shouldn't come home."

"But you—"

"It's all right," I tell him. "I want you to stay."

"Are you sure?"

I nod. "Mamey would be proud."

"Well, I'm hardly sailing around the world," he says with a smile. "But perhaps Boston is a start."

Sam, as promised, escorts me to the station and puts me on a train. He looks so young and handsome and happy standing on the platform, waving good-bye as the train pulls away.

As Boston recedes into the distance, the domestic concerns that have receded from my thoughts swim back into focus: How is Mother's health? Has she been sleeping well? Did she manage the cooking? I think about the dirt I'll find in the corners of the kitchen, the piles of laundry that no doubt await, the ashes piled up in the range. The mule, the cows, the chickens, the pump behind the house . . . I look out at the horizon—horizontal bands of color, black to blue to russet to orange, a line of gold and then blue again. Heading north is like going back in time. When the train pulls into Thomaston it's cold and muddy and gray, exactly how Boston looked when I arrived there several weeks ago.

A FEW MONTHS after I've returned, Mother sits me down at the dining room table, a letter in her hand. Papa stands behind her in the doorway. "Sam and Ramona would like for you to go back to Boston to be evaluated. The Carles know a very good doctor who—"

"Yes, she mentioned it," I interrupt. Now that I'm home again, back to my familiar routines, Boston seems very far away. The disruption of my chores, the effort of the journey, not to mention the almost certain painfulness of the procedure and the far from certain outcome: It's hard to imagine why I would put myself through such an ordeal. "I said I'd consider it. But honestly, I don't think there's any point."

Mother reaches for my wrist and grasps it before I can pull away. She turns it over, revealing raised red strips on my arm. "Look. Just look at what you've done to yourself."

I've started using my elbows, my wrists, my knees to lift heavy pots, balance the teakettle and fill it with water from the pump, lug it to the range. My forearms are striped with burns. Partly for this reason and partly because over the years my arms have become thinner and more sticklike, I hide them as often as I can in voluminous sleeves. I yank my arm away, slide the sleeve down to cover it. "There's nothing anyone can do about it."

"We don't know that."

"I get along fine, Mother."

"If it continues getting worse, you will not be able to walk. Have you thought about that?"

I busy myself brushing some crumbs on the table into a pile. Of course I've thought about it. I think about it every day when I navigate the fourteen-foot-long pantry by using my elbows along the walls.

"Do you think you'll get along fine when your legs don't work at all?" she persists.

"It's decided," Papa says abruptly. We both turn to look at him. "She's going to Boston, and that's the end of it."

Mother nods, clearly surprised. Papa rarely asserts his opinion with such force. "You heard your father," she says.

It seems there's no use arguing. And who knows, maybe they're right—maybe something can be done to reverse or at least slow my decline. I pack two equally weighted bags to help me keep my balance, and Al borrows a neighbor's car to drive me to Portland so I won't have to change trains by myself. When I reach Boston, Sam and Ramona pick me up in Harland's brand-new sky-blue Cadillac sedan and drive me to City Hospital on Harrison Avenue in the South End—a stately brick building with giant columns and a turreted dome—where I'm admitted for a week's "observation."

A hen-breasted nurse pushes me in a wheelchair into an elevator, accompanied by Sam and Ramona, and up to a small private room on the eighth floor with an iron bed and a view of the neighboring rooftops. It smells of paint thinner.

"When are visiting hours?" Ramona asks.

The nurse consults my chart. "No visitors."

"No visitors? Why on earth not?" Sam asks.

"The prescription is rest. Rest and solitude."

"That hardly seems necessary," Ramona says.

"Doctor's orders," the nurse says. "I'll leave you alone with her for ten minutes. Then you need to let her settle in. You can come back to collect her in a week." Looking over at me, she lifts her beak. "There's a hospital gown on the bed for you to wear. The doctors will do their rounds later in the afternoon. Any questions?"

I shake my head. No questions. Except—"What is that smell?"

"Ether," Ramona says. "Horrid. I remember it from when I had my tonsils out."

"And overcooked peas," Sam adds.

When the nurse leaves, Ramona pulls a book out of the bag she's carrying and places it on the nightstand. *My Ántonia*. "I haven't read it, but apparently it's all the rage. Country life in Nebraska." She shrugs. "Not my cup of tea, but if you get bored . . ."

Looking at the book jacket, gold with bronze lettering, I realize that this must be the third in Cather's prairie trilogy. I read the other two at Walton's suggestion. A line from *O Pioneers!* pops into my mind: "People have to snatch at happiness when they can, in this world. It is always easier to lose than to find . . ."

"We'll ask the nurse exactly when you're being discharged so I can be here to pick you up," Sam says.

"I'll be counting the minutes," I say.

"If you finish that book, I can bring more," Ramona says. "Sherwood Anderson has a collection of stories everybody's talking about."

Once a day a gaggle of doctors, gooselike in their white coats, march into the room and gather around my bed, led by a specialist I come to think of as "Big Bug" because of his eyes, enormous behind oversized spectacles. The doctors instruct me to stand up, wave my arms, and stomp my legs, and then, muttering among themselves, troop back out again. They act as if I don't have ears, but I hear everything they say. The first few days they speculate that perhaps electricity will help. By day four they decide that electricity would be disastrous. Nobody seems to have the slightest idea what's wrong with me. On the seventh day, Big Bug releases me into the care of Sam and Ramona with a sanctimonious smile and a prescription.

"You should go on living as you've always done," he declares, steepling his fingers at me while the other doctors scribble notes on their pads. "Eat nourishing food. Live out of doors as much as you can. A quiet country life will do you more good than any medicine or treatment."

"I don't suppose she needed to travel all the way to Boston to learn that," Ramona mutters under her breath.

On the train home I squint out the window at a silver-dollar moon framed in a blue-velvet sky. I've done what my parents wanted me to do. They don't have to fret about a cure we didn't seek. This disease—whatever it is—will advance as it will. I think about the destructiveness of desire: of wanting something unrealistic, of believing in the possibility of rescue. This stint in

Boston only confirms my belief that there is no cure for what ails me. No matter how long I hold a stick with fluttering rags above my head, no trawler in the distance will be coming to my rescue.

Though I am only twenty-five, I know in my bones that my one chance for a different life has come and gone.

I pull the now-dog-eared copy of *My Ántonia* out of my satchel—I've read it twice—and leaf through the pages, looking for a line that comes near the end. Ah—here it is: "Some memories are realities and are better than anything that can ever happen to one again." Maybe so, I think. Maybe my memories of sweeter times are vivid enough, and present enough, to overcome the disappointments that followed. And to sustain me through the rest.

IF ALVARO HAD been born in a previous generation, he would have been a ship captain like our ancestors. His stoic temperament is ideal for sailing. His passion for the sea—up before dawn in all kinds of weather, out on the ocean as light seeps into the sky—is in his blood. But when Papa's hands stiffen and gnarl, when Sam shows no sign of returning from Boston and Fred gets a job at a dry goods store in Cushing and moves to an apartment in town, Al is the only one left to run the farm.

"This farm is in fine shape," I overhear Papa telling him one spring morning. "I've managed to save more than two thousand dollars. The horse team and the equipment are paid off. Now it's up to you to keep it going."

Later that morning Al clips our mare, Tessie, to the runner, guides her down to the shore, and loads up his dory—the boat he goes out in every day. He brings it up to the house, hauls it into the shed attached to the kitchen, and stores it upside down, high in the haymow, with all his fishing gear. Then he dry-docks his sailboat, the *Oriole*, on the tip of the point of Little Island.

"What are you doing?" I ask him. "Why put the boats away?"

"That time is past, Christie."

"But maybe someday—"

"I'd rather not be reminded," he says.

Over the next few months, thieves pillage the dry-docked

sailboat, stealing the fixtures and lanterns and even pieces of wood, leaving its decimated carcass to rot in the grass. The fish house behind the barn falls into disrepair, the tools inside languishing like relics from a long-ago era: decoys, bait barrels, boat caulking, lobster traps as dry and bare-boned as fossils.

In the late afternoon, when his chores are done, I sometimes find Al in the shed, fast asleep beneath the dory on a pile of horse blankets. I feel badly for him, but I understand. It's painful to hold out hope for the things that once brought you joy. You have to find ways to make yourself forget.

ONE DAY A deliveryman from Rockland shows up with a wheelchair, and from then on Papa is rarely out of it.

"What do you need that thing for?" I ask him.

"We should get you one, too," he says.

"No, thank you."

Papa's bones ache, he says, when he tries to do just about anything. His arms and legs have thinned and weakened; they're contorted in a way that's familiar to me. But he calls his condition arthritis and refuses to believe it has anything to do with mine.

Both of us are proud, but we wear our pride differently. Mine takes the form of defiance, his of shame. To me, using a wheelchair would mean that I've given up, resigned myself to a small existence inside the house. I see it as a cage. Papa sees it as a throne, a way to maintain his fleeting dignity. He finds my behavior—my limping and falling—undignified, shameless, pathetic. He is right: I am shameless. I am willing to risk injury and humiliation to move about as I choose. For better or worse, I think, I am probably more Hathorn than Olauson, carrying in my blood both intractability and a refusal to care what anybody thinks.

I wonder, not for the first time, if shame and pride are merely two sides of the same coin.

In a fit of optimism—or perhaps denial—Papa buys a car, a black Ford Runabout, for $472 from Knox County Motor Sales in Rockland. The car, a Model T, is shiny and powerful, and though Papa is proud of it, he is too infirm to drive it. I am too. So Al becomes the family chauffeur, taking Papa and the rest of us where we need to go. He drives to the post office every day, whatever the weather, and picks up the mail for our neighbors along the road, distributing it on his way back. He does errands for Mother in Thomaston and Rockland. The car provides Al a measure of freedom: he starts going out at night now and then, usually to Fales, where a group of men can be counted on for a card game, old Irving Fales making a dime or two barbering in the middle of it.

During one such evening, Al hears about a treatment in Rockland that supposedly cures arthritis, administered by a Doctor S. J. Pole. The next day he drives Papa into Rockland to find out more. The two of them come back talking animatedly about apples and surgery-free treatments, and at supper we pore over the contract Papa has been given to sign. The gist of it is that he will be required to eat many apples. There's a small orchard behind our house that he planted fifteen years ago; the trees are laden with shiny red and green apples. But these, apparently, are not the right kind. He has to eat a specific variety, one he can only get in Thomaston for five cents apiece.

I flip through the pages of the contract. "It is fully understood by me that while S. J. Pole believes that he can help and perhaps cure me, he in no way guarantees anything," it reads. "It is mutually agreed that no money paid by me for his services shall be refunded. I am of lawful age."

"Fifty-seven. That's lawful age, isn't it?" Papa laughs.

Mother purses her lips. "Has this worked for other people?"

"Dr. Pole showed us page after page of testimonials from people he cured," Al says.

"Katie," Papa says intently, putting her hand on Mother's, "this could be the remedy."

She nods slowly but doesn't say anything more.

"How much money is it, exactly?" I ask.

"It's reasonable," Papa says.

"How much?"

Al looks at me steadily. "Papa hasn't had hope for a long time."

"So what does it cost?"

"Just because nothing worked for you, Christie . . ."

"I can't understand why we have to buy apples when we have a perfectly good orchard full of them."

"This doctor is an expert. Papa could be cured. You don't want that?"

I once read a story about a man named Ivan Ilych who believes he has lived justly and is outraged to discover that he must suffer a horrible fate, an early death of unknown cause.

My father is like this. He is furious that he has become a cripple. He has always believed that industry and cleanliness equal moral rectitude, and that moral rectitude should be rewarded. So I'm not surprised that he is so eager to believe this preposterous story about a cure.

Papa signs the contract and pays for thirty sessions over thirty weeks, the minimum required. Every Tuesday Al helps him into the passenger seat of the Model T and drives to Rockland. At each appointment—which, as far as I can tell, consists merely of paying more money for mysterious tablets and cataloging his intake of those expensive apples—a divot is punched in his contract.

Papa has always run the farm with a firm hand, selling blueberries and vegetables, milk and butter, chickens and eggs, cutting ice and managing the fishing weir for extra money. He's always stressed the importance of saving. But now he seems willing to spend whatever this doctor tells him to in the hopes of getting well.

One Tuesday morning, about four months into the treatment, only an hour after Al and Papa have left for the weekly trip to Rockland, I hear a car door slam and look out the kitchen window. They're back. Al has a grim look on his face as he helps Papa get out of the car. After taking him upstairs to his room, Al comes into the kitchen and sits down heavily. "Oh Lord," he says.

"What happened?"

"It was all a ruse." He rubs his hand through his hair. "When we got to Pole's office, the whole building was shuttered. A few days ago, they told us, he was chased out of town by angry patients. A lot of people lost their shirts."

Over the next few months, the severity of our situation becomes starkly clear. Papa's two thousand dollars in savings are gone. We can't pay our bills. More infirm than ever, Papa is listless and depressed and spends all his time upstairs. I try to be sympathetic, but it's hard. Apples. The fruit that tempted Eve lured my poor gullible father, both seduced by a sweet-talking snake.

IT'S A CHILLY Thursday morning in October when Papa asks Al to carry his wheelchair down to the Shell Room. An hour later, a sleek four-door maroon Chrysler glides up to the house and a woman in a trim gray suit steps out of the back. The driver stays in the car.

Hearing a knock on the front door, I make a move to answer it, but Papa says gruffly, "I'll handle it."

From the back hallway I can hear some of their conversation: . . . *generous offer* . . . *wealthy man* . . . *desirable shorefront* . . . *doesn't come twice* . . .

After the woman leaves—"I'll let myself out," she says and does; I watch out the window as she ducks into the backseat of the Chrysler and taps the driver on the shoulder—Papa sits in the Shell Room for a few minutes by himself. Then he wheels awkwardly into the kitchen. "Where's Alvaro?"

"Milking, I think. What was that all about?"

"Fetch him. And your mother."

When I'm back from the barn, Papa has wheeled himself into the dining room. Mother, who spends most of her time upstairs, sits at the head of the table, a shawl around her shoulders. Al troops in behind me and stands against the wall, grimy in his overalls.

"That lady brought with her an offer from an industrialist by the name of Synex," Papa says abruptly. "Fifty thousand dollars for the house and land. Cash."

I gape at him. "What?!"

Al leans forward. "Did you say fifty?"

"I did. Fifty thousand."

"That's a hell of a lot of money," Al says.

Papa nods. "It's a hell of a lot of money." He pauses for a few moments, letting the news sink in. I look around—all three of us are openmouthed. Then he says, "I hate to say this, but I think it would be wise for us to accept this offer."

"John, you can't be serious," Mother says.

"I am serious."

"What an absurd idea." She sits up straight, pulling the shawl tight around her shoulders.

Papa raises his hand. "Hold on, Katie. My savings have been spent. This could be a way out." He shakes his head. "I hate to say it, but our options at this point are few. If we don't take this now . . ."

"Where would you—we—go?" Al asks. I can tell as he stumbles over the words that he's trying to assess Papa's state of mind, wondering if he and I factor into it at all.

"I'd like a smaller house," Papa says. "And with the money I could help you set up your own homes."

We are all quiet for a moment, contemplating this. Except for the time with Walton—which seems to me now like a fever dream, hallucinatory and indistinct, unrelated to my life before or after—I have lived in this house like a mollusk in its shell, never imagining that I might be separated from it. I've taken for granted my existence here—the worn stairs, the whale-oil lamp in the hall, the view of the grass and the cove beyond from the front stoop.

Mother rises abruptly from her chair. "This house has been in my family since 1743. Generations of Hathorns have lived and died here. You don't walk away from a house simply because someone offers to buy it."

"Fifty thousand." Papa raps his misshapen knuckles on the table. "We will not see an offer like this again, I can tell you."

She tugs at her dress, her jaw clenched, the veins on her neck like rivulets of water. I have never seen the two of them in conflict like this. "This is my house, not yours," she says fiercely. "We will stay on."

Papa's face is grim, but he doesn't speak. Mother is a Hathorn; he is not. The conversation is over.

Papa will spend the next fifteen years confined to a wheelchair in a small room on the ground floor of the house he was so eager to sell, rarely venturing outside. Al and I, with the help of our brothers, will scrape and save, learn to live with even less. We'll manage, just barely, to save the farm from bankruptcy. But sometimes I will wonder—all of us will wonder—whether it would have been better to let it go.

IN JULY OF 1921 Sam, laughing, gathers our family together in the Shell Room. Clasping the hand of his bespectacled choir-leader girlfriend, Mary, he announces that he has asked for her hand in marriage.

"Of course I said yes!" Mary beams, holding out her left hand to show us the modest engagement ring she inherited from her grandmother.

This news isn't a complete surprise: the two of them met in Malden, where Mary grew up, when Sam stayed to work for Herbert Carle, and have been together for several years. I watch as he moves closer and whispers something, as she blushes and he brushes her hair behind her ear. "I'm so happy for you both," I tell them, and though I feel a pang of sadness for myself witnessing their casual intimacy, I mean it. Dear kind Sam deserves to find love.

Sam and Mary's wedding is held on the "lawn," as Mary calls it, though we Olsons have never thought of it as anything but the field. Al and Fred build a pergola and set up two rows of twenty chairs borrowed from the Grange Hall. Over several days I bake rolls, blueberry and strawberry pies, and a wedding cake, Sam's favorite: lemon with buttercream frosting. Mary wears a lacy dress and veil; Sam is dashing in a dark gray suit. A three-piece band from Rockland plays on the bluff above the shore, where Fred has organized a clambake at the water's edge.

After their honeymoon, the newlyweds move into our family homestead to save money for a house of their own. I like having another woman around, particularly one as young and friendly as Mary, who is solid and kind and laughs easily. She is good company in the house, helping me cook and clean.

Sam and Mary settle into a bedroom on the third floor, away from the rest of the family, and soon enough, Mary is with child. Unlike Ramona—as reported in her letters—she has no morning sickness. We sit by the hearth as she knits blankets and I sew frocks for the baby, talking about the weather and the crop yield and the people we know in common, such as Gertrude Gibbons, who was married recently herself. (She sent an invitation to the wedding, but I didn't go.)

"That girl's got some border collie in her blood. Can't help herding and nipping. But she's all right," Mary says.

The image makes me smile, both because it's exactly what Gertrude does and because Mary says it so matter-of-factly, without rancor. I don't mention my waspish comment to Gertrude at the dance. It's hard to feel proud of that.

MONTHS LATER, WOKEN in the middle of the night by a low moan, I lie in the darkness of my bedroom, my breathing the only sound. Sitting up, I strain to listen. Minutes pass. Another moan, louder this time, and then I know: it's time for the baby to be born. I hear Sam's heavy footsteps down two flights of stairs and out the front door. The Ford engine revs; he's on the way to get the midwife.

I bend and unbend my legs, as I do every morning, and carefully swing them over the side, holding onto the spindle frame as I reach for my dress on the peg on the back of the door. In the darkness I pull on stockings and lace my feet into shoes, then make my way downstairs, leaning on the banister. Papa is in the foyer in his wheelchair, bumping around, muttering under his breath in Swedish, trying to navigate the doorways to get to the kitchen. He must've roused himself from bed, a task Al usually helps him with.

I fill the kettle from the urn of water on the floor, fire up the Glenwood, and take out oats for porridge and bread for toast as the sun rises in the sky. After some time, I see the car pull up in front of the house. The midwife steps out, carrying a large tapestry bag. Then the back door opens and Gertrude Gibbons emerges. What is she doing here?

"Look who I found," Sam says, stepping into the kitchen. "Mary thought it might be useful to have another set of hands."

"How are you, Christina?" Gertrude says, just behind him, smiling brightly.

"I'm fine, Gertrude," I say, trying to keep my voice neutral. We haven't seen each other since that long-ago dance, and it feels stiff and awkward between us.

"I know you have difficulty with those stairs, and your mother isn't well," she says. "I'm honored to fill the gap. Where is dear Mary?"

When everyone has trooped upstairs, I step out into the cool air of the backyard, shadowed at this early hour by the house. Al has been plowing the garden plot, and the dirt smells fresh and damp from yesterday's rain. Tessie neighs in a distant field. Lolly winds between my legs, pressing against my calves. Sinking onto the stone step, I pull her into my lap, but she yowls and slinks away. I feel low, heavy, weighted to the earth. Earlier in the spring a birth announcement arrived from Ramona and Harland: a girl named Rose, seven pounds, nine ounces. In June, Eloise married Bill Rivers, and Alvah eloped with Eva Shuman a few weeks later. I'm glad for Sam and Mary, for all of them, but every ritual—weddings, births, christenings—reminds me of how alone I am. My own life so barren in contrast.

Tears well in my eyes.

"Why, there you are!" Glancing over my shoulder, I see Gertrude's face cross-hatched in the screen. "I've been looking for you all over. The midwife doesn't need me at the moment. She says Mary is a natural."

I wipe my face with the back of my hand, hoping she didn't see, but nothing gets past Gertrude. "What on earth is wrong? Are you hurt?"

"No."

She tries to open the screen, but I'm sitting in the way. "Did something happen?"

"No."

"Can I come out there?"

The last thing I want to do is explain my tears to Gertrude Gibbons. She is here out of curiosity, after all, and boredom, and her endless desire to know what's going on. "Please, just give me a minute."

But she will not. "Mercy, Christina, if—"

"I said," I tell her, my voice rising, "leave me alone."

"Well." Affronted, she pauses. Then she says coldly, "I was coming down to help with breakfast. But I see you have let the fire go out."

I stand up unsteadily. Then I yank open the door, startling her, tears clouding my vision. I lurch into the kitchen. My awkwardness irritates me even further; everything is a blur, and Gertrude is looking at me in her usual obtuse, judgmental, pitying way.

I hate her for it. For seeing me clearly, for not seeing me at all.

I careen through the pantry, forcing her to step back against the wall. I want to be upstairs in my bedroom, with the door shut, but how can I navigate the stairs without her watching? And then I realize I don't care. I just need to get there. Leaning against the wall, I pull myself along the hallway until I reach them. I use my forearms and elbows to hoist myself up the narrow stairs, stopping to rest every few steps, knowing that Gertrude is listening to every grunt. When I reach the landing at the top, I look down. There she is, standing in the foyer with her hands on her hips. "Honestly, Christina, I do not under—"

But I won't listen. I can't. Turning away, I wrench myself along the floor to my bedroom, where I kick the door shut behind me.

I lie on the floor of my bedroom, breathing heavily. After a few minutes, I hear footsteps plodding up the stairs.

Then a rap on the door.

"Christina?" Gertrude's voice is laced with affected concern.

Scooting backward I grasp the bedpost, then turn around and

heave myself up onto the mattress, trying to slow my pounding .
heartbeat. Her presence on the other side of the door radiates a
nasty heat; I am flushed with it.

Another rap.

"Go away."

"For mercy's sake, let me in."

There's no lock. After a moment, I watch the white porcelain
knob turn. Gertrude steps into the room and shuts the door, her
doughy face pinched with pantomimed worry. "What is wrong
with you?"

I wish I could dart around her, but my only recourse is words.
"I did not invite you here."

"Well, your brother asked me to come. Honestly, with three of
you infirm in this household I should think you'd be grateful for it."

"I assure you, I am not."

For a moment we glare at each other. Then she says, "Now
listen. You make breakfast for this family every single day of the
year. You need to pull yourself together and prepare some food
right this minute. Why are you being so hateful?"

I'm not sure I understand it myself. But my flinty anger feels
good. Better than sadness. I don't want to let it go. I cross my
arms.

She sighs. "We are about to welcome this wonderful new
life—this baby! I'm sorry to be blunt, but you are acting like a
child. Maybe nobody else is saying this to you, but I assure you
they're thinking it." She runs her hands down the bedspread
near my leg, smoothing the wrinkles. "Sometimes we all need a
good friend to tell us what's what."

I flinch from her hand. "You are not a friend to me. Much less a good friend."

"Why . . . how can you say that? What do you mean?"

"I mean that . . ." What do I mean? "You take pleasure in my misfortune. It makes you feel superior."

Her neck reddens. She puts a hand to her throat. "That is a terrible thing to say."

"It's how I feel."

"I invited you to my *wedding*! Which—let me remind you— you did not attend. Nor send a gift."

I feel a little twinge. I'd forgotten about the gift. But I'm in no mood to apologize. "Let's be honest, Gertrude. You didn't want me at your wedding."

"Do not presume to know what I want or don't want!" she says, her voice rising in a hiss. Then she pokes at the ceiling and puts a finger to her lips. "Shh!"

"You're the one raising your voice," I say evenly.

"Christina, this is foolishness," she says, suddenly imperious. "No doubt it was devastating for you, what happened with that man. Walton Hall." Hearing his name on her lips makes me shudder. "But it's time to move on. You have to stop stewing in your misfortune. Don't you wish the best for your brother and Mary? Now let's forget this ever happened and go make some food for those hungry people."

Bringing up Walton is the final straw. "Get out of my room."

She gives a little disbelieving laugh. "Why, I—"

"If you don't leave my room this minute, I swear I will never speak to you again."

"Now, Christina—"

"I mean it, Gertrude."

"This is outrageous. In all my days . . ." She looks around as if some unseen presence in the room might come to her aid.

I shift on the bed, turning my body away from her.

She stands in the middle of the floor for a moment, breathing heavily. "You have a very cold heart, Christina Olson," she says. Then she wrenches open the door and walks out into the hall, slamming it behind her. I hear her hesitate on the landing. Then heavy footsteps down the stairs.

Muffled voices. She is speaking to Papa in the dining room. The screen door opens with a creak and swings shut.

WHAT PROMISES I *make, I keep,* Walton once said. His words were empty, but mine are not. Despite the fact that we live in a small place and are bound to run into each other, I keep my promise to Gertrude Gibbons. I will never speak to her again.

By the time my nephew—John William, given his grandfather's American name—is born on the third floor a few hours later, I've made my way downstairs to the pantry, where I wash my face with a cool cloth and tame my hair with a horsehair brush. I coax the fire back to life and lay a table with sliced turkey and pickled beans and fried apple cake. When my brother Sam places the small bundle in my arms, as warm and dense as a loaf of bread fresh from the oven, I look down into the face of this child. *John William*. He stares up at me intently with dark eyes, his brow furrowed, as if he's trying to figure out who I am, and my melancholy lifts, lightens, evaporates into the air. It's impossible to feel anything for this baby but love.

THORNBACK

1946–1947

Only traces of white remain on the sun-bleached, snow-battered clapboards and shingles of this old house. Inside, wood smoke, fuel oil, and tobacco have darkened the wallpaper. Sometimes it feels as if Al and I are living in a haunted house with the ghosts of our parents, our grandparents, all those sea captains and their wives and children. I still keep the door between the kitchen and the shed open for the witches.

Ghosts and witches, all around. The thought is oddly comforting.

Much of the time, these days, the house is quiet. I've come to think of silence as another kind of sound. After all, the world is never totally silent, even in the middle of the night. Beds creak, a wolf howls, wind stirs the trees, the sea roars and shushes. And of course there's plenty to see. In springtime I watch the deer, noses to the wind, trailed by speckled fawns; in summer rabbits and raccoons; in autumn a bull moose loping across the field; a red fox vivid against December snow.

Hours accumulate like snow, recede like the tide. Al and I drift through our routines. Get up when we want to, go to bed when light drains from the sky. Nobody's schedules to attend to other than our own. We hunker down in the fall and winter, slow our heartbeats to a hibernating rhythm, struggle to rouse ourselves in March. People from away arrive in cars laden with bags and boxes in June and July and head out in the opposite direction in August and September. One year melts into the next. Each season is like it was the year before, with minor variations. Our conversations often revolve around the weather: Will this summer be hotter than last; can we expect an early frost, how many inches of snow by December?

This life of ours can feel an awful lot like waiting.

In the summer I'm usually up before sunrise, lighting the Glenwood range and making porridge. (I rarely sleep through the night on my pallet; my legs throb, even in my dreams.) I'll scoop a cup for myself and eat it in the dark, listening to the sounds of the house, the gulls cawing outside. When Al comes into the kitchen, I'll hand him a cup of porridge and he'll take it to the counter and sprinkle sugar on it from Mother's cut-glass bowl.

"Well, I suppose it's milking time," he says when he's finished. He carries the cup to the sink in the pantry and dredges water from the pump.

"I can wash that," I sometimes protest. "You've got chores."

But he always rinses his cup, and my cup too. "It's no trouble."

When Al heads out to the barn, I sit in my old chair looking out the window toward the road to town in one direction and the St. George River, and beyond it the sea, in the other. The sun shimmers on the water and the wind carves patterns in the high grass. Around mid-morning Andy usually shows up, disappears upstairs, emerges for lunch, leaves in the late afternoon. With the door propped open, Topsy and the cats come and go as they please. Sometimes a friendly porcupine climbs up the steps, waddles across the kitchen, and disappears into the pantry. I might drift to sleep and wake to purring, which sounds to my sleep-clotted brain like a faraway motor. Lolly, seeing my eyes flicker, stretches toward my face, her paws digging into my shoulder. I reach under her rib cage, feeling through her warm skin the quick thrumming of her heart.

Later in the day I'll weed and prune my flower garden, brilliant with color—poppies and pansies and an assortment of sweet peas, pale blue, peach, magenta. Red geraniums grow fat and healthy in the window in their Spry shortening cans and old blue-painted pots. I fill vases with the white lilacs that have grown beside the shed for a hundred years alongside Al's favorite pink roses. The cats sprawl in the sun, blinking lazily. I can't imagine anywhere I'd rather be.

But in the winter, when it's so cold in the early morning that you can see your breath as you lie in bed, when getting to the barn requires a hoe to cut through the icy crust on top of the snow, when the wind slices branches off the trees and the sky is as dull as a stone, it's hard to see why anyone would live here if they have a choice. Heating this old house is like heating a lobster trap. The three woodstoves must be fed constantly or we will freeze. It takes eleven cords of wood to keep the fires burning until spring. Darkness comes early without electricity. Before turning in, Al banks the stoves high with firewood to keep the embers glowing through the night. I heat bricks in the oven to wrap in towels and slide under the covers. Many nights we are in bed by eight o'clock, staring at the ceiling in separate rooms.

Do our natures dictate the choices we make, I wonder, or do we choose to live a certain way because of circumstances beyond our control? Perhaps these questions are impossible to tease apart because, like a tangle of seaweed on a rock, they are connected at the root. I think of those long-ago Hathorns, determined beyond all reason to leave the past behind—and we, their descendants, inheritors of their contrarian tenacity, sticking it out, one generation after the next, until every last one of us ends up in the graveyard at the bottom of the field.

THE POSTCARD, STAMPED Tokyo, features a scenic view of an arched bridge leading to a mansion with a curved roof. "Nijubashi: The Main Entrance to the Imperial Palace," the caption says, in English, on the front, next to a string of Japanese characters. Though it's not unlike the half-dozen postcards I've received in the past few months of 1945, the scrawled message from John on the other side is a surprise: "Finally, Aunt Christina—I'm coming home!"

My old friend Sadie Hamm also has reason to celebrate: her son Clyde was injured, but he is coming home with only a flesh wound to his upper arm and some shrapnel in his legs. She's teary when she tells me the news. "It could've been so different for us," she says. "When I think about what others have to endure . . ."

The postmistress Bertha Dorset's two sons were drafted into the army, and her youngest died in France. And Gertrude Gibbons's nephew, who grew up in Rockland and was trained as a fighter pilot, was killed over the Pacific. I never would have guessed, seeing the soldiers on Boston Common all those years ago, that another world war would engulf us. I couldn't have imagined how much more there was to lose.

"You could drop Gertrude a note, you know," Sadie says gently. "I'm sure it would mean a lot to her."

"I could," I say.

"A lot of time has passed."

"It has."

But though I feel a pang of sadness for Gertrude, I know I won't reach out. I am too old, too stubborn. Her meddlesome insensitivity was something I could not—cannot, in the end—forgive.

And if I'm honest, there's something else. Gertrude has become a stand-in for anyone who ever pitied me, didn't try to understand me, abandoned me. She gives my bitterness a place to dwell.

IT TAKES SEVERAL weeks for John to travel by boat from Japan to Treasure Island in the South Pacific and, from there, by ferry to San Francisco, and another five days on a train to Boston, where he is officially discharged from the navy on Christmas Eve, 1945. He shows up at our house in uniform on Christmas Day with a chestful of medals, colorful packets of pastel-colored hard sugar candies called Konpeito that I don't care for, and a newly acquired, un-Olson-like propensity to hug.

John is taller, thinner, and flinty featured, but still as mild-mannered as ever. "I can't wait to pull my lobster boat out of the shed and get out on the water," he tells me. "I've missed this place."

He doesn't waste any time getting settled. By spring 1946 he's engaged to a local woman named Marjorie Jordan. "You'll come to the wedding, won't you, Aunt Christina?" he implores, taking my hand.

How will I ever get to a wedding when I can barely walk? "My land, you don't need me at your wedding."

"I most certainly do. You're coming if I have to carry you there myself."

I motion for him to come closer. I don't know what to say, but I want to say something. I'm touched that he wants me there. "I'm glad you survived," I tell him when he crouches down beside me.

Laughing, he kisses me on the cheek. "I'm glad I survived, too. So you'll come?"

"I'll come."

Sadie claps her hands together when I tell her the news. "What fun! All right, then, we need to find you a dress. I'll take you into Rockland."

"Not store-bought. I'm going to make it myself."

She looks at me doubtfully. "How long has it been since you sewed anything?"

"A while, I guess." I hold my gnarled hands out, palms up. "I know they look frightful, but they work just fine."

Sighing, she says, "If you insist, I'll take you to get some fabric."

The next morning Sadie helps me into her cream-colored Packard sedan and drives me to Senter Crane in Rockland. On the ride I begin to worry. How is she going to maneuver me inside? When she parks the car, Sadie leans over and pats my knee. As if reading my mind, she says, "Why don't you let me go in and get you some samples? What would you like?"

I let out a breath I didn't know I was holding. "That's probably best. Maybe a flowered silk?"

"You got it."

I watch her whisk through the revolving door. She spins out ten minutes later with a dress pattern and three squares of fabric. "Thanks to rationing, no silk," she says. "But I found some decent options." She hands me the squares: a sky-blue dotted Swiss, a floral rayon, and light pink cotton broadcloth. I choose the pink, of course.

At home, in the dining room, I spread the fabric across the table and study the picture on the cover of the pattern: a thin, elegant woman who looks nothing like me in a dress with a fitted bodice and a long paneled skirt. I take the flimsy folded pattern out of its envelope and lay it over the cloth, find the pincushion in my sewing basket, and attempt to secure it. I'm startled to find that my fingers are shaking badly. Only with laborious effort do I manage to pin a section of the pattern to the cloth. I slice into it with my heavy silver scissors, but the line is jagged. When I open the sewing machine, I sit at it for a few minutes, running my hand over its curves, touching the still-sharp needle with my finger.

All at once I'm afraid. Afraid I'll ruin the dress.

I sit back in my chair. It's not just the dress, or my wretched hands; it's all of it. I'm afraid for my future—a future of inevitable debilitation. Of increasing reliance on others. Of spending the rest of my years in this broken shell of a house.

When Sadie stops by a few days later, she runs her finger along the erratic line of the pins. Inspects the ragged cut. "You made a start," she says gently. "Shall I take it over to Catherine Bailey in Maple Juice Cove to finish it up?" She doesn't look in my eyes; I can tell she doesn't want to embarrass me. When I nod, she says, "Right, then," and carefully folds the pattern with the fabric, gathers the spools of pink thread and the instructions. Unfurling the yellow measuring tape from my sewing box, she encircles my waist, my hips, my bodice, scratches the numbers on a scrap of paper, and tucks it all into a bag.

SEVERAL WEEKS LATER I'm sitting in the kitchen, wearing my new dress, about to leave for the wedding, when Andy shows up, unannounced as usual, at the door.

Stopping abruptly in the doorway, he says, "My God, Christina." He strides over and runs his hand down my sleeve, whispering to himself, "Magnificent. Like a faded lobster shell."

1922–1938

In the summers, now, I make my way to the Grange Hall in Cushing most Fridays, but instead of swaying with the music and chatting with friends as they jostle on and off the dance floor, joking and laughing and carrying on, the bolder ones smoking cigarettes outside and tippling from a flask, I am consigned to the role of fruit-punch server, pound-cake cutter, molasses-cookie arranger. I pick up soiled napkins and wash dirty glasses in the sink behind a partition. Most of the women who play this role are older than I am and married. Only a few are my age: the unchosen and childless.

I have not gotten used to it. I'm not sure I ever will. For a while I continue to bring my dress shoes in a bag, as I always have, and put them on as soon as I arrive. But one evening when the hall is particularly hot, I excuse myself from the serving table, go outside, roll my stockings down, slip them off my feet, and put my flat-heeled walking shoes back on. What does it matter?

It's a damp Friday in August and I'm walking to the Grange Hall with Fred and his fiancée, Lora, wearing a white dress I finished sewing hours earlier from a new McCall's pattern, when I slip in a rut in the road. I put my hands out to stop my fall, but my arms aren't stable enough to support my weight. I drop heavily into the muck and gravel, tearing my sleeves, scraping my chin.

"Oh!" Fred shouts, leaping toward me, "Are you all right?"

My chin drips blood, my wrists throb, I am facedown in the wet, soiled dress it took me weeks to sew. The skirt is bunched up round my hips, my bloomers and misshapen legs exposed. Lifting myself slowly on my elbows, I survey my torn bodice. All at once I am so tired of this—of the constant threat of humiliation and pain, the fear of exposure, of trying to act like I'm normal when I'm not—that I burst into tears. No, I am not all right, I want to say. I am fouled, degraded, ashamed. A burden and an embarrassment.

"Can you get up?" Lora asks kindly, standing over me. She crouches down. "Let me help you."

I turn my face away.

"Doesn't seem to be a break," Fred murmurs, running his expert farmer's hands over my wrists and ankles. "But you'll have some bruises and swelling, I'm afraid. Poor thing." He tells me to flex my hands, not the easiest maneuver even when I'm not in pain. When I grimace, he says, "Probably a nasty sprain. No fun at all, but it could be worse."

Lora waits with me while Fred jogs back to the house to get the car. At home the two of them carry me through the front door and upstairs to my room, where Lora finds my nightgown on a peg and discreetly helps me undress and Fred gently washes my face and arms. Once they've shut the door behind them, I burrow into my blankets and turn toward the wall.

How did I go from being the maiden in a fairy tale to a wretched old maid so quickly? It happened almost without my realizing it, the transition to spinsterhood. Mamey said that in her day a woman who had not married by the age of thirty was called a thornback, named after a flat, spiny, prehistoric-looking fish. It's what they called Bridget Bishop, she said. *Thornback.* That's what I have become.

WHEN MOTHER'S HEALTH becomes so precarious that she and Papa need separate bedrooms, I offer to give up mine. She's in pain; her kidney issues are worse, her legs puffed with fluid. She has started sleeping upright in a parlor chair. I move downstairs, where my bed is a pallet on the dining room floor that I roll up each morning and tuck in the closet. It's not so bad; I'm closer to the kitchen and the privy, secretly relieved not to have to navigate the stairs.

In the mornings I prepare the noon meal and carry it through the narrow pantry to the round oak table in the dining room for Al and Papa and me, making a separate plate for Al to carry upstairs for Mother. Baked or boiled potatoes, green beans, roast chicken or turkey or ham, a stew of beef and carrots and onions and potatoes. Every few days I make bread with the sourdough starter. Watch the bread rise, punch it down, watch it rise again. In the summer and fall I can the berries Al rakes from their bushes and the strawberries he grows in the garden for jams and jellies, cakes and pies.

We mark the days by the chores that need to be done, the

way farm families have always done. Al feeds the hens and horses and pigs, splits wood in the fall, slaughters a pig when the weather turns cold, cuts ice in the winter. I collect eggs from the laying hens and Al drives me into town to sell them. He times the planting so that by the Fourth of July we'll have new peas and by September there's a whole field of corn. Gulls lunge for a feast, ravaging the crop, so Al kills a few and hangs them from poles as warning. During haying season in midsummer, I see him from the dining room window in his visored cap, scything the hay by hand with six hired men walking abreast, forking the newly mown hay onto the hayrack. They haul the hay to the barn, where a block-and-tackle hoist lifts it into the mow. Swallows, disrupted from their nests, swoop in and out.

In late July and August, blueberry season, Al uses a heavy steel hand rake to harvest the small dark berries from their low bushes. It's grueling work, stooping over those low bushes in the hot sun, dumping the berries into a wooden box to be winnowed and weighed, and all summer the back of his neck is burnt and peeling, his knuckles scraped and scarred, his lower back constantly sore.

Aside from the Grange Hall socials, the sewing circle I go to now and then, and the occasional visit with Sadie, I don't see many people. Most of my old friends and acquaintances are busy with their new husbands and new lives. At any rate, I have little in common with most of the girls I went to school with who are married and having children. I can tell, when we're together, that they are self-conscious talking about their husbands and pregnancies. But this difference only highlights what has always been true. I've never shared either their fluid ease of movement or their quick laughter. My wit—such that it is—has always been more sardonic, stranger, harder to recognize.

Now and then I leaf through the small blue volume of Emily Dickinson poems that my teacher, Mrs. Crowley, pressed into my hand. I remember her words to me when I left school: *Your mind will be your comfort.*

It is, sometimes. And sometimes it isn't.

With no one to talk to about the poems, I have to try to parse the meanings myself. It's frustrating not to be able to discuss them with anybody, but also strangely freeing. The lines can mean anything I want.

> Much Madness is divinest Sense—
> To a discerning Eye—
> Much Sense—the starkest Madness—
> 'Tis the Majority
> In this, as all, prevail—
> Assent—and you are sane—
> Demur—you're straightaway dangerous—
> And handled with a chain—

I imagine Emily sitting at her small desk, her back to the world. She must've seemed very odd to those in her orbit. A little unhinged. Even dangerous, perhaps, asserting, as she does, that it's the people who lead conventional lives who are the mad ones.

I wonder about that chain that held her. I wonder if it's the same as mine.

❧

MY CATS, AS cats will do, have kittens. Al takes boxes of them into town and gives away as many as he can, but before long I'm feeding a dozen. They swarm underfoot, mewling and jumping and sometimes hissing at one another. Al grouses about it, pushes them off the table with an open palm, kicks at them when they wind around his legs, mutters about solving the problem with a rock-heavy sack in the pond. "It's too many, Christie, we've got to get rid of them."

"Oh? And then what, I'll go around talking to an empty house?"

He chews his lip and goes back out to the barn.

LATE ONE EVENING, I'm lying on my pallet in the dark in the dining room when I hear a commotion upstairs, directly above me. Mother's bedroom. I sit up quickly, fumble for a candle and match, and make my way to the foyer. "Mother?" I call. "Are you all right?"

No answer.

Al is out with Sam, playing cards. Papa is sound asleep in his room. (There's not much point in waking him; he's frailer than I am.) I haven't been upstairs in months, but I know I have to get there now. I haul myself up the stairs as quickly as I can on my elbows, sweat dampening my neck from the effort. When I reach the top, I pull myself to my feet and grope my way down the hall to Mother's door, push it open. In the moonlight I see that she is on the floor on her knees, fumbling at the quilt in a kind of panic, trying to claw her way up back onto the bed, her nightgown bunched around her thighs.

She turns and gives me a bewildered look.

"I'm here, Mother." Stumbling forward in the dark, I collapse on the floor beside her. I try to help her up with my hands, my elbows, even my shoulder, but her weight is like a sack of flour, and I can't get any traction.

She begins sobbing. "I just want to go to bed."

"I know," I say miserably. I feel helpless and angry: at myself for being so feeble, at Al for going out. After a few minutes, her sobbing turns to whimpering, and she rests her head on my lap. I pull her nightgown down over her legs and stroke her hair.

Some time later—fifteen minutes? Half an hour?—the front door opens downstairs. "Al!" I shout.

"Christie? Where are you?"

"Up here."

Footsteps pound up the stairs, the door slams open. I see the confusion in Al's eyes as he takes in the sight of Mother collapsed on the floor, me cradling her head in my lap. "What is going on?"

"She fell off the bed, and I couldn't lift her."

"Lord a mercy." Al comes over and gently hoists Mother up onto the mattress, then pulls the quilt over her and kisses her on the forehead.

After he's helped me down the stairs and onto my pallet in the dining room, I say, "That was terrible. You can't leave me alone with her like that."

"Papa's here."

"You know he's no help."

Al is silent for a moment. Then he says, "I need a life of my own, Christie. It's not too much to ask."

"She could've died."

"Well, she didn't."

"It was hard for me."

"I know." He sighs. "I know."

SEVERAL MONTHS LATER, about a week after Thanksgiving, I wake early, as usual, to stoke the fire in the kitchen and begin the process of making bread. The floorboards above my head creak with the ordinary sounds of Al getting up and dressed and going to Papa's room to check on him, the muffled sounds of Papa's deep bass and Al's higher tenor. I scoop flour into the earthenware bowl and add a sprinkle of salt, my hands going through the motions while my head is free to plan the day: pickled beets and sliced ham, warmed in the oven, for the noontime meal; gingerbread cookies if I have time, a pile of mending . . . I add a scoop of yeasty starter, a dollop of molasses, warm water from the saucepan on the range, and start kneading, folding in the flour.

Upstairs, Al knocks on Mother's door—or perhaps I only think I hear it, so accustomed am I to his routine. And then I hear, sharply, "Mother." Furniture scrapes along the floor.

I feel it before I know it. I look up at the ceiling with my hands in the dough.

Al clatters down the stairs. Materializes, panting, in the kitchen.

"She's gone, isn't she?" I whisper.

He nods.

I sink to my knees.

The next day Lora brings a mourning bouquet to hang on the front door. It's round and black, with long streamers and artificial flowers pasted in the middle. Mother would've hated it. She didn't like fake flowers, and neither do I.

"It's to show the community that this is a house of mourning," Lora says when she sees me scowling.

"I suspect they know that," I say.

The wind blew so hard all night it swept most of the snow into the sea. Neighbors swoop toward the house like crows, in groups of two and three, black scarves and coats flapping. They rap on the front door, hang their coats on hooks in the foyer, file past Mother's body in the Shell Room. The women bustle into the kitchen. They know what to do in a situation like this: exactly what they've always done. Here is Lisa Dubnoff, unwrapping a loaf of spice cake. Mary-Violet Verzaleno, slicing turkey. Annabelle Weinstein, washing dishes. The men jam their hands in their pockets, talk about the price of lobster, squint out at the horizon. I watch some of them out the kitchen window smoking cigarettes and pipes in the yard, stamping their feet and hunching their shoulders as they pass around a flask.

These neighbors leach pity the way a canteen of cold water sweats in the heat. The slightest inquiry is freighted with words unsaid. *Worried about you . . . feel sorry for you . . . so glad I'm not you. . . .* The women in the kitchen stop talking as soon as I come in, but I hear their whispers: *Lord help her, what will Christina do without her mother?* I want to tell them, My mother hasn't actually been present for a long time; I'll get along fine. But there's no way to say this without sounding harsh, so I stay quiet.

In the late afternoon of the third day, we huddle around Mother's burial plot in the family graveyard, strafed by the wind, the sky as yellow gray as a caul. Reverend Carter from Cushing Baptist Church opens his bible, clears his throat. When you live on a farm, he says, you are particularly aware that God's creatures are born naked and alone. Given only a short time on this earth. Hungry, cold, persecuted, afflicted, released. Each one of us experiences moments of doubt, of despair, of feeling unduly burdened. But there is solace to be found in giving yourself to the Lord and accepting his blessings. The best we can do is appreciate the wonders of God's green earth, try to avoid calamity, and put our faith in him.

This sermon sums up Mother's life perhaps all too well, though it does little to improve the general mood.

Before we leave the gravesite, Mary sings Mother's favorite gospel hymn:

> Oh, what joy it will be when His face I behold,
> Living gems at His feet to lay down;
> It would sweeten my bliss in the city of gold,
> Should there be any stars in my crown.

Mary's lovely voice rises and lingers in the air, and by the end of the song most of us are crying. I am too, though I still don't know what those stars are meant to represent. My mistake, I suppose, is in thinking they should mean something.

ONE MORNING IN July I'm sitting in my chair in the kitchen, as usual, when there's a rap on the window. A slip of a girl with straight brown hair and large brown eyes is staring at me. The side door is open, as it always is in the summer. I nod at the doorway and she comes to the threshold and steps cautiously inside.

"Yes?"

"I'm hoping I might impose on you for a glass of water." The girl is wearing a white shift dress, and her feet are bare. She is watchful but clearly unafraid, as if accustomed to walking into the homes of strangers.

"Help yourself," I tell her, motioning toward the hand pump in the pantry. She sidles across the room and disappears around the corner. From my chair I hear the screech of the heavy iron arm moving up and down, the chortle of water.

"Can I use this cup here?" she calls.

"Sure."

She comes back around the corner, drinking noisily from a chipped white mug. "That's better," she says, setting the cup on the counter. "I'm Betsy. Staying up the road with my cousins for the summer. And you must be Christina."

I can't help smiling at her forthrightness. "How did you know that?"

"They told me there's only one woman living in this house, and she's named Christina, so I figured."

Lolly, who's been winding around my feet, leaps into my lap. The girl strokes her under the chin until she purrs, then glances at the other cats milling around the kitchen. It's time for their breakfast. "You sure have a lot of cats."

"I do."

"Cats only like you because you feed them."

"That's not true." Lolly sinks down, exposing her belly to be rubbed. "I'm guessing you don't have a cat."

"No."

"A dog?"

She nods. "His name is Freckles."

"Mine is Topsy."

"Where is he?"

"Probably out in the field with my brother Al. He doesn't like cats much."

"The dog, or your brother?"

I laugh. "Both, I guess."

"Well, that's no surprise. Boys don't like cats."

"Some do."

"Not many."

"You seem awfully sure of your opinions," I tell her.

"Well, I think about things a lot," she says. "I hope you won't mind my asking: What's wrong with you?"

I have spent my life bristling at this question. But the girl seems so frankly curious that I feel compelled to answer. "The doctors don't know."

"When I was born, my bones were kind of deformed," she says. "I had to do all kinds of exercises to get better. I'm still a little crooked, see? Kids made fun of me." She shrugs. "You know."

I shrug back. I know.

The girl raises her chin at the pile on the sideboard. "Look at that pile of dirty dishes. You could use some help." She goes over to the sideboard, makes a pile of dishes, and carries them over to the long cast-iron sink in the pantry.

And then, to my surprise, she washes them.

WHEN PAPA DIES at the age of seventy-two in 1935, he has been so unwell and so unhappy for so long that his death comes as a relief. For decades I did my best to care for this man who ended my schooling at twelve, who squandered the family fortune, such that it was, on a crackpot scheme, who expected his only daughter—possessed of an infirmity as debilitating as his own—to manage the household, and never once said thank you. I fed him, cleaned up after him, washed his soiled clothes, inhaled his sour breath; and his own discomfort was all he could see.

I have to remind myself that once I saw this man as kind and just and strong.

When my brothers and their wives arrive at the house, we go through the familiar motions of mourning, serving cake and tea and slicing ham, accepting condolences, singing hymns. The body in the Shell Room, the burial in the family plot. As I stand at Papa's grave I think of how he was at the end, miserable in his wheelchair in the front parlor, clutching a chunk of anthracite in his fist and gazing out through the window toward the sea. I don't know what he was longing for, but I can guess. His robust youth. His ability to stand and walk. His family of origin in the land of his birth, to which he never returned. A clear sense of where he belonged, and to whom, and why. Did he regret the calculations and miscalculations he made that opened up the world to him and eventually narrowed it to this point of land?

Though I lived with this man for my entire life, I never really knew him. He was like a frozen bay himself, I think—an icy crust, layers deep, above roiling water.

AFTER ALL THE mourners leave, I am struck by the vast emptiness of this house, stretching up three floors to the dormers. All these unused rooms. Sam and Fred have started their own family farms and gone into business together, manufacturing lumber and hay. Now it's just Al and me—and the wheelchair, taking up space in the middle of the Shell Room.

"It's yours if you want it," Al says. "Still in pretty good shape."

I look at the nasty contraption, with its sagging stained seat and rusted wheels. "I hate that chair. I never want to see it again."

His eyes widen. I guess it's the first time I've said that aloud. He stands there for a moment, sucking on his pipe. Then he goes over to the woodstove, knocks the ashes out of his pipe, and says, "All right. Let's get rid of it, then."

I watch as Al drags the wheelchair out the front door and down the steps, where it teeters to its side and crashes over. He disappears into the barn and comes back a few minutes later with Tessie hitched to the small wagon. Pulling on her harness, he leads her close to the wheelchair and heaves it into the wagon, then doffs his hat to me with a smile and leads the horse and wagon down to the cove.

About half an hour later I see Al through the window, trudging back up the field with Tessie. The wagon is empty.

"What'd you do with it?" I ask when he comes through the kitchen door.

He sits in his chair, takes off his cap, sets it on the bench in front of him. Fiddles inside his jacket, pulls out his old brown pipe and a pouch of tobacco. Finds a matchbook in his trouser pocket. Takes a pinch of tobacco, packs it into the pipe, tamps it down with his finger. Adds more tobacco, tamps it down again. Sticks it in his mouth and lights it, cupping a hand around it to protect the flame. Shakes out the match. Sits there inhaling the smoke and blowing it out.

I know better than to rush him. Anyway, we have all the time in the world.

"You know the boulder by the Mystery Tunnel? That drop-off below?" he says after a while.

I nod.

He sucks on the pipe. Takes it out of his mouth and blows a stream of smoke. "I rolled that wheelchair up to the top of the rock and dumped it over."

"Gone," I say. "Good riddance."

"Good riddance," he says.

For the rest of my life I will think of that wheelchair lying smashed and rusting in the salty water near Mystery Tunnel, a place that once opened me to a world of magic, of possibility, but that over the years has come to mean something else. A place where Walton spun his false promises. A path strewn with anticipation that ends at a pile of rocks. A repository for my broken dreams, the treasure vanishing as soon as I reach for it.

The wheelchair, fool's gold, in the depths below.

SADIE IS STANDING in my kitchen, dropping off a chicken dish, when she says, "Are the rumors true? I hear Al's got his eye on that new teacher at the Wing School."

My skin prickles. "What are you talking about?"

"Angie Treworgy, I think her name is. She's boarding with Gertrude Gibbons."

Boarding with . . . Gertrude Gibbons? "I haven't heard a thing about it."

"He would make some lucky girl a wonderful husband, don't you think?"

"No, I do not think," I say stiffly.

Al has started going out three or four nights a week, usually to join the card game at Fales. He knows I don't like being left alone at night, but still he goes. On Saturdays he often drives to Thomaston, where the stores and bars stay open until nine. Or at least that's what he tells me. Now I wonder if he's going instead to Gertrude Gibbons's.

I don't mention what I've heard about the teacher, but for several days I give Al the silent treatment. He doesn't ask why.

I hear no further news of any woman until a few weeks later, when Al mentions casually that he's going to help out a man who lives with his daughter down near Hathorn Point. "They could use some firewood," he says. "I told him I'd cut some logs for them later in the week."

"How old's the daughter?" I ask.

"What?"

"You heard me."

"Why do you want to know?"

"I just wonder."

He gives me a look and scratches his head. "Old enough that it's rude to ask her age."

"As old as you are?"

He shifts his feet. "Well, no."

"Is she even in her forties?"

"I'd say not."

"Married?"

Sighing heavily, he says, "Divorced, I believe."

"I see." A few days later, I ask Sadie, "So who's that divorcée down on Hathorn Point?"

"You mean Estelle Bartlett?"

I shrug.

"Lives with her father?"

"That's the one."

Sadie leans close. "Word is she's been married three times, each time to someone older and wealthier. Who knows, it could be idle gossip. But she does appear to be well-off. Bought her father a brand-new Pontiac. Why do you ask?"

"Al's doing some odd jobs for her father."

Sadie's eyes shine. "She's a pretty lady. Wavy brown hair. That devil, your brother! Good for him."

Al keeps to his routine. He does his chores in the house, in the barn. But more and more these days he comes and goes as he pleases.

It's a sunny Fourth of July, the day of the annual clambake down at the shore near Little Island. My sister-in-law Mary's in charge—she pickled carrots and made wild rhubarb pies; Lora fried chicken and made yeast rolls. They've gathered blankets and bonnets and cutlery and dishes and piled them into baskets to be transported to the beach. My only task this year is drop biscuits, which I could make in my sleep. I start on them early in the morning. By the time people start showing up, just before noon, five dozen biscuits are cooling on racks in the pantry. I've had time to change my apron, which I can never help soiling (a dousing of flour, a smear of lard), and I'm sitting in the kitchen when they arrive.

"You look well, my dear!" Lora says.

"Doesn't she?" Mary says.

I know they mean to be kind, but their chipper tone makes me feel like I'm a hundred years old.

While Lora packs up the biscuits, Mary helps me into the car. She drives to the grassy area above the water, where they set up a chair for me away from the treacherous rocks. A gaggle of children, my nieces and nephews and some of their friends, are already on the beach, skipping rocks far out into the sound, competing to see whose goes the farthest, whose skips the most, their voices rising and mingling with the cawing of gulls.

My fourteen-year-old nephew, John, the oldest of the bunch, climbs up from the beach to sit with me for a while. We watch the others play games in the grass: Red Rover and Red Light/ Green Light and Giant Steps and hide-and-seek. They climb pine trees and gaze out at the small islands like Al and I used to do, sailors on the mast of a ship, the fields below a yellow ocean. The adults lounge on wool blankets, poke at the fire, pour fruit punch, squint up at us with a wave and a smile. Only Al is absent.

After some time, I hear the familiar clacking of the old Ford engine up near the house. The motor cuts off. I twist around to see Al climb out, go around to the other side, open the passenger door. Out steps a slim smiling woman with light brown pin curls.

Estelle—it must be. My stomach lurches. He did not mention a word to me about bringing her here.

"Well, look at that," John says. "Al's got a girl."

Here they come, now, down the path, Al in front, grinning shyly, wearing a crisp white shirt I've never seen before, the woman behind in a blue dress, sure-footed, laughing, dimple-cheeked, swinging a basket in one hand and a straw bonnet in the other. I want to run away, but I can't. I am caught like a fox in a trap, squirming, panicked, stuck.

"Beautiful day, isn't it?" Al says. As if we were acquaintances running into each other at the hardware store.

"Sure is," John says.

I gaze at Al steadily, saying nothing.

Color creeps up his neck. He clears his throat. "Christina, this is Estelle. I think I told you I've been doing some work for her father."

"There's work that needs to be done at our house," I say.

Estelle's smile fades.

"How about we head down and see the others?" Al says to her.

She looks at him, then inclines her head toward me and John. "Nice to meet you," she says in a tiny voice.

"Likewise," John says.

They turn and pick their way down to the rocks.

John cracks his knuckles. "Well, guess I'll grab another slice of rhubarb pie."

I nod.

"You okay, Aunt Christina?"

"I'm fine."

"Can I bring you anything?"

"No, thank you."

When John goes back to the clambake, I watch Al and Estelle, smiling and chatting and pointing at a sailboat, accepting plates of food. I sit glowering above them like a hot coal.

Lora clambers up to sit beside me, then my brother Fred, bearing offerings from below: an ear of corn, still warm in its charred green husk, a bowl of clams, a slice of blueberry cake. I shake my head. No. I will not eat. Their voices falsely cheerful, they exclaim over the blue sky, the glassy water, those delicious drop biscuits, what a lovely dress.

It was on this very bank that I sat with Walton—how many years ago? I know what everyone is thinking. *Poor Christina. Always left behind.*

I feel myself battening down, fortressing.

Sam climbs up and sits on the grass beside my chair. "What's going on?" he asks, patting my knee.

I look down at his hand on my knee and then at him. He removes his hand.

"Nothing's going on," I say.

He sighs. "This is no good, Christina."

"I don't know what you're talking about."

"You are ruining this picnic."

"I'm doing no such thing."

"You are, and you know you are. And you're making Al very unhappy."

"If he's going to bring that—that gold digger—" I blurt.

Sam puts his hand over mine. "Stop. Before you say something you'll regret."

"He's the one who's going to regret—"

"Come on," he says sharply. "Don't you think Al deserves to be happy?"

"I thought Al was happy."

He sits back on his heels. "Look, Christina, you know that Al has always been here for you. And he always will be. To begrudge him this—this relationship feels a little . . . well . . . mean-spirited."

"I'm not begrudging him anything. I'm just questioning his judgment."

Sam sits with me a minute longer, and I know he wants to say more. The words are sitting on his tongue. I can guess what they are. But he seems to think better of it. He pats my knee again and stands up, goes back to the others.

A few minutes later Al and Estelle climb the bank and up to the Ford, looking away when they pass me. Even the children seem wary, giving me a wide berth as they play their games in the grass. Within the hour Lora and Mary are packing up blankets and putting food into hampers. When they pick me up and help me into the car, they don't say much, but their faces are grim.

Mary and Lora settle me into my chair in the kitchen and go back to the car for some foil-covered leftovers—"to tide you over for a few days," Mary says. After carefully placing the dishes in the icebox under the floorboards, she gives me a small strained smile. "You're all set?"

"I'm fine."

"Well. Happy Fourth."

"Happy Fourth," Lora echoes.

I nod. None of us seem very happy.

After they leave, I scoop Lolly into my lap. I notice that the geraniums have wilted in their blue pot with the crack running up the side. The fire in the range has died out. The air is damp, rain is on the way. And all at once I have the peculiar sensation of watching myself from above, in the same spot where I have sat nearly every day for the past three decades. The geranium, the cracked pot, the cat in my lap, the fire that must be fed, rain on the horizon, the road to town in one direction and the St. George River in the other, stretching all the way to the sea.

I don't know how much time has passed when I hear Al's car crackling up the drive. The door creaking open, slamming shut. Footsteps to the kitchen stoop, the squeak of the screen door.

He flinches when he sees me. "Didn't know you were in here."

"Yep."

"It's dark."

"I don't mind."

"Want me to light the lamp?"

"It doesn't matter."

He sighs. "Well, okay, then. Guess I'll turn in." He hangs his cap on the hook beside the door and turns to leave.

"She's been married three times," I say. My heart is thumping in my chest.

"What?"

"Did you know that?"

He inhales sharply. "I don't think—"

"Did you know that, Al?"

"Yes, of course I know that."

"And I hear she's . . . ambitious."

"What's that supposed to mean?"

"Her motivations are questionable. I'm told."

He winces. "Who told you that?"

"I'm not at liberty to say." I know I'm hurting him, but I don't care. I like the sharpness of the words. Each one of them a dagger. I want to wound him for wounding me.

"What 'motivations' could Estelle possibly have?" he says quietly, hands on his hips. "I have nothing to offer. Except myself."

"She probably wants this house."

"She doesn't want this house!" he spits. "Nobody wants this house. I sure don't."

I feel like I've been slapped. "You can't mean that. We have a responsibility. Our family . . . the Hathorns. Mother—"

"Mother is dead. To hell with the Hathorns. And damn it, we should've sold this house when we had the chance. It's become a prison, can't you see that? We're inmates. Or maybe you're the inmate and I'm the warden. I can't do this anymore, Christie. I want a life. *A life.*" He slaps himself on the chest, a dull thwack. "Out there in the world." He sweeps his arm toward the window.

I don't think I've ever heard him string so many words together at a time. I hold my breath. Then I say, "I never knew you felt that way."

"I didn't used to. But now I see . . . I see that maybe things could be different for me. You know what that feels like, don't you?"

Al has never spoken to me so directly. I think I've assumed he didn't feel things as deeply as I do—but obviously I was wrong. "That was a long time ago. This is different."

"Why? Because it's not about you?"

I flinch. "No," I snap. "Because we're older. And this is where we belong."

"No, it isn't. It's just where we ended up."

His voice sounds choked. I think he might be crying. I'm crying too. "So what about me? I've spent my whole life cooking and washing and cleaning for this family. And now you'd just—throw me out with the trash?"

"Come on," he says. "Of course not. You'd be welcome with me wherever I go, you know that."

"I'm not a charity case."

"I never said that."

"This is my home, Alvaro. And yours."

"Christina . . ." His voice is weary, leaden. By the time I realize he isn't going to say anything further, he has already left the room.

IN THE MORNING I wake to silence. My first thought is: Al is gone. But when I look out the window, I see the Ford in the same place where he parked it last night. I go about my morning routine as usual, and as usual Al comes in from the barn for the noonday meal. He doesn't say a word until he clears his plate, and then he says thank you and heads back outside. As I'm setting newly churned butter in its earthenware pot in the shed, my eye is drawn to the dory, high in the rafters.

We should've sold this house when we had the chance. You're the inmate and I'm the warden. The words hang in the air between us. But as long as neither of us mentions them, we can pretend they were never said.

For the next few months, each morning when I wake up, I think he'll be gone.

Al doesn't bring Estelle to the house again. He doesn't speak her name. One day Sadie casually mentions that she heard Estelle met a man with two kids and moved to Rockland.

Over time, Al and I settle back into our old ways. But he is changed. A bird flies into a windowpane on the second floor, breaking the glass, and instead of fixing it he stuffs a rag in the hole. He leaves the old Model T to rot behind the shed. He rarely cleans out the woodstoves anymore, just shoves the ashes back to make room for new logs. Long winters strip the white from the house, exposing gray boards underneath, and he doesn't bother to paint. One after another the fields go fallow, farm equipment abandoned to rust. Within a couple of years, Al is farming only one small patch.

It's as if he has chosen to punish the house and land for needing him. Or maybe he's punishing me.

CHRISTINA'S WORLD

1948

In the middle of the field the earth smells like sourdough. Each sharp blade of grass is separate and distinct. Dainty yellow cowslips hang on their stems like tiny wilting bouquets; a yellow-and-black tiger swallowtail butterfly hovers overhead. It's a mild May afternoon, and I'm on my way to visit Sadie in her cottage around the bend. She offered to come and get me in her car, but I prefer to make my own way. It takes about an hour to get there, pulling myself along on my elbows, hitching my body forward. My cotton knee pads are frayed and grass stained. This close to the ground, the only sound is my own rough panting and the chirp of crickets. Blackflies circle, nipping my ears. The air tastes of salt and lavender and dirt.

I can't walk at all anymore. My chair has worn a deep groove into the kitchen floor between the table and the Glenwood range. I will not use a wheelchair. So I have a choice: I can stay inside, in the security of the kitchen and my pallet on the dining room floor, or I can get where I need to go as best I can. That's what I do. Once a week or so I visit Mother and Papa, crawling through the yellow expanse of grass to the family graveyard where they are buried, overlooking the sound and the sea. On mild afternoons I take a small pail with me and pick blueberries.

I like to rest in the grass and watch the fishing vessels as they pull away from Port Clyde, out past Monhegan Island and into the open ocean.

When I arrive at Sadie's, she's on the front porch waiting for me. "Mercy," she says with a wide smile. "Look at you. I'll bet you could use a glass of iced tea."

"That'd be nice."

Sadie disappears inside the cottage while I drag myself up the steps and lean against the wooden railing, breathless from the effort. She comes back out with a bowl of berries, a pitcher of iced tea with mint, two glasses, and a wet washcloth on a large tray.

"Here you go, my dear." She hands me the cool cloth. "So glad you came for a visit, Christina."

"It's a lovely day, isn't it?" I say, wiping my face and neck.

"It surely is. I hope we have a temperate summer like last year, not like the one two years ago. Remember that? Even nighttime was miserable."

"It was," I agree.

Sadie and I don't talk about much. A lot of our time is spent in companionable silence. Today the water in the cove shimmers like broken glass in the late-afternoon sun. The lilacs beside the porch smell like vanilla. We eat the raspberries and blackberries that she plucked earlier in the day, and drink the iced tea, the cool tingle of mint leaves slipping into our mouths like wafers.

The older I get, the more I believe that the greatest kindness is acceptance.

ANDY HASN'T ASKED me to pose since I complained about the portrait in the doorway. But one mild afternoon in early July, out of nowhere, he comes into the kitchen and says, "Will you sit for me in the grass? Just for twenty minutes. Half an hour at most."

"What for?"

"I have an idea in my head, but I can't envision it."

"Why not?"

"I can't get the damned angle right."

He knows I don't want to. I feel shy, self-conscious. "Ask Al."

He shakes his head. "Al's done posing, you know that."

"Maybe I am too."

"You're always posing, Christina. It's not as hard for you."

"What are you talking about?"

"Al is restless. You know how to be still."

Patting the arms of my chair, I say, "Let's face it, Andy, I don't have much choice."

"That's true, I suppose. But it's more than that." He strokes his chin, thinking. "You know how to be . . . looked at."

I laugh a little. "What an odd thing to say."

"Sorry, that does sound odd. What I mean is I think you're used to being observed but not really . . . seen. People are always concerned about you, worried about you, watching to see how you're getting on. Well-meaning, of course, but—intrusive. And I think you've figured out how to deflect their concern, or pity, or whatever it is, by carrying yourself in this"—he raises his arm as if holding an orb—"dignified, aloof way."

I don't know how to respond. No one has ever spoken to me like this, telling me something about myself that I didn't know but understand instantly to be true.

"Right?" he says.

I don't want to give in too soon. "Maybe."

"Like the queen of Sweden," he says.

"Come on."

He smiles. "Ruling over all of Cushing from your chair in the kitchen."

"You're just teasing me now."

"I swear I'm not." He reaches out his hand. "Pose for me, Christina."

"Are you going to make me look like death warmed over?"

He laughs. "Not this time. I promise."

AFTER ANDY LEAVES the kitchen to get his painting supplies, I slide off my chair, pull myself along the floor to the open door, and winch down the steps to a shaded spot in the grass. It feels cool and springy under my fingers. I rest there, waiting, propping myself on my arms. When Andy comes to the doorway and sees me, he squints. Walks down the steps and circles me slowly, cocking his head. Directs me: "Like this. Tucked under. Leg back." I feel like a heifer at the livestock fair. He has a pencil in one hand and the sketch pad in the other. Then he opens the pad, settles with a grunt on the stoop ten feet away, and starts to draw.

After a while, my back starts to feel sore. I say, "It must've been at least an hour already."

"It's not so bad, is it? Out here in the sunshine?" Andy looks at me and back at the pad, sketching.

"You said twenty minutes."

Holding the piece of charcoal aloft, he gives me a big smile. "Come on, Christina. You know a boy will say anything when he's trying to seduce you."

"That's for sure."

He raises his eyebrows.

I don't say anything more.

A few minutes later he says, "Hey, where is that pink dress? The one you wore to John's wedding?"

"In the hall closet."

"Would you put it on?"

"Right now?"

"Why not?"

I'm tired. My legs are throbbing. "We've already been out here longer than you promised. This is enough for today."

"Tomorrow then."

Though I roll my eyes, we both know I'll agree.

Early the next morning, I ask Al to get the pink cotton dress from the closet. He lays it on the dining room table and I shoo him out of the room before wriggling into it and pulling it down over my hips, then call him back in to fasten the buttons. When he's done he says, "I always did like that color."

Al's not one for compliments. This is as good as it gets. I give him a smile.

When Andy appears in the distance an hour later, I watch from the kitchen window. He makes his way up the hill with his tackle box, hitching one leg forward, pivoting slightly, grunting with the effort, and I find myself oddly moved by his sweet mix of bravado and vulnerability.

Strangely, my hands are clammy. Like a girl waiting for her date.

"Oh, Christina!" He gives a low whistle when he comes through the door. "You are—marvelous."

Despite myself, I blush.

"It's a nice day to be outside. Let's get something for you to sit on so you'll be more comfortable." He sets his tackle box on a chair. "I saw a pile of quilts in one of the front bedrooms." He disappears upstairs, emerging a few minutes later with an old double wedding-ring I made over one arm and his rickety easel and sketch pad under the other. "I'm taking these outside. Shall I come back and get you?"

"Well . . ." Ordinarily I would say no. But dragging myself down the steps and across the grass in this dress might ruin it. "I suppose."

I watch as he sets up his easel in the same patch of grass as the day before. He unfolds the quilt and lays it on the ground, pulling the scalloped edges to smooth it. Then he comes back inside to get me, standing very close, and puts his shoulder under mine as he pulls me up from my chair. I haven't been this close to a man I'm not related to since I was with Walton. I am acutely aware of my body next to Andy's, my fragile bones and papery skin against his warm solid chest, his muscular arm clasping my gaunt one. My senses suddenly sharpen; I possess the eye of an eagle, the ear of a cat, the nose of a dog. His breath on my face is sickly sweet. I hear a faint click between his teeth. My stomach lurches as my brain registers the smell. "Is that . . . butterscotch?"

"Sure is."

He doesn't notice that I turn my head away.

With his arms wrapped around me, under my elbows, to support my weight, he half walks, half carries me outside. My heart is beating so loudly I almost wonder if he can hear it. Gently he sets me on the quilt—adjusting my legs, smoothing my dress, tucking my hair behind my ear—before rooting around in his jacket pocket. He pulls out a cellophane bag filled with the wrapped amber candies. "I warn you, they're addictive."

"No, no—I don't want one," I say, putting up my hand. "I can't abide the smell. Much less the taste."

"How can that be? Everybody likes butterscotch."

"Well, not me." The memory is so painful I have to catch my breath: Walton's scratchy cheek against mine, one hand on the small of my back, his breath on my neck as we dance at the Grange Hall . . . "Someone I knew was always . . . sucking on them."

"There's a story," he says, tucking the cellophane bag back into his pocket. "Let me guess. The boy you alluded to yesterday?"

I look away. "I didn't allude to any boy."

He spits the butterscotch into his hand and flicks it into Al's rosebush. Adjusts the easel, props his pad on it, opens the tackle box. "I'm sorry to tell you this," he says, pulling out his pens and brushes, "but I suspect we'll be here for more than an hour today as well. In case, you know, you're concerned you won't have time to tell me about him."

For a while I am silent. I listen to Andy's pen scratching the paper. Then I take a deep breath. "It was . . . a summer visitor."

"One summer?"

"Four. Four summers."

"How old were you?"

"Twenty, the first year."

"Around the age I was when I met Betsy," he says, holding his hand out in an L shape and squinting at me through it. "Was it serious?"

"I don't know." I swallow hard. "He promised me that . . . that we would be together."

"You mean that you'd get married?"

I nod. Is that what he promised? I'm not quite sure.

"Oh, Christina." Andy sighs. "What happened?"

Something in his manner makes me want to confide things to him I've never told anyone. Even painful things, shameful things.

I didn't know how badly I wanted to share them.

"HONESTLY, CHRISTINA," ANDY says, shaking his head, when I finish telling him the story. "That man sounds very dull. Very conventional. What in the world did you see in him?"

"I don't know." I think, again, of my mother opening her

front door to a Swedish sailor, the stuff of fairy tales: Rapunzel letting down her hair, Cinderella sliding her foot into the glass slipper, Sleeping Beauty awaiting a kiss. All were given one chance to step into a happily ever after—or at least it must've seemed that way. But was it the prince who attracted them, or merely the opportunity for escape?

How much of my love for, obsession with, Walton was about my fantasy of rescue—a fantasy I didn't even know I harbored until he came along?

"I suppose I just wanted . . ." To be loved, I almost blurt. But I'm ashamed to say it. "A normal life, I guess."

Andy sighs. "Well, that's the problem, isn't it? Look, I don't mean to be rude, but you could never have a normal life, even if that's what you thought you wanted. You and me, we're not 'normal.' We don't fit into conventional boxes." Shaking his head again, he says, "You dodged a bullet, if you ask me. If that man lives to be a hundred, he'll never know the strength of his convictions."

I swallow the lump in my throat. "He knew he didn't want me."

"Pah. He was weak. Easily swayed. Believe me, you avoided a lifetime of misery. That man would've chipped away at your heart bit by bit until there was nothing left. It may have been bruised, but at least it's whole."

He may be right; my heart might be whole. But I think about the people I've kept at arm's length, even those I love. I think about how I treated Al and Estelle. What I said, and meant, to Gertrude, who had come only to help that morning during my nephew's birth: *I swear I will never speak to you again.* Maybe she was right when she told me I had a cold heart. "I feel as if . . . as if it's been encased in ice."

"Ever since?"

"I don't know. Maybe it always was."

He caps the pen in his hand. "I can see why it might feel that way. But I don't believe it. You're guarded, perhaps, but that's understandable. Jesus, Christina, you've been dealt a rough hand. Taking care of your family your whole life. Your goddamn legs that don't work the way they're supposed to." He looks at me intently, and again I have the uncanny sense that he can see straight through me. "It's obvious to me—it's always been obvious—that you have a big heart. Just watching you with Betsy, for one thing. The affection between you. And your love for your nephew—there's no mistaking that. But most of all, you and Al, in this house. Your kindnesses to each other. This guy—this guy *Walton*," he says, mocking his name, "has no consequence here. You scared the poor bugger off." He laughs drily. "What did Al think of him?"

"Not much."

"Didn't think so." Closing the sketchbook, he says, "Al knows what's what."

My heart—bruised, battered; who knows, possibly thawing—constricts. *Your kindnesses to each other.* Andy doesn't know the whole story.

He's right about one thing, though: Al does know what's what. Has always known. And I rewarded his empathy, his loyalty, by taking him for granted, by ruining his relationship with a woman who probably would have been good for him. Who would've changed his life. I can picture the small, neat cottage that the two of them might've lived in. His pale pink roses on another trellis. Al up before dawn and out on the water in his lobster boat, checking traps, calculating the yield with a tug. Home in mid-afternoon to a cozy kitchen, wingbacks by the fire, a child to play a game with, a wife to ask about his day . . .

In my own grief and panic, I denied him the respect he has always given me. What right did I have to deny him his one chance for love?

"I NEED TO say something, Alvaro," I tell him in the kitchen at dusk, when we are drinking tea by the range. "Not that it will make any difference now. But . . . I had no right to force you to stay."

I can barely make out his features, but I see him flinch.

"I am sorry."

He sighs.

"You could have been happy with her."

"I'm not unhappy." His voice is so quiet I can barely hear it.

"You loved her, didn't you." I choke out the words. "I kept you here."

"Christie—"

"Will you ever forgive me?"

Al rocks back and forth in his creaky chair. Reaches into his pocket and pulls out his pipe, tamps down the tobacco, swipes a match against the oven door and lights it. Mumbles something under his breath.

"What?"

He sucks in the smoke and blows it out. "I said, I let myself be kept."

I think about this for a moment. "You felt sorry for me."

"It wasn't that. I made a choice."

I shake my head. "What choice did you have? I made you feel like you were abandoning me, when you were just trying to live your life."

"Well." He swipes at the air with his hand. "How could I leave all this?"

It isn't until he gives me a wry grin that I realize he's making a joke.

"Nobody else knows how I like my oatmeal," he says. "And anyway. You would've done the same for me."

I wouldn't have, of course. Al is being kind, or maybe it's easier for him to believe this. Either way, it doesn't excuse what I did. Here we are, the two of us, not partners but siblings, destined to live out our lives together in the house we grew up in, surrounded by the phantoms of our ancestors, haunted by the phantom lives we might've lived. A stack of letters hidden in a closet. A dory in the rafters of the shed. No one will ever know, when we're gone to dust, the life we've shared here, our desires and our doubts, our intimacy and our solitude.

Al and I have never hugged, that I can remember. I don't know the last time we've touched, except when he is helping me get around. But here in the murky darkness I put my hand over his, and he lays his other hand over mine. I feel the way I do when I lose something—a spool of thread, say—and search for it everywhere, only to discover it in an obvious place, like on the sideboard under the cloth.

I think of what Mamey told me long ago: there are many ways to love and be loved. Too bad it's taken most of a lifetime for me to understand what that means.

A FEW DAYS after Andy started sketching me in the pink dress in the grass, he takes his drawings upstairs. I work in the kitchen all morning, scraping my chair around the floor. I leave biscuits cooling on the counter, a pot of chicken soup on the range. At noontime he comes downstairs and helps himself, scooping a biscuit through his bowl of soup, gulping water from the pump in the pantry, wiping his mouth with the back of his hand. Heads back upstairs. In the afternoon I bake a blueberry pie, cut a warm slice, push it ahead of me on a plate to the stairs, and call for him to come and get it. It's worth the effort for the grin on his face.

He rows home at dusk. Comes back the next day and troops upstairs, his heavy thudding footsteps the only sound in the quiet house. I hear him pacing around up there, opening doors, shutting doors, walking into different rooms.

This goes on for weeks.

One month, then two.

There are traces of Andy everywhere, even when he's gone. The smell of eggs, splatters of tempera. A dry, splayed paintbrush. A wooden board pocked with color.

The weather cools. He's still working. He doesn't leave for Pennsylvania as usual at the end of August. I don't ask why, half afraid that if I speak the words aloud, they'll remind him that it is past time for him to return home.

While he's upstairs I go through the motions of my routine. Heat water for tea. Knead the bread. Stroke the cat on my lap. Watch the grasses sway out the window. Chat with Al about the weather. Settle in to enjoy the sunset, as vivid as a Technicolor movie. But all the time I'm thinking of Andy, tucked away in a distant room like a character in a fairy tale, spinning straw into gold.

One October morning Andy doesn't show up. I haven't seen Betsy in weeks, but the next day, when I'm darning socks, she pops her head in the kitchen door. "Christina! Will you and Al come to dinner?"

"To your house?" I ask with surprise. They've never invited us before.

She nods. "Andy talked to Al, and they agreed Al can bring you in the car. Please tell me you'll come! Just a simple meal, nothing fancy. We'd adore it. A nice send-off before we head back to Chadds Ford."

"Andy's finished for the season, then?"

"Finally," she says. "It'll be nice to have some peace and quiet, I'll bet."

"We don't mind. We have a lot of peace and quiet."

IT'S LATE IN the afternoon a few days later when Al—wearing a light-blue collared shirt I made for him years ago that I rarely see him in—lifts me out of my chair in the kitchen and carries me down the steps and into the back of the old Ford Runabout. It's been a long time since I've been anywhere in a car—since

I've been anywhere except Sadie's, in fact. I'm dressed in a long navy cotton skirt with forgiving panels and a white blouse—an old uniform, but at least it isn't torn or stained. Hair smoothed back and tied with a ribbon.

The backseat of the car is dark and cool. As we bump down the drive I lean back and close my eyes, feeling the vibrating thrum of the motor against my legs and a flutter of nervousness in my stomach. I've never seen Andy anywhere except in our house, with his paint-spattered boots and pockets bulging with eggs. Will he be a different person in his own home?

Al turns right at a stop sign, then drives mile after mile on a smooth road. I hear the loud blinker; we make a slow right turn. Then the crackle of gravel. "We're here, Christie," he says.

I open my eyes. White clapboard cottage, trellis of white clematis, dark windows, neat green arborvitae. I knew they'd moved out of the horse stalls, but seeing the cottage reminds me anew: Betsy got her house after all.

And here she is, standing on the porch in slim black pants, a mint-green blouse, a red-lipped smile, waving. "Welcome!" Behind her, Andy waves too. It is strange seeing him here, out of context, wearing a crisp white shirt and clean, unsullied trousers and shoes, his hair neatly combed. He looks like a nice, ordinary man in a nice, ordinary house. The only hint of the Andy I know is his hands stained with paint.

Al gets out and opens my door. He and Andy cradle me up the steps and into the house. Betsy holds the door open; two young boys dart back and forth like minnows.

"Nicholas! Jamie!" Betsy scolds. "You two go play upstairs. I'll bring you some cake if you're good."

Al and Andy carry me into a sparsely furnished room with a long red couch, a low oblong wooden table in front of it, and two striped wingback chairs. They settle me onto the couch while Betsy disappears through a swinging door and emerges with a tray of radishes in a small bowl, a platter of deviled eggs, and a little jar of green olives with red tongues. (I've seen olives like this before, but never tried one.) She sits beside me and directs Andy and Al to sit across from us in the wingbacks.

Andy seems a little jittery. He shifts in his chair and gives me a funny smile. Al glances above my head and then looks at Andy. He seems jittery too.

"Toothpick?" Betsy offers.

I take one and spear an olive into my mouth. Briny. Texture like flesh. Where to put the toothpick? I see a small woodpile on Andy's plate and balance the toothpick on my own. Looking around the room, I see Andy's familiar pictures in frames all over the walls: a watercolor of Al raking blueberries, his pipe and cap in profile. A charcoal sketch of Al sitting on the front doorstep. The large egg tempera of Mamey's lace curtains in a third-floor room billowing in the wind.

"They look nice in frames," I tell Andy.

"That's Betsy's domain," he says. "She names them and frames them."

"We divide and conquer," Betsy says. "A glass of sherry, Christina?"

"No, thank you. I only drink at the holidays." I don't want to say it, but I'm afraid I might spill on my blouse.

"All right. Al?" Betsy asks.

"A drink would be nice," he says.

Al and I, not used to being served, are stiff and formal. Betsy's doing her best to put us at ease. "It's supposed to rain tomorrow, I hear," she says as she hands Al a tiny glass of sherry.

"Good thing, we can use it," Al says and takes a sip. He winces. I don't think he's ever tasted sherry before. He sets the glass on the table.

I glance at Betsy, but she doesn't seem to notice. Laughing lightly, she says, "I know rain is good for the farm, but it's no fun to be stuck inside with the children on a rainy day, let me tell you."

Al gives Andy a droll look. "You should get them painting," he says.

Andy shakes his head. "Finger painting is more like it. Actually, Nicholas seems to have no aptitude for it whatsoever, but Jamie—I think he might actually have some talent."

"For heaven's sake, he's two years old," Betsy says. "And Nicky's only five. You can't know that already."

"I think maybe you can. My father said he saw that spark in me when I was eight months old."

"Your father . . ." Betsy rolls her eyes.

Spearing another olive, I ask, "So you're headed back to Pennsylvania in a few days?"

Betsy nods. "Starting to pack up. It's always hard to leave. Though we stayed longer than usual this year."

"It feels like you just got here," I say.

"Goodness, Christina, you can't mean that! With Andy bothering you day in and day out?"

"It wasn't a bother."

"Except when I made her pose." Andy catches my gaze. "Then it was a big bother."

I shrug. "I didn't mind it so much this time."

"Glad he didn't ask me again," Al says.

Andy laughs, shaking his head. "I learned my lesson."

"Well," Betsy says, standing up, "I need to go up and check on the boys. Andy, can you clear these plates?"

I see a look pass between them.

"Yes, ma'am," he says. When Betsy leaves the room, he gathers the bowls and puts them back on the tray. "You two will have to entertain each other. I'm just the hired help." We watch him shuffle backward through the swinging door, holding the tray aloft.

"Nice house, isn't it," Al says when it's just us.

"Very nice." We're artificial with each other, unaccustomed to small talk. "I could get used to those olives."

He grimaces. "I don't care for them. Too—rubbery."

This makes me laugh. "They are kind of rubbery."

As we sit in strained silence I see Al's gaze rise up the wall above my head again. He looks at me for a moment, then back at the wall.

"What?" I ask.

He lifts his chin.

I shift on my seat, craning my neck to see what he's looking at.

It's a painting, a large painting, and it fills almost the entire wall above my head. A girl in a yellow field wearing a light pink dress with a thin black belt. Her dark hair blows in the wind. Her face is hidden. She's leaning toward a shadowy silver house and barn balanced on the horizon line, beneath a pale ribbon of sky.

I look at Al.

"I think it's you," he says.

I look back at the painting. The girl is low to the ground but almost appears to float in space. She is larger than everything around her. Like a centaur, or a mermaid, she is part one thing and part another: my dress, my hair, my frail arms, but the years on my body have been erased. The girl in the painting is lithe and young.

I feel a weight on my shoulder. A hand. Andy's hand. "I finally finished it," he says. "What do you think?"

I look closely at the girl. Her skin is the color of the field, her dress as bleached as bones in the sun, her hair stiff grass. She seems both eternally young and as old as the land itself, a line drawing in a children's book about evolution: the sea creature sprouting limbs and inching up from shore.

"It's called 'Christina's World,'" he says. "Betsy titled it, like she always does."

"Christina's world?" I repeat dumbly.

He laughs. "A vast planet of grass. And you exactly in the middle."

"It's not quite . . . me, though, is it?" I ask.

"You tell me."

I look at the painting again. Despite the obvious differences, this girl is deeply, achingly familiar. In her I see myself at twelve years old, on a rare afternoon away from my chores. In my twenties, seeking refuge from a broken heart. Only a few days ago, visiting my parents' graves in the family cemetery, halfway between the dory in the haymow and the wheelchair in the sea. From the recesses of my brain a word floats up: synecdoche. A part that stands in for the whole.

Christina's World.

The truth is, this place—this house, this field, this sky— may only be a small piece of the world. But Betsy's right: It is the entire world to me.

"You told me once you see yourself as a girl," Andy says.

I nod slowly.

"I wanted to show that," he says, gesturing at the painting. "I wanted to show . . . both the desire and the hesitation."

I reach for his fingers and draw them to my lips. He's startled, I can tell; I've never done this before. It surprises me too.

I think about all the ways I've been perceived by others over the years: as a burden, a dutiful daughter, a girlfriend, a spiteful wretch, an invalid . . .

This is my letter to the World that never wrote to Me.

"You showed what no one else could see," I tell him.

He squeezes my shoulder. Both of us are silent, looking at the painting.

There she is, that girl, on a planet of grass. Her wants are simple: to tilt her face to the sun and feel its warmth. To clutch the earth beneath her fingers. To escape from and return to the house she was born in.

To see her life from a distance, as clear as a photograph, as mysterious as a fairy tale.

This is a girl who has lived through broken dreams and promises. Still lives. Will always live on that hillside, at the center of a world that unfolds all the way to the edges of the canvas. Her people are witches and persecutors, adventurers and homebodies, dreamers and pragmatists. Her world is both circumscribed and boundless, a place where the stranger at the door may hold a key to the rest of her life.

What she wants most—what she truly yearns for—is what any of us want: to be seen.

And look. She is.

AUTHOR'S NOTE

WHEN I WAS EIGHT YEARS OLD, growing up in Bangor, Maine, my father gave me a woodcut by a local artist inspired by Andrew Wyeth's *Christina's World*. It reminded him of me, he said, and I understood why: our shared name, the familiar Maine setting, the wispy flyaway hair. Throughout my childhood I made up stories about this slight girl in a pale pink dress with her back to the viewer, reaching toward a weathered gray house on a bluff in the distance.

Over the years I came to believe that the painting is a Rorschach test, a magic trick, a slight of hand. As David Michaelis writes in *Wondrous Strange: The Wyeth Tradition*, "The down-to-earth naturalism of Wyeth's paintings is deceptive. In his work, all is not as it seems." Andrew Wyeth's paintings always have an undercurrent of wonder and mystery; he was fascinated with the darker aspects of human experience. You get glimpses of this in the arid, dry-as-bones grasses rendered in startlingly precise detail, the wreck of a house on a hill with a mysterious ladder leading to a second-story window, a lone piece of laundry floating like an apparition in the breeze. At first glance the slim woman in the grass appears to be languidly relaxed, but a closer look reveals odd dissonances. Her arms are strangely thin and twisted. Perhaps she is older than she appears. She seems poised, alert, yearning toward the house, and yet hesitant. Is she afraid? Her face is turned from the viewer, but she appears to be gazing at a darkened window on the second floor. What does she see in its shadows?

After I finished writing my novel *Orphan Train*, I began to look for another story that would engage my mind and heart as completely. Having learned a great deal about early-to-mid-twentieth-century America as part of my research, I thought it would be fruitful to linger in that time period. I'd become particularly interested in rural life: how people got by and what emotional tools they needed to survive hard times. As with *Orphan Train*, I liked the idea of taking a real historical moment of some significance and, blending fiction and nonfiction, filling in the details, illuminating a story that has been unnoticed or obscured.

One day, several months after that novel came out, a writer friend remarked that she'd seen the painting at the Museum of Modern Art in New York and thought of me. Instantly, I knew I'd found my subject.

For the past two years I've immersed myself in Christina's world. I sat in front of the actual painting for hours at the Museum of Modern Art in New York, listening to the enthused, perturbed, intrigued, dismissive, passionate comments of passersby from all over the globe. (My favorite, from a Danish woman: "It's just so . . . creepy.") I studied the work of all three famous-artist Wyeths—N.C., his son Andrew, and Andrew's son Jamie—to get a sense of the rich and complex family legacy. In Maine I became intimately familiar with the Farnsworth Museum in Rockland, which has an entire building devoted to Wyeth art, and the Christina's World homestead in Cushing, an old salt-water farm that is now part of the Farnsworth. I interviewed art historians and American historians and was lucky to get to know several tour guides from the Olson house, who sent me articles and letters I never would have discovered on my own. I read biographies, autobiographies, obituaries, magazine and newspaper articles, art histories, art books, and criticisms. I read more than I needed to about the Salem Witch Trials, which play a role in the family's history. (So interesting!) I collected postcards and even bought a print of *Christina's World* to hang on my wall.

Here's what I discovered. Christina Olson, descended on one side from the notorious chief magistrate in the Salem Witch Trials and on the other from a poor Swedish peat-farming clan, was uniquely poised to become an iconic American symbol. In Wyeth's painting she is resolute and yearning, hardy and vulnerable, exposed and enigmatic. Alone in a sea of dry grass, she is the archetypal individual against a backdrop of nature, fully present in the moment and yet a haunting reminder of the immensity of time. As MoMA curator Laura Hoptman writes in *Wyeth: Christina's World*, "The painting is more a psychological landscape than a portrait, a portrayal of a state of mind rather than a place."

Like the silhouetted figure in James Whistler's *Whistler's Mother* (1871) and the plain-featured farm couple in Grant Wood's 1909 painting *American Gothic*, Christina embodies many of the traits we have come to think of as distinctively American: rugged individualism and quiet strength, defiance in the face of obstacles, unremitting perseverance.

As I did with *Orphan Train*, I tried to adhere to the actual historical facts wherever possible in writing *A Piece of the World*. Like the real Christina, my character was born in 1893 and grew up in an austere house on a barren hill in Cushing, Maine, with three brothers. A hundred years earlier, three of her ancestors had fled from Massachusetts in midwinter, changing the spelling of their family name to Hathorn along the way, to escape the taint of association with their relative John Hathorne, the presiding judge in the Salem Witch Trials and the only one who never recanted. On the scaffold, one of the convicted witches put a curse on Hathorne's family, and the specter of the trials clung to the family through generations; it was said among the townspeople of Cushing that those three Hathorns had brought the witches with them when they fled. Another relative, Nathaniel Hawthorne—who also changed the spelling of his name to obscure the family connection—wrote about his great-great grandfather Hathorne's unremitting ruthlessness in *Young Goodman Brown*, a tale about how those who fear the darkness in themselves are the most likely to see it in other people.

Another true story became an equally significant part of my novel. For generations, the house on the hill was known as the Hathorn house. But early in the winter of 1890, in the midst of a raging snowstorm, a fishing vessel bringing lime to make mortar and bricks became stuck in the ice of the nearby St. George River channel, and a young Swedish sailor named Johan Olauson was stranded. The ship captain, a Cushing native, offered to take him in. Olauson walked across the ice to Captain Maloney's cottage, where he hunkered down for the winter, waiting for the thaw to melt the ice so he could put back to sea. Just up the hill from the cottage was a magnificent white house belonging to a respected sea captain, Samuel Hathorn. Johan soon learned the story of the family on Hathorn Hill: they were on the brink of "daughtering out," meaning that no male heirs had survived to carry on the family name. Within several months, the young sailor had taught himself English, changed his name to John Olson, and made his presence known to the "spinster" Hathorn daughter, Kate—at 34, six years his senior. In a one-month span, Samuel Hathorn died and John Olson married Kate, taking over the farm. Their first child, Christina, was born a year later, and the big white homestead became known as the Olson house. The Hathorns had daughtered out.

BY ALL ACCOUNTS, from an early age Christina was an active and vibrant presence. She had a lust for life, a fierce intelligence, and a determination not to be pitied, despite the degenerative disease that stole her mobility. (Though she was never correctly diagnosed in her lifetime, neurologists now believe she had a syndrome called Charcot-Marie-Tooth, a hereditary disorder that damages the nerves to the arms and legs.) Christina refused to use a wheelchair; as she became increasingly immobilized she took to dragging herself around. Several years ago the actress Claire Danes portrayed Christina Olson in an hour-long tour-de-force dance performance that emphasized her ferocious desire to move freely despite her devastating disease.

Quick of wit and sharp of tongue, Christina was a force to be reckoned with. Late in life—with her straw-like hair and hooked nose, her spinsterhood and independent nature—she was rumored among some of the townspeople of Cushing to be a witch herself. Andrew Wyeth variously called her a "witch" and a "queen" and "the face of Maine."

Wyeth first appeared at Christina's front door—along with Betsy James, his future wife, who'd been visiting the Olson farm since she was a girl—in 1939. He was twenty-two, Betsy seventeen, Christina forty-six. He began coming around almost daily, talking with Christina for hours, and sketching and painting landscapes, still lifes, and the house itself, which fascinated him. "The world of New England is in that house," Wyeth said "—spidery, like crackling skeletons rotting in the attic—dry bones. It's like a tombstone to sailors lost at sea, the Olson ancestor who fell from the yardarm of a square-rigger and was never found. It's the doorway of the sea to me, of mussels and clams and sea monsters and whales. There's a haunting feeling there of people coming back to a place."

In time, Wyeth began incorporating Christina into his paintings. "What interested me about her was that she'd come in at odd places, odd times," he said. "The great English painter John Constable used to say that you never have to add life to a scene, for if you sit quietly and wait, life will come—sort of an accident in the right spot. That happened to me all the time—happened lots with Christina."

For the next thirty years, Christina was Andrew Wyeth's muse and his inspiration. In each other, I believe, they came to recognize their own contradictions. Both embraced austerity but craved beauty; both were curious about other people and yet pathologically private. They were perversely independent and yet reliant on others to take care of their basic needs: Wyeth on his wife Betsy and Christina on Alvaro.

"My memory can be more of a reality than the thing itself," Wyeth said. "I kept thinking about the day I would paint Christina in her pink dress, like a faded lobster shell I might find on a beach, crumpled. I kept building her in my mind—a living being there on a hill whose grass was really growing. Someday she was going to be buried under it. Soon her figure was actually going to crawl across the hill in my picture toward that dry tinderbox of a house on top. I felt the loneliness of that figure— perhaps the same that I felt myself as a kid. It was as much my experience as hers."

"In Christina's World," Wyeth said, "I worked on that hill for a couple of months, that grass, building up the ground to make it come toward you, a surge of earth, like the whole planet . . . When it came time to lay Christina's figure against the planet I'd created for her all those weeks, I put this pink tone on her shoulder—and it almost blew me across the room."

In becoming an artist's muse—a seemingly passive role—Christina finally achieved the autonomy and purpose she craved her entire life. Instinctively, I believe, Wyeth managed to get at the core of Christina's self. In the painting she is paradoxically singular and representative, vibrant and vulnerable. She is solitary, but surrounded by the ghosts of her past. Like the house, like the landscape, she perseveres. As an embodiment of the strength of the American character, she is vibrant, pulsating, immortal.

For many reasons, this was the most difficult book I've ever written. Christina Olson was a real person, as were—and are—many of the people in this novel, and I did a tremendous amount of research into her life, her family, and her relationship with Andrew Wyeth. But at a certain point I had to let the research go and allow my characters to move the story forward. Ultimately, *A Piece of the World* is a work of fiction. Biographical facts regarding the characters in this book should not be sought in these pages. I hope readers intrigued by the story I tell here will explore the nonfiction accounts I mention in the acknowledgments. And above all else, I hope I have done this story justice.

ACKNOWLEDGMENTS

I WAS BORN in Cambridge, England, and spent my early years with my parents and younger sister in a small nearby village called Swaffham Bulbeck, in a house built in the thirteenth century. When you stood in the living room and looked up, you could see the circular outline of what had once been the hole in the roof above the space where the original inhabitants had built fires. There was no refrigerator or central heating; we used an icebox and a small gas heater that required coins to operate. Several years later we moved to Tennessee and lived on an abandoned farm, in an unheated house that had only recently been wired for electricity. Eventually we moved to Maine, into a normal house with basic amenities. But we spent weekends, holidays, and summers at a camp my father built on a tiny island on a lake with an outdoor pump for water, gas lanterns and candles for light, a fireplace for warmth, and an outhouse. We snow-shoed across the frozen lake in the winter and chipped ice from the front door to get inside. My sisters and I would huddle in our coats around the hearth until the fire my parents built was robust enough to warm us.

So I want to thank my father, William Baker, and my late

mother, Christina Baker, who taught their four daughters that living close to the elements can make you more attuned not only to the world around you, but to the world within. I have no doubt that my unusual childhood shaped me as a writer. And in my last two novels, *Orphan Train* and now this one, I've drawn explicitly from those early experiences to create characters who live simply, without the modern-day amenities that most of us have come to expect.

One sunny afternoon in July 2013 I took a tour of the Christina Olson house in Cushing, Maine, led by a young woman named Erica Dailey. Erica noticed that I was taking notes and asked if I was writing an article; I confessed that I was thinking about writing a novel. As I was leaving the house, another docent, Rainey Davis, pulled me aside, slipped her card into my hand, and told me to reach out if I had more questions. I did— and Rainey and I became fast friends. We met in Rockland, Maine and even Sarasota, Florida, where she has a house and I was giving a lecture. Some months later, another docent, Nancy Jones, sent me an email offering to introduce me to some people close to Christina. Through her, I met Andrew Wyeth's nephew David Rockwell, whose knowledge about the Wyeths and the Olson House is encyclopedic; Jean Olson Brooks, Christina's niece, who knew her intimately for many years; ninety-year-old Joie Willimetz, a distant cousin of Christina's who shared her childhood memories of visiting Christina in the 1930s and '40s; and Ronald J. Anderson, M.D., a Harvard Medical School professor who, in *The Pharos* medical journal, argued persuasively that Christina had a hereditary motor sensory neuropathy called Charcot-Marie-Tooth disease. Nancy and I attended his lecture "Andrew Wyeth and Christina's World: Clues to Christina's Secret Illness" at the National Society of Clinical Rheumatology conference in 2015 that happened to be in Maine.

As I worked on this novel I read everything I could get my hands on about the Wyeths and the Olsons. Two biographies were my touchstones: *Christina Olson: Her World beyond the Canvas* by Jean Olson Brooks and Deborah Dalfonso, and *Andrew Wyeth: A Secret Life* by Richard Meryman. Both books became so tattered that I needed to buy multiple copies. (Special thanks to Elizabeth Meryman and Meredith Landis, Richard's wife and daughter respectively, for their help along the way.) Betsy James Wyeth's beautiful book of paintings, pre-studies, and reminiscences, titled simply *Christina's World*, was also tremendously important to my research. Other relevant sources were *Andrew Wyeth: Autobiography*, with an introduction by Thomas Hoving; *Andrew Wyeth, Christina's World, and the Olson House* by Michael K. Komanecky and Otoyo Nakamura; *Wyeth: Christina's World*, a MOMA publication by Laura Hoptman; *Rethinking Andrew Wyeth*, edited by David Cateforis; *Wondrous Strange: The Wyeth Tradition*, with a foreword by David Michaelis; and *Andrew Wyeth: Memory and Magic* by Anne Clausen Knutson. For details about Christina's life and rural life in general, I turned to *John Olson: My Story*, as told to his daughter, Virginia Olson; *Old Maine Woman* by Glenna Johnson Smith; *We Took to the Woods* by Louise Dickinson Rich; and *Farm Appliances and How to Make Them* by George A. Martin, among others.

ACKNOWLEDGMENTS

A number of videos were useful to me, including *Christina's World*, a Hudson River Film & Video documentary narrated by Julie Harris; *Bernadette*, the story of a contemporary young woman named Bernadette Scarduzio afflicted with Charcot-Marie-Tooth disease; a BBC film titled *Michael Palin in Wyeth's World*; and a Boston Museum of Fine Arts video in which Jamie Wyeth, Andrew's son, talks about his creative process while working on a painting titled *Inferno*.

My trusted friend John Veague, a gifted writer and editor, read the manuscript long before anyone else—and not once, but over and over. (I'd wake up in the morning to emails time-stamped 3 A.M. saying, "I've just thought of one more thing . . .") The manuscript is stronger as a result of his rigor and thoughtfulness.

My three sisters, Cynthia Baker, Clara Baker, and Catherine Baker-Pitts, are my ideal readers; their notes on my manuscript were sharp and intelligent. I'm indebted to Michael Komanecky, Chief Curator at the Farnsworth Art Museum, for patiently answering my many questions and giving the manuscript a shrewd and incisive read. Rainey Davis, Nancy Jones, and David Rockwell fact-checked the novel; Anne Burt, Alice Elliott Dark, Louise DeSalvo, Pamela Redmond Satran, and Matthew Thomas improved it in ways large and small. Marina Budhos gave me the germ of the idea. My husband, David Kline, cheered me on and provided invaluable notes. Laurie McGee did such a brilliant job copyediting my last novel that I requested her again (and once again benefited from her thoroughness and exactitude). My wry, savvy agent, Geri Thoma, has supported me every step of the way; Simon Lipskar and Andrea Morrison at Writers House were also hugely helpful.

I've been working with my editor, Katherine Nintzel, for a long time. With each novel, my admiration for her grows. In her calm and gentle way, she is relentless. This book is infinitely better as a result of Kate's skillful guidance and perceptive editing. I also want to thank my team at William Morrow/HarperCollins for their unstinting support: Michael Morrison, Liate Stehlik, Frank Albanese, Jennifer Hart, Kaitlyn Kennedy, Molly Waxman, Nyamekye Waliyaya, Stephanie Vallejo, and Margaux Weisman.

On a personal note, I am so grateful for my husband David and my sons Hayden, Will, and Eli, without whom my own small piece of the world would be barren indeed.

CREDITS

Grateful acknowledgment is made for permission to reprint the following:

THE POEMS OF EMILY DICKINSON: VARIORUM EDITION, edited by Ralph W. Franklin, Cambridge, Mass.: The Belknap Press of Harvard University Press, Copyright © 1998 by the President and Fellows of Harvard College. Copyright © 1951, 1955 by the President and Fellows of Harvard College. Copyright © renewed 1979, 1983 by the President and Fellows of Harvard College. Copyright © 1914, 1918, 1919, 1924, 1929, 1930, 1932, 1935, 1937, 1942 by Martha Dickinson Bianchi. Copyright © 1952, 1957, 1958, 1963, 1965 by Mary L. Hampson.

The epigraph and quotes in the Author's Note attributed to Andrew Wyeth are drawn from Richard Meryman's biography of the artist, *Andrew Wyeth: A Secret Life* (Harper, 1996). Used with the permission from the Andrew Wyeth Estate.

me every step of the way; Simon Lipskar and Andrea Morrison at Writers House were also hugely helpful.

I've been working with my editor, Katherine Nintzel, for a long time. With each novel, my admiration for her grows. In her calm and gentle way, she is relentless. This book is infinitely better as a result of Kate's skillful guidance and perceptive editing. I also want to thank my team at William Morrow/HarperCollins for their unstinting support: Michael Morrison, Liate Stehlik, Frank Albanese, Jennifer Hart, Kaitlyn Kennedy, Molly Waxman, Nyamekye Waliyaya, Stephanie Vallejo, and Margaux Weisman.

On a personal note, I am so grateful for my husband David and my sons Hayden, Will, and Eli, without whom my own small piece of the world would be barren indeed.

CREDITS